K. A. S. QUINN

The Queen Alone

Chronicles of the Tempus

CORVUS

Published in paperback and e-book in Great Britain in 2014
by Corvus, an imprint of Atlantic Books Ltd.

10 9 8 7 6 5 4 3 2 1

A CIP catalogue record for this book is available
from the British Library.

Paperback ISBN: 978 1 84887 056 7
E-book ISBN: 978 1 78239 454 9

Printed in Great Britain.

Corvus
An imprint of Atlantic Books Ltd
Ormond House
26–27 Boswell Street
London
WC1N 3JZ

www.corvus-books.co.uk

The Queen Alone

Chronicles of the Tempus

K. A. S. Quinn was born and raised in California and studied History and English at Vassar. For ten years she was the publisher of the *Spectator*. She has written for *The Times*, the *Telegraph*, the *Independent* and the *Wall Street Journal*, as well as appearing on *Any Questions*, *A Good Read*, *Famous Lives* and *Broadcasting House* for the BBC. An enthusiast of the Victorians, she enjoys speaking at schools on this topic, and the trials and joys of writing. She and her husband live in London with their two boys.

Also by K. A. S. Quinn

Chronicles
of the Tempus

The Queen Must Die
The Queen at War

We begin with family and we end with them.

To my family:
Charles Sanders, Genevieve Sanders, Lugene Sanders Solomon, Marvin Solomon, Jennifer Solomon, Stephen Quinn…
… and with hugs and kisses to William Quinn and Lorcan Quinn

The Cast of Characters: Where three worlds meet . . .

Modern Day New York City

Katie Berger-Jones-Burg: A typical New York kid, who just happens to be part of the Tempus Fugit.

Mimi: Her mother.

Dolores: The housekeeper, but much more.

Reilly O Jackson: A new friend.

The Victorians

Queen Victoria: She reigns from 1837 to 1901. The emblem of a powerful industrial nation and a great empire – though as a person, she has her flaws . . .

Prince Albert: Also known as the Prince Consort. Queen Victoria's husband.

Princess Alice: Queen Victoria and Prince Albert's second daughter, and Katie's best friend.

Bertie, Vicky, Louise, Leopold: Children of Queen Victoria.

Sir Brendan O'Reilly: Doctor O'Reilly, the Royal Household physician newly ennobled by Queen Victoria.

James O'Reilly: Sir Brendan's son and an important friend to Katie and Princess Alice.

Jack O'Reilly: Sir Brendan's eldest son and James's brother, killed in the Charge of the Light Brigade.

Grace O'Reilly, Riordan O'Reilly: Other children of Sir Brendan.

John Reillson: As Civil War rages in the United States of America, he comes to London to promote the cause of the Northern States and the abolition of slavery.

Florence Nightingale: A national heroine due to her nursing during the Crimean War.

Mary Seacole: A Jamaican Creole, she ran a hotel in the Crimea during the war and nursed the sick and wounded.

Those Who Live in No Time

Lucia: The Leader of the Verus. She must keep history in balance, and make certain our world moves forward, in order to harvest our communication skills for her own people.

Lord Belzen: The Leader of the Malum. He longs for war, greed and violence. He and his followers feed off brute force. He has a way with snakes.

The Little Angel: The child who brings peace. She understands Katie and the Tempus.

The Man of All Time

Bernardo DuQuelle: Prince Albert's Private Secretary, old flame of Lucia, tormentor and saviour of Katie. An enigma.

Windsor Castle:
21 December 1860

'Thump!' Princess Alice looked up from her writing to the wintry window. A snowball, she decided, the work of her brother Bertie. She glanced towards her father, but he continued to toil at his desk, stopping only to adjust the green shade of his lamp.

Christmas was coming, and it was snowing. The battlements of Windsor Castle were cloaked in soft white flakes, its towers transformed into fairytale turrets. It was bleak midwinter; the shortest day of the year, yet the snow captured what light there was, bathing the gardens in a moon-like glow. Outside there was ice-skating on the pond, sleigh rides and snowmen on the East Terrace. Inside, beech-log fires blazed in every room, adding to the cheer of the red carpets and damask curtains. There were whispery giggles as gifts were wrapped and shouts of joy as snowballs hit their targets. A dozen Christmas trees were hung with gifts and sweets. Down below in the kitchens, huge barons of beef were being prepared for the holiday feasts.

At Windsor Castle everyone was making merry – everyone except Princess Alice and her father, Prince Albert, the Prince Consort. Together they worked in the study facing the gardens. The Prince, at his desk, ploughed methodically through the papers filling a large red-leather box, embossed with the Royal Cypher of his wife, Queen Victoria. Occasionally he passed something to his daughter, murmuring 'Alice, if you would . . .' and she began the laborious task of copying, precisely and neatly. The day progressed; the snow still fell. At 4 p.m. the lamps were lit, yet their work went on, a stream of correspondence, memorandum, reports and petitions.

It was tedious work for a girl her age. But Alice needed to watch over her father. Prince Albert was not well. The handsome Prince the Queen had married at age twenty now looked older than his forty-one years. His face was puffy, his hair lank and receding. The Prince, once known for his fine figure and dignified carriage, stooped like a man of eighty. He had a noticeable paunch around the waist.

Dark rings surrounded his eyes. 'He is so tired,' Alice thought. 'He works much too hard.' And she redoubled her own efforts, writing as fast as neatness would permit, in an attempt to lighten her father's burden.

The red boxes with the work of the government never stopped arriving. Prince Albert was the Queen's husband, friend, guide, moral compass and Private Secretary. He was the king in everything but name. For many years the people of Britain had resented him, a foreigner from the German states, marrying their queen and influencing her decisions. But he had begun to win the public over and was rewarded for his toils with a new title, Prince Consort. Princess Alice was proud of her father; but was it worth the sacrifice of his health? She stared at the paper before her until the words blurred, wondering.

A shout of merriment outside was followed by a hail of snowballs. Princess Alice shook off her worries and, rising, peeped out the window. Most of her family were enjoying the unusually heavy snowfall. The Queen was seated on a bench, snug in her furs, with her youngest child, little Beatrice, on her lap. Prince Leopold was swathed in blankets, his invalid's bath chair under a tree. This was a rare treat. Leopold suffered from haemophilia, the bleeding disease, and was not usually allowed out in the cold.

But it was Bertie, Alice's oldest brother, who led the fun. He darted about, pelting their sister Louise with snowballs. He shouted with joy as he caught Louise in the face, and she dashed up the steps of the East Terrace to hide behind a large snowman. As Bertie ran for more ammunition, he stumbled against the wheels of Leopold's bath chair, tipping him into the snow. The Queen leapt to her feet. Leopold was so fragile; with even the tiniest cut or scrape he could become seriously ill.

'Really, Bertie,' the Queen exclaimed, 'typical, typical, such immature, such unthinking behaviour . . .' Bertie's bright face clouded over. He was a constant disappointment to his mother.

'I d-d-didn't mean any harm,' he stuttered, trying to pick his brother up, but dropping Leopold in his agitation.

Alice was about to run outside to help, when she saw that James O'Reilly was with them. James, the son of the Royal Physician, was certain to make things right. Indeed, he set to work immediately, brushing the snow from Leopold, checking him for cuts and bruises, and settling him comfortably back into the bath chair.

James had been raised within the Royal Court and Princess Alice had known him from infancy, perhaps the only commoner she really knew. 'James is so competent, always quietly caring for others. I don't know another person like him,' Alice thought, not realizing she shared the same traits.

'There's no harm done, Mother.' Leopold said, pulling the blankets close. 'Please don't make me go inside; the snow is so much fun.' He begged until the Queen relented, though the shadows lengthened on the East Terrace and the sky began to glow as red as little Beatrice's knitted cap.

Princess Alice pulled the heavy curtain shut and returned to her corner of the room. Her father heard no shouts of laughter. He had completely missed the crisis with Leopold. Wrapped up in his work, he had scant time for his wife and family. He'd forgotten Christmas, the decorated tree in his study, even his serious daughter working quietly in the corner – all forgotten, swept away in the onslaught of papers. Princess Alice was puzzled: was it just the work or was there something else? Was there some secret trouble that so absorbed her father?

Prince Albert sighed and rubbed his eyes. 'Mein Kopf schmerzt so . . . oh, but my head does ache . . . this pain will be the death of me.'

Princess Alice was not the only person to hear her father. Standing in the doorway was Bernardo DuQuelle. He hardly cut a Christmas figure, with his ashen white face and sombre black clothing, yet DuQuelle came into the room with a jaunty step and an exaggerated low bow. Prince Albert looked up from his work, and winced. Bernardo DuQuelle was a useful Private Secretary, a brilliant man. He knew all of society's secrets, every skeleton in every closet. The man was competent . . . eerily competent . . . and helpful . . . irritatingly helpful. He was not to be trusted.

How long had Bernardo DuQuelle been standing in the doorway? A Royal must never show weakness, and DuQuelle was certain to have heard Prince Albert's complaints in both German and English. Language was no barrier. Bernardo DuQuelle had an unnerving ability with languages – he conversed in German, as well as French, Russian, Italian, Spanish, Portuguese, Mandarin, Cantonese, Arabic, Persian, Hindi, Urdu, Pashto and Tagalog. He could read and write in Latin, ancient Greek and Sanskrit. He was considered the world's leading scholar on the ancient Hebrews. Prince Albert shuddered. There was something of the vampire in Bernardo DuQuelle's greed for communication.

Yet Prince Albert could not rid himself of this man. Bernardo DuQuelle's grasp of language and lack of morals meant he could flatter the Queen beyond every other courtier – and the Queen adored flattery. Prince Albert's head pounded. At times like these he was acutely aware that he was the Consort, the Prince and not the ruler. He loathed Bernardo DuQuelle and yet he needed him, particularly now.

Prince Albert spoke stiffly, 'DuQuelle, I wish to take you into my confidence.' Neither man seemed to notice Princess Alice in her corner. Bernardo DuQuelle's face was impassive, mask-like; yet Princess Alice could see a smile hovering at the corners of his mouth.

I wish to take you into my confidence the Prince had

said, but DuQuelle knew perfectly well there were few things Prince Albert wished for less. DuQuelle bowed in response. 'This is for me an honour.'

Prince Albert hesitated, growing more uncomfortable with each passing moment. He sometimes fancied that Bernardo DuQuelle could read his mind, that he understood his thoughts and feelings. Could DuQuelle see the mistrust, the uneasiness and the endless weariness? Prince Albert shook his head to dislodge this fancy. 'I am so tired,' he thought. 'It is making me paranoid. I am so very tired.'

'You are so very tired, Sir,' DuQuelle echoed. 'I am grateful for the opportunity to help.'

The Prince paused, and when he did speak, he knew he sounded defensive. 'You, DuQuelle, are unique. Foreign to the ways of the court and yet you understand everyone. You have a gift for motive.'

DuQuelle remained silent and bowed his head to acknowledge – not quite a compliment – a recognition of his skills.

Prince Albert continued. 'I have received a report from Sir Richard Mayne of the Metropolitan Police, which I would like you to consider. There has been a series of crimes. Ships set on fire at St Katharine Docks, burglaries in some of the foreign embassies and violence in the streets. They seem to be separate episodes, but Sir Richard is linking them to the United States of America.

He thinks the crimes relate to potential civil war in that country.'

Bernardo DuQuelle examined the tip of his walking stick, as if the answers might be found there. 'A civil war is the most terrible kind of war: the tearing of a country in two. Family will fight family, brother against brother. But the Northern States and the Southern States of America will not see eye to eye.'

Prince Albert rummaged through the red box and found a letter, embossed with the eagle and stars of the office of the President of the United States of America. 'I feel for this newly elected President, Abraham Lincoln,' he said. 'He was elected because of his opposition to slavery, yet this very issue just might destroy his nation.'

DuQuelle sighed. 'The enslavement of one man by another leaves a bad taste in the mouth. Yet without slaves, the American South could not produce cotton. Our own industry depends on this. Britain buys five million bales of cotton from the Southern States each year. Our textile mills in the North of England would grind to a standstill without the Southern Americans and their slaves.'

Prince Albert did not hesitate to reply. 'Then our textile mills must stand still. Britain will not support slavery. I am the President of the Society for the Extinction of the Slave Trade. I take this position seriously.'

'All right-thinking men abhor slavery,' DuQuelle

agreed. 'Yet the South believes we will join them in war. The Southern States call themselves King – King Cotton. They think that Britain's need for industry and love of money will force us to support them. You say you will not support the American South, but this does not mean you will support the American North.' It was useless to withhold information from DuQuelle.

'I am in favour of neutrality,' the Prince admitted. 'This coming war is not our war . . .'

'That is not the opinion of the Prime Minster, Lord Palmerston. He is always up for war . . . and decidedly backs the American South,' DuQuelle commented drily.

Prince Albert disliked the Prime Minister even more than he distrusted Bernardo DuQuelle. He had no desire to discuss one with the other.

'For now, let us address the problem before us – this particular one in Sir Richard Mayne's report,' the Prince cut across Bernado DuQuelle. 'I desire that you keep this as private as possible. The report is not pleasant reading.'

Prince Albert might have forgotten his daughter, but DuQuelle was all-seeing, all-knowing. He glanced towards her in the corner. She was pretending to write, but was listening with all her might. Bernardo DuQuelle admired Princess Alice as much as he could admire any human being. Best leave her quietly in the corner, without reminding the Prince.

Prince Albert flipped through the pages of the thick

document. 'Here is a most gruesome find, a body, floating in the Thames. The corpse was slit from chin to groin, the body filled with a toxic, tar-like substance. It took an age to identify; the doctors assigned to the corpse kept falling ill. The dead man turned out to be, like you DuQuelle, a Private Secretary – but to the American Ambassador. In his report, Sir Richard links this to a handful of crimes perpetuated against American ships, American residencies and American citizens. Some of them are quite distressing . . .'

Prince Albert's voice trailed off at the horror of the story, but DuQuelle listened quietly, as if to a weather report, or the cricket scores. Prince Albert continued, 'Maynes writes that he has seen this type of attack before.' DuQuelle's glance flickered to Princess Alice.

From her corner of the room, Princess Alice felt rising alarm. She knew what her father was talking about, and that no one would understand better than Bernardo DuQuelle. Yet DuQuelle feigned confusion, running his fingers through his black curls. 'Let me think . . . can I remember . . . oh yes . . . Fräulein Bauer . . . and perhaps . . . Sir Lindsey Dimblock . . . wasn't there a nasty incident on London Bridge? Hushed up, of course. I remember the tar like substance. It turned out to be quite toxic to the touch. Were there any witnesses?' he spoke casually, but Alice knew this was not a casual question.

Prince Albert looked again at the report. 'Maynes says

the few witnesses are useless to the case, babbling idiots – practically out of their minds. They talk of "visions of pure evil". They call it the "prelude to the end of the world".' He paused and glanced at the Christmas tree in his study, a golden angel crowning the top. 'If I didn't know better, I'd think there was some element to this that is beyond man . . . dare I say it . . . beyond God.'

Bernardo DuQuelle stood very still. The Prince Consort had hit the mark; these were not the crimes of man, but of someone, or something, far worse. DuQuelle again exchanged glances with Princess Alice, dread flickering deep in his green eyes. But only for a moment. Soon his face was its usual sphinx-like mask. It was best to underplay this situation, no matter how desperate it really was. The last thing anyone needed was panic.

'They are noxious cases, but they are nothing more than violence, the baser instincts of mankind,' DuQuelle finally answered. 'There is no mystery . . . and I would take Sir Richard's memorandum with a pinch of salt. This is, after all, the man who has just outlawed the throwing of snowballs by children in public areas.'

To DuQuelle's relief, Prince Albert laughed. 'I'd forgotten about the snowballs in public. Sir Richard can be a bit dramatic, and draconian, at times.'

A shrill squeal from outside caught the Prince's attention, and for the first time he looked out of the window to the drifts of snow, shot through with a bright red sunset. 'Sir Richard's snowball laws,' he continued chuckling. 'I am afraid my own son will end up in prison. Bertie is pummelling Princess Louise at this very moment.'

He continued to watch his children in the snow. 'There is so much work to do,' he said to himself. 'I had almost forgotten it is Christmas. What I would give to be a child again, playing with my brother Ernst at our home in Coburg. I cannot be a child again, but I have children of my own. I see them from this window, and they are growing up quickly. Yet there is still time for us to play together. A vigorous snowball fight might do much to clear my head and raise my spirits.' Prince Albert's back became straighter, his eyes brighter as he pulled on his coat and wrapped a scarf around his neck. Soon he was outside, laughing, running and throwing snowballs like a child himself.

Bernardo DuQuelle looked out of the window, at the large happy family playing in the snow. He did not smile, but shivered. Only now did he address Princess Alice.

'You have heard,' he said.

She nodded and asked, 'Do you think my father knows?'

DuQuelle contined to watch as the Prince Albert ran across the terrace, sweeping his youngest daughter, Princess Beatrice, into his arms. 'The Prince has a broad mind, but it does not extend to the more grotesque reaches of the imagination. He knows, but not enough – at least I hope that is the case.' DuQuelle turned from the window and looked at Princess Alice. She had always seemed old for her age; she had such quiet purpose, such a sense of duty. Now he realized, with a pang of regret, that her childhood was almost over. 'And what do you think of that memorandum from Sir Richard Maynes?' he asked.

She countered with her own question. 'You will know, better than any of us, for you are one of them. The Malum, Lord Belzen – are they back?'

DuQuelle looked at the Princess, with her soft brown hair and gentle face. He looked at the cosy room with its roaring fire, red carpets and evergreen Christmas tree. He looked out of the window at the dazzling snow and the laughing family. He took it all in, as if to record this moment in his memory.

'Yes,' he said. 'Lord Belzen has returned. He leads the Malum. They are stronger than ever. We must talk and we must decide. You will find James O'Reilly outside with your family. If you please, bring him to me immediately. I fear we have little time.'

Chapter One

The Core of Darkness:
Lord Belzen

'Drip . . . drop . . . droplet.' How could a place be so wet and yet so icy cold? The dark seemed limitless. There were no boundaries, there was no time; for in the dwelling of the Malum time did not exist. And there was certainly no Christmas. What did the birth of a baby matter in a place like this? As for snow, there was wet and ice enough to freeze the heart, but nothing as downy and dancing as snow. This was a place without fancy or merriment, a place only for brute force and aggression: those were what the Malum needed to exist.

Gathered in the core of darkness were Lord Belzen

and his followers. Some were human, or had been. Some were shaped like people, but never would be human. Lord Belzen took a surprising form. He appeared to be an elegant aristocrat, wrapped in the finery of the upper classes, really very handsome. Yet there was something about him – the strange wavering sway of his slender body, the oddly blunted nose starting high in his forehead. His close-set glittering eyes were hypnotic; his slightly lisping voice could hold one captive. He bore a strong resemblance to the snakes that lolled and lapped about his polished boots. Lord Belzen was dangerous to know.

'What stands in our way?' he asked those around him; and, as usual, answered his own question. 'It is Britain, a peaceful Britain.' Lord Belzen hissed the word 'peaceful' as if it were repulsive to him. 'And why must we suffer through peace? Again, the problem is Britain. A strong and unified nation which has become rich, with an expanding Empire abroad. All this strength, all this stability – it cannot halt the Malum, but it is slowing us down.'

Around him, a muted response stirred the chill air, hoarse muttered words mixed with yips and grunts and, underneath it all, a terrible hissing. It was the soundtrack to a nightmare.

Lord Belzen's head jerked upwards, as if it had a life of its own, separate from his neck and torso. 'And what is the key to this wonderful, growing, peaceful Britain? It is Prince Albert, the Prince Consort.' He spat the words with venom. 'A ridiculous man, with a ludicrous title. He thinks that with his pure white soul, his moral strength, his knowledge and his ceaseless toil, he can rule Britain wisely and bring his knowledge and influence to other nations. He can do much good in his world, but he has not considered that there are other worlds.'

The noise around him grew, an unnerving flapping and hissing and smacking of lips. Lord Belzen's eyes glittered wetly.

'The Prince is weakened already. All that goodness takes its toll.' He was met with an appreciative laugh. 'It will be easy to kill him off. We will be able to extinguish him and his good influence on the Queen. Then she is vulnerable. There is someone in her service, vain and weak, who is much in my debt. He can destabilize the Queen, subdue her. With such a fragile, insecure Queen, the Empire they are building will collapse into chaos. The effects will echo through the world. We will be able to lure Britain into war.'

With the word 'war', a jolt of power throbbed through the core of darkness. The fiends around him gasped with joy and the snakes writhed in ecstasy.

With a sweep of his long undulating arms, Lord Belzen sent a globe spinning above them. It whirled and leapt, lit from within – a replica of the earth, joining in the dance of death. It stopped at the Western Hemisphere, where an ugly red light pulsed through the United States of

America. Belzen reached up and, taking the globe, traced the Americas with his long, webbed fingers. They left a glistening trail of wet behind. 'There it is,' he murmured, 'The United States of America, spiralling down, down, down, into a civil war. Britain will enter this war, France and Russia will follow. We will set the entire world on fire with this war.'

The cries became louder, as they realized what this meant. 'It will be most potent!' one of them hissed.

'Yes,' Belzen responded, 'the creation of brute force, the animal fierceness we need to survive. Our source of energy. We cannot be stopped. We will create unceasing war in this world. The Malum will harvest the ugly power of man, unchained from humanity.'

Lord Belzen had such authority; it was difficult to interrupt him. And most of his disciples made a point of agreeing. But one voice did speak out above the howls and jeers, the hissing in the chill darkness. 'We can be stopped,' it said. '*She* knows everything. She has thwarted us before. She and the Tempus Fugit, they are always a threat. And beyond that, there are her friends. They are beginning to understand. Just one or two, but that is dangerous enough. The Prince we so despise, he has his doubts. And then there is Bernardo DuQuelle, Lucia, Flo—'

Lord Belzen drew his breath in, dropping his attractive mask. His nostrils lengthened strangely, long dark slits cut into his face. The questioning voice was cut short and replaced by a sharp shriek of pain, as something whipped through the darkness and slashed at the speaker.

'You are ridiculous,' Belzen's elegant voice became high and angry. 'DuQuelle?' he hissed. 'A puppet. Lucia? She is blinded, paralysed by her beliefs. Both are ineffectual. The Verus and all their goodness, their futile attempts to make this world a place of peace – all for what? So that they can use words, take communication from this weak, silly world. We will wipe out the Verus with one swipe.' There was another strange slap and yelp and the questioner was felled.

'Are you such a coward, that *she* would scare you?' Lord Belzen scoffed. 'We will use her for our own advantage. It is easy enough to lure her here – under the pretence that her friends are calling. We know the words that will bring her. I will plant the seeds within her mind: doubt, jealousy and loneliness. *She* will come and we will make her ours.'

No one dared speak, but Belzen could feel the questions in the chill air. '*She* is no longer a child,' he continued, 'but she is still the child who can bring war or peace. We will make certain it is WAR she brings. She lives in America, the focus of war; if not in the same time, at least in the same place. America is the heart of her temporal life. We shall use this, and her, to lure Britain into her nation's war. She will turn against her friends. When they ask for her help, she will refuse. This girl will weaken the Prince and help us destroy the Royal Family. Their heroine? Their saviour? Hardly. She will bring the war that ends the world.'

Whomever or whatever surrounded him in the dark liked what they were hearing, and voiced their approval in shrill cries and foul language.

For a moment Lord Belzen allowed himself to sway and hiss along with them. 'This is only the beginning,' he exhorted. 'We must set the stage in the household of the Queen.' He tossed the globe lightly into the air. Again it spun and flashed. Its walls transformed into clear glass.

Inside the globe, the entire world resolved into a single scene. It was a family, playing in the falling snow. A small plump woman smiled upon them and nodded her fur-trimmed bonnet, while her husband tossed their youngest daughter into the air. The small girl shrieked with joy and her red hood went flying. An older girl, with shining brown hair, caught snowflakes in her hand and brought them to her sickly brother in his bath chair. 'See,' she said, 'no two snowflakes are alike.'

'I know that,' the boy replied with the pettish irritation of the invalid. But still, he looked at the flakes with interest and squeezed the girl's hand. A young man shouted with laughter, and as he ran from flying snowballs, collided with a large grinning snowman.

Lord Belzen watched them all at play, within his circling glass globe, and then he reached out a webbed finger to give the globe a poke. The snow fell more heavily. The earth trembled, ever so slightly, beneath the feet of the playful family. 'How happy they are,' he hissed softly. 'This year they are so happy. The Queen, how the Queen loves her Prince.'

Lord Belzen's hissing voice transformed to the womanly tones of the Queen. 'My precious Albert, he has made the Christmas season perfect,' he cooed. 'It is true Christmas and the dear, sweet children are beside themselves with the joy of the snow. Albert joins them with great spirit. Such a merry, joyful time, all due to my beloved Albert.' Belzen's mimicry had a cutting edge. 'Albert! Oh, my dear Albert! You are everything to me!'

Around Belzen there was cruel laughter as he poked again, harder, at the floating snow globe. 'Soon, little Queen, your *everything* will become *nothing*. This year there is Christmas cheer, but next year – grief. Your heart will be in darkness. The Malum shall prevail. Katie . . . Katie . . . the time has come to play your part . . . we are calling you.'

Raising his arm, Lord Belzen gave the globe a clout with the palm of his hand, leaving a wet mark. The snow globe shuddered. It was not just the little white flakes, but the people within that began to revolve. The Queen, Prince Albert and Princess Alice floated and swirled in chaos . . . and the dancing white flakes turned to black.

Chapter Two

New York City, 21 December: Here and Now

'Hooonnnnkkkk!' Was every taxi driver in New York City leaning on his horn? Katie Berger-Jones-Burg turned her head towards the terrace. The snow swirled outside the windows of Apartment 11C, looking almost black, as an early night set in. December 21st, the shortest day of the year. A day of panic. School had ended and time was running out – fast. Christmas was coming, at avalanche speed, and New Yorkers were bracing themselves. Trees needed to be decorated, lights hung in the windows, family feasts planned. Ahead lay the long car trips to Ohio or Virginia or Connecticut (even Long Island seemed an endless trip with the kids in the backseat, squabbling.) And of course there was the shopping, shopping, shopping, for nobody shops like a New Yorker.

They were crushed together on the sidewalks, scouring the stores for something, anything, to buy. It was a battlefield out there. The streets were wet and icy and crunched with salt and grit. The sidewalks became trenches, with huge mounds of dirt and snow on either side. Postal delivery vans were double- and triple-parked. Taxis honked, buses moved at a snail's pace and the subway was a tangle of wet, exhausted, irritated passengers. It was a good day to stay inside. But Katie Berger-Jones-Burg would rather have been outside, with the crowds, with anyone. School was out, her mother Mimi was gone and she was the only New Yorker in the world with nothing to do.

She lay flat on her back on the big cream sofa. The window was boring, so she turned her eyes to the Christmas tree. Well, not really a Christmas tree. Her mother Mimi had given strict instructions; it was to be referred to, at all times, as the Tree of Peace. It was flocked in some kind of white spray-on junk. Miniature Menorahs, little Buddhas, and the Islamic star and crescent hung from the branches. Ribbon garlands carried Mimi's favourite slogans: *Give Peace a Chance! Just Say No! Live the Life*

You Imagined! And largest of all, the name of Mimi's new fragrance: FOREVER YOUNG!

That morning, the tree had been photographed for a press release 'Happy Holidays from pop's eternal role model: Mimi rocks with her multi-cultural Tree of Peace.'

'The Tree of Peace, my foot,' Katie said to herself. The house was anything but peaceful. George, the door-man, buzzed up every five minutes with more and more packages. There were endless gifts . . . for Mimi. Bribes from fashion companies who wanted her to wear their size-zero creations, stacks of designer handbags, swathes of sandals with eight-inch heels that looked like instruments of torture – and barrels full of scented candles; it seemed this was the year that everyone introduced a scented candle.

Mimi greeted each gift with childlike enthusiasm. She loved stuff. An entire room in Apartment 11C was dedicated to Mimi's clothes. A light- and temperature-controlled room. The handbags each had their own velvet-lined case, labelled with their names: *The Sofia* – Louis Vuitton, *The Jackie* – Gucci, *The Granville* – Dior, *The Anya, The Kelly, the Birkin gold . . . the Birkin turquoise, the Birkin rose...*Their housekeeper Dolores said Mimi's handbags lived a better life than most of the world's population.

Among the millions of Mimi gifts was the odd package for Katie. She knew already what would be inside.

Technology. Endless techi-things. The latest, most talked about stuff on the market. Mimi hired someone to 'handle her technology' – 'the nails darling, one must be very careful of the manicure . . .' – but viewed Katie as the pioneer girl of the IT age.

'This is your future,' Mimi would lecture. 'Life is so much easier with these . . . these . . . miracles of science! You don't have to read, you don't have to write, you don't have to look things up or figure out where you are going. You'll never have to decide on a restaurant, a shop, a friend. These wonderful things can do all this for you.' Katie sometimes worried whether there was any thinking or personal choice in this wonderful new world of Mimi's.

Katie rolled off the sofa, and began to rummage under the Tree of Peace. Maybe her father had sent her something she might like, or her stepfather, or her other stepfather . . . When your name is Katie Berger-Jones-Burg, there are a lot of fathers who might send you a sensible gift, maybe even a book . . . She pushed aside several glittering packages, stopping to snort at one in a clear acrylic case. It was a silver and crystal evening bag shaped like a microphone. '*To Mimi: The Voice of Our Time*' the card read.

Dolores pushed open the door from the kitchen and, bustling through the room, began to pick up the litter of diet cola cans and crummy plates. She stopped briefly to stare at the package Katie held. 'Those handbags!' she snorted. 'Mimi's always going on about the poor. What's that song she sings? "Feed the World"? Well, she could feed a village in Africa for a year out of the price of one of those handbags!'

'"Feed the World" was a hit,' Katie weakly defended her mother. 'And she doesn't buy the handbags. They just give them to her.'

'Giving,' Dolores harrumphed as she restacked the gifts under the tree. 'There's no such thing as giving in that world of Mimi's. They get their money's worth out of her.'

'Mimi might give one of those handbags to you,' Katie commented slyly. She'd seen Dolores dusting Mimi's handbags with a sneaking look of admiration. Dolores was female, after all.

'I don't need no $10,000 handbag, I've got a perfectly serviceable black one for church already,' Dolores said. 'And I don't want any more of Mimi's cast-offs. *Give me a handbag.* I know Mimi's idea of giving me a gift. She just switches cards on a couple of those packages. You remember last year? She gave me a mink jacket. A MINK JACKET. In size zero. With the lining personalized. *Mimi* it says, all embroidered in pink. She doesn't buy gifts for people. She doesn't pick them out. She doesn't even hire one of those people of hers to buy 'em.' Dolores did her Christmas shopping at Target. She lined up at 6 a.m. on a Saturday morning to get into the store before the crowds descended.

Katie flopped back on the sofa and closed her eyes. Even with the traffic and the bustle she could hear

Dolores muttering . . . 'mink, size zero, Mimi, really,' as she swept back into the kitchen to tackle the ironing. Despite this, Katie felt that tiny bit more secure. Dolores might grumble, but she was the closest thing Katie had to a caring parent. She knew Dolores wasn't going anywhere; there was no new 'final tour' with a pop band, no cheesy fragrance to launch. Dolores had been looking after Katie . . . and Mimi . . . for years. And though Katie might grow up (there was little hope for Mimi) Dolores had no intention of stopping – or holding her tongue.

Had there ever been a Mr Dolores? Not that Katie could remember. There was a son, Tyrell, and a daughter, Sonia. Katie often heard stories about them as she hung out in the kitchen. Tyrell spent time with his friends, was wild about computer games and basketball, pretty much a glorious human boy. He was about to go to college and study sports physiotherapy.

Sonia was a nurse and worked long hours. She was married, with children, and lived in the Bronx. Sonia and her husband were both good church-goers. Dolores thanked God for every night, on her knees. Sonia might have married early, but she'd finished nursing college. Tyrell didn't belong to a gang and didn't take drugs. Just a few more years for Tyrell and they'd both be in that safe harbour most mothers dream of.

Katie thought about Dolores. She seemed to be in

charge of everyone . . . Sonia, Tyrell, Katie, Mimi. After finishing a long day in Manhattan, Katie knew Dolores took the train out to the Bronx and helped Sonia with the children. All this didn't come without a lot of sacrifice. Mimi was a great believer in *me time*. Well, it seemed like Dolores only had *you and you and you time*. Dolores poked her head back around the kitchen door. 'Honey, I hate to tell you, but you've got to get ready for that doctor's appointment.' This time her voice was soothing, though her face looked worried.

All was not right with Katie Berger-Jones-Burg. It had started with the attack. Their neighbour, ex-boyfriend of Mimi's and resident psychopath Professor Diuman, had broken into Apartment 11C. Mimi had been brutally beaten. The police had found Katie locked in the bathroom. She seemed to have slept through the entire thing.

For once Mimi's plastic surgery was necessary rather than voluntary. But she made a miraculous recovery. She looked great, and it had been a shot in the arm for her career. *Plucky Mimi Fights off Attacker!* The headlines had screamed. *Mimi Recovers from Near Death Experience: Long Live Mimi!* Katie had to admit, Mimi might not have much of a voice, but she had a terrific agent. They cut a deal with one of the big cosmetic firms and Mimi launched her own fragrance: FOREVER YOUNG! Between the television appearances, the endless interviews and the national tour, she was in seventh heaven.

Katie hadn't suffered even a scratch from the attack, yet she wasn't doing nearly as well. She just couldn't seem to bounce back. She lacked Mimi's exuberance, or perhaps it was Mimi's lack of reflection. Katie was worried and anxious. No one understood why Professor Diuman had suddenly turned violent. Sure, he'd gone out with Mimi, years ago, but they'd maintained a perfectly good friendship. Diuman was incapable of explaining. He wasn't in prison, but in Bellevue Mental Hospital – totally bonkers. He spent the day talking, talking, talking, until he lost his voice. 'The walking stick . . .' he cried over and over, 'the walking stick!'

It was as Katie had suspected. The walking stick always spelled trouble. It had arrived at Apartment 11C years before, addressed to Katie Berger-Jones-Burg, with a card engraved with just two words: Aide-memoire. There was no name, no signature, and no explanation. Aide-memoire – to help her remember.

And the worst thing was, she could remember. Just snippets, flashes of memory. Strange things were going on in Katie Berger-Jones-Burg's brain. Images and people, sights she'd never seen before and voices she'd never heard. She hated what was happening in her head. And she hated the effect it had on the people around her. Dolores was worried sick, she knew it. And Mimi – the enthusiastic, loud, dramatic Mimi – now became quiet, almost frightened, when her daughter was in the room.

Katie continued to lie on the sofa, eyes closed, worry lines etched between her brows. Dolores came in and stroked Katie's head with her worn, warm hand. 'Come on, sweetheart,' she encouraged Katie. 'Let's get you up and out. Talking to that doctor, it really should help.' But Katie had her doubts. Would anything really help?

Chapter Three

The Doctor's Office

No matter how many times Katie sat in the doctor's reception, it never got easier. She hated the tasteful light-brown leather sofa, the piles of *National Geographic* magazines and the latest copy of *Vogue* on the coffee table. There were some foam puzzles for younger patients to put together – nothing with sharp corners, of course. The paintings on the walls were designed to be neutral, peaceful and unchallenging. It was all too careful. It gave itself away. It was a room designed for people on the edge, about to go over.

Usually, everyone sat as far apart as possible; each person believing 'I am actually well, and I don't want to catch crazy from anyone here . . .' But today a boy, really a young man, came in and sat down right next to Katie. She started to get up and find another seat. But something about him caught her attention and made her stay.

He was older than Katie, quite tall, with square shoulders, a strong nose and thick brown hair standing every which way atop his head. Everyone else in the room looked at a magazine, or a picture on the wall or twisted their hands in their laps. This boy looked right at Katie, with bright blue eyes. He had the air of someone who'd just heard a good joke. He seemed to want to share this joke with Katie. She felt a jolt, and a wave of joy surged through her.

'Katie,' he said. And she felt a different kind of jolt. Her stomach turned over. How did he know? She'd never seen him, had she? But then she remembered; her name was monogrammed on her canvas school bag.

'You don't know I'm Katie,' she said defensively, picking up the bag and hugging it to her chest. 'It could just be some designer's name. A designer handbag. The latest Katie.'

'But you are Katie,' he replied, still fixing her with his bright eyes. 'No one else could be. And besides, there is no Katie designer label – Kate Spade, yes, but no Katie. Trust me. If you had my mother . . . I learned to read tracing designer labels on her handbags.'

Katie laughed. 'Do you think she's my mother's twin sister?' The other patients in the doctor's office looked up, offended by her laughter. The boy gave them a cheery wave and they glanced away, as if he had made an obscene gesture.

'Reilly Jackson,' he introduced himself. 'Well, actually Reilly O Jackson.'

'What does the O stand for?' Katie asked, before she could stop herself.

Reilly shook his head. 'The O stands for O,' he said, and mimicking a breathless ingénue voice quoted:

'O brave new world, that has such people in't.'

He really did laugh this time. 'Before the designer hand-bags and the soap operas, my mother used to be quite a good actress. She did lots of Shakespeare.'

'*The Tempest*,' Katie said. 'My mother went through a Shakespeare phase too. We have the complete works, bound in cream suede to match the living room. Mimi thinks it gives the apartment some depth.'

To Katie, this Reilly O Jackson seemed nearly perfect. There must be some catch. 'What's wrong with you?' she asked, and then wanted to bite her tongue off. After all, she was sitting in a psychiatrist's office too. Reilly didn't seem to mind her bluntness at all.

'I want to save the world,' he explained, 'and the world seems to think this is bonkers.' For the first time she looked up, directly into his clear blue eyes.

'That's the least bonkers thing I've ever heard,' she said, then wished she hadn't. Katie looked down at her hands twisting in her lap, like the other patients in the room, at her bitten fingernails. 'I'm, like, so much crazier than you are,' she confessed. 'At least you say something that makes sense. I write – and write – and write – and it's all nonsense.'

Reilly didn't look suspicious, or distrustful. He didn't look worried, the way Dolores did when she found Katie's scribbles, or frightened, like Mimi. He just looked incredibly interested.

'What do you write?' he asked. 'One person's nonsense is another person's masterpiece.'

'It's just gibberish,' Katie said. 'Like I'm taking notes in a classroom, at some kind of lecture or something. Here, I can show you,' she said. Rummaging through her rucksack, she pulled out a tattered piece of paper, covered in words, scrawled in her own handwriting.

Visions – mirror – walking stick – DuQuelle – Alice – James – Tempus – Occidit – Fugit – Verus – Malum – Lucia – Belzen – Grace – Corset – Angel – fleas – Felix – Florence – Seacole – Russell – salve – charge – charge – CHARGE – Jack – Jack – Jack . . .

'I don't even know when I do it,' Katie explained. 'Mimi, that's my mother, and Dolores, our housekeeper, find piles of them. And then I keep seeing . . .' Katie trailed off. She'd shared enough with Reilly O Jackson. Too much in fact.

Reilly read through the paper. When he looked up at Katie, his eyes were serious, a deeper blue. 'It could be automatic writing,' he suggested, 'like writing in a trance. You could be tapping into your unconscious . . . or . . . the spirit world . . . or . . .' He turned redder and Katie understood. There were certain things you think, particularly at night, that you just don't say out loud.

It had been a long time since Katie met anyone she liked as much as Reilly O Jackson. But the time had come to shut up. Why should she talk to him about all this stuff; she wasn't even telling the doctor. She couldn't tell anyone. It was too weird.

The crazy endless writing was bad enough. And then there were the visions. The worst thing was, it all made much more sense than she wanted to admit to anyone, even to herself. In the depths of her being, she was remembering. The visions that came to her weren't of her time. The people who appeared wore old-fashioned clothes. The men rode on horses and the women wore long skirts. But the people themselves, strange as they appeared, were not strangers to Katie. The pretty girl with the serious grey eyes, the studious boy who rubbed his hair until it stood on end – they seemed like old friends. And the tall pale man in the black silk top hat. She knew the glitter in his green eyes, and recognized his walking stick. It was exactly like hers.

Was it all just a trick of her mind? Or was there a reason? She realized she'd been staring into space for a long time, but this didn't seem to bother Reilly O Jackson.

'Here,' he said, handing back her scrawled paper. 'Keep the papers, and take care of them. I think they're important. I think they'll tell an amazing story one day. Somehow, some day, you'll understand them.'

The receptionist looked up from her gossip magazine. Katie cringed when she saw a photograph of Mimi on the cover. 'Reilly Jackson,' the receptionist called out, as the doctor hovered in the doorway, visibly alarmed at the two teenagers together.

'Jack!' the doctor greeted him with practised familiarity. The boy gave him a guarded look, suddenly quite a different person. 'Jackson,' the doctor corrected himself, 'Reilly Jackson, how good to see you.' Reilly Jackson obviously didn't share these feelings. The square shoulders slumped and the brown hair fell over his blue eyes. With a parting, almost pleading look at Katie, he slouched towards the door. He wasn't going to give the doctor anything.

'Jack,' Katie thought. 'The doctor called him Jack.' And there he was, in her mind's eye. Jack: in a blue and gold military tunic, sabre at his side, the unkempt hair replaced by a neat trim and some rather fantastic sideburns. Jack: a dashing soldier of another time. The visions. Why the visions? Katie shook her head slightly, and this figure merged with the retreating back of the boy in the psychiatrist's office. Jack.

Chapter Four

The Snow Globe

A s Katie walked home, jostled on the busy streets, she felt giddy, almost light-headed. At last, a sprinkling of Christmas spirit. She had managed to talk to the doctor for a full hour, sounding frank and open, but without telling him anything important. And she'd met someone who made sense to her: a boy, a funny, kind boy, who just happened to be a co-crazy. But as the doorman swung open the glass doors to 50 East 89th Street, she realized she might never see Reilly O Jackson again. He'd never been in the doctor's reception room before. Katie thought hard. 'I'll tell Mimi that I'm beginning to open up emotionally,' Katie decided, shaking snow from her boots and whistling 'Jingle Bells'.

Mimi loved doctors, especially the ones that were paid to listen to her talk. She'd been waiting for Katie's breakthrough for a long time.

George was sitting behind the front desk, as he had been for the past twenty-five years. 'I've lived through lots of Mimi's Christmases,' he called out to Katie, 'but this one is the limit.' He lifted yet another bundle of packages – wrapped gifts, orchids, cupcakes – all for Mimi.

'Send the orchids to Mount Sinai Hospital,' Katie instructed, an old pro at dealing with Mimi's gifts, 'and eat the cupcakes yourself. Mimi will shriek if she sees all those carbs. I'll take the packages up. I'm sure we'll all be glad when the holidays are over.'

George gave her a wink. He'd known Katie since she was a baby.

Dolores had been watching out for Katie, but she wasn't happy to see the packages. 'MORE, I can't believe there's MORE,' she grumbled. 'Not even the baby Jesus deserves this much stuff.'

'Maybe we'll have to move,' Katie said thoughtfully, as she placed the packages under the laden tree. 'I don't think Mimi has enough room in her wardrobe for this stash. But look on the bright side. It might all be tax-deductible. I mean, it is part of Mimi's job . . . being fawned over . . . and she has to wear all these clothes . . .'

Dolores sniffed. 'I don't see her wearing A LOT of clothes up there on stage. It's get'n shameful, at her age.

Just a few spangle beads and feathers . . .' Katie sat down by the tree, making room for the new gifts. One tumbled into her lap. The card on top said *Katie Berger-Jones-Burg*: written in the most elaborate penmanship, all swirls and curls. As Katie stared down at the package in her lap, her Christmas cheer evaporated and tears sprang to her eyes. *Katie Berger-Jones-Burg*: the name of a girl with a much-married mother. A girl who receives every gift but the one she really needs.

'Well, that's one fancy gift,' Dolores said. Katie dabbed at her eyes with the winter scarf still around her neck. She picked up the box and examined it more closely. 'I think it's come far,' she said. 'It's got that funny travelling smell – kind of burnt, kind of electric. It smells like your clothes when they've been on an aeroplane too long.'

Dolores harrumphed. 'My clothes don't fly around on aeroplanes. My clothes stay right in the Bronx where they belong. We're not budging from New York. We're staying right here in the USA.'

'But where did you come from?' Katie asked Dolores. 'I mean, most Americans come from somewhere else. Your parents or grandparents must have chosen America, and come here from another country.'

Dolores put her hands on her hips and looked at Katie with disbelief.

'Choose! We didn't choose. Haven't you ever looked at the colour of my skin, child? We were dragged here, captured in some raid on a village, some African war. We came as slaves. Choose! No one chooses to be a slave.'

Having had her say, Dolores swept into the kitchen for a bout of ironing and television. Katie felt even more miserable. All she really had was Dolores, and now she'd made her angry. 'So much for happy holidays,' she said to herself.

The strange package in her lap was wrapped in thick cream paper, beautifully marbled in crimson and blue. The large curving bow shimmered like spun gold. 'It really is beautiful,' Katie murmured. Mimi had promised to be home for Christmas, but who could tell with Mimi? Why not open a present now. Just one; this one pretty package. Katie gave the bow a tug.

Nothing happened. She pulled again, harder. Still, the bow would not give way. Katie tried sliding the bow off the package. She got scissors out of Mimi's 'writing desk'. But the bow would not budge. Who would send her such a stubborn package? Strange, but the envelope with her name slipped easily from under the ribbon. Carefully, she opened it. Inside, in the same elaborate script it said:

Where is the book?

So the card asked questions. Katie knew she should be surprised. But somehow it seemed the most natural thing a card could do. The real question was: what book?

Katie had hundreds of books. She read and read; for her it was a means of escape. Thick paperbacks, cloth-bound hardbacks, the occasional leather-bound fancy ones – but they were always real books. Mimi found this very eccentric. Almost every book in the house was in Katie's bedroom, and the majority of these were under her high, Victorian canopy bed. Placing the package back under the tree, she ran to her room and crawled under the bed.

Since early childhood, this had been her refuge. Somehow it was safe under the bed. She kept her treasures in a cardboard box: a broken Swiss army knife her father once gave her, some dried flowers from a rare walk in the country . . . Mostly though, it was the books. She scanned the titles: *Beowulf, The Mysteries of Udolpho, Girl, Interrupted, Germ Theory and Disease, Dealing with Death, The History of Milk* . . . her reading tastes were nothing if not diverse.

And then it came to her with great clarity. There, shoved under *Wuthering Heights*, was the book. A very old and possibly very dangerous book. Professor Diuman had lent it to her, way before he had attacked Mimi and ended up in a loony bin. She could smell the book almost before she could see it. The same strange, burnt, musky smell, just like the package under the tree. '*Tempus Fugit, Libertati Viam Facere*' was written on the cover page. She'd looked it up in her Latin textbook: '*Time Flies, Making a Road to Freedom*'.

Grabbing the book, she took it back to the tree. Still, the package would not open. She placed it on the book, she tapped the package with the book, and she read aloud, in Latin, from the book. Nothing. Katie was about to toss the gift back under the tree, when the card caught her eye. It was the same swirling script, only the message had changed:

. . . and the walking stick.

Always a puzzle, and so annoying, that walking stick. The police had taken it as evidence in Professor Diuman's attack. Then they'd lost it. But months later the walking stick appeared at 89th Street, a knobbly package addressed to Katie. She had her suspicions that someone other than the police had sent it back to her. Dashing to her closet, Katie rummaged through the debris until she found it. A long ebony cane with a silver tip. She ran her hands over it, her fingers caressing the strange symbols carved deep into the wood. She had a hundred questions about the walking stick, but she knew one thing for certain – it was the answer to the package.

This time she didn't run back but slowly approached the tree. Seating herself with crossed legs, she placed the book in her lap and the package on top. Taking up the walking stick, she gently tapped the bundle. The ribbon slipped away and she could easily open the wrapping. Inside was a simple wooden box containing a Christmas ornament: a glass globe. Katie felt a rush of disappointment. It was pretty and it was interesting, but it didn't seem to warrant the *Alakazam* of ancient books and magical wands.

Katie looked at it carefully. Actually, it was a snow globe. Inside was a family scene of Christmas in Victorian times. The father, mother, sons and daughters were clustered around a Christmas tree, their long hooped skirts and velvet jackets fitting for the time of year. Katie peered more closely. There was so much detail. A fire crackled in the fireplace and on the mantle a large clock was surrounded by evergreen branches. Deep-red curtains hung around windows that were filled with painted snow. A small brass plaque was attached to the base of the globe. It read: *CHRISTMAS, 1860*.

Dolores bustled back from the kitchen; she could never stay angry with Katie. 'I brought you some hot chocolate, honey,' she said, setting it down on the coffee table. 'Now that's a dainty little thing,' she added, peering at the glass globe. 'Let's shake it up and make it snow.' Obediently Katie shook the globe, but it wouldn't snow.

'How strange,' Dolores said. But Katie had figured it out: this globe wouldn't snow with the shake of a hand, because it wasn't a normal snow globe. It wasn't even a gift. The snow globe had something to tell her: like a message in a bottle, washed to shore from sea. It needed the book and the walking stick in order to tell its story.

Tap, tap, tap – Katie could feel it in some inner recess of her mind. '*Tempus Liberatati*,' she whispered. ' . . . No . . . *Tempus Vaim* . . . damn . . . no . . . *Tempus Fugit, Libertati Viam Facere*.' She finally got it right and tapped on globe. 'The words,' she tried to explain to an increasingly worried Dolores. 'It's always the words.'

She found herself muttering, almost involuntarily, 'their time, our time, passing time, all time, no time, out of time'. All was still. The pretty Victorian family was frozen in time, quietly celebrating in their safe world of glass. And then the snow began to fall. She could see it, through the window in the snow globe. Not the plastic flakes, put in a ball of water and glycerine by a Chinese manufacturer. These were not '*Made in China*' flakes. These were real.

The snow continued to fall and now the figures stirred as well. At first all did seem merry. The fire crackled, the candles twinkled on the tree. Then the clock began to whirl, the hands moving faster and faster. The windows flashed from light to dark – from snow to rain to sun. Leaves splattered against the panes and then again, the steady fall of snow.

The little brass plaque on the base of the snow globe changed as well. It now read: CHRISTMAS, 1861. A year had passed within the globe. The miniature family had been filled with Christmas spirit, but now grew more sombre. The father sat down, then lay flat on the sofa. He seemed to be in pain. The mother kneeled beside him, holding his hand. A young man came through the door – where had the door come from? – and one of the daughters ran towards him, her shining brown hair streaming behind her. The two were soon deep in conversation, heads together. With growing unease, Katie realized she knew these people. She held the globe closer; so close that she could see the worry lines between the girl's serious grey eyes.

Some sort of debate was going on. The two young people turned – could Katie really hear the rustle of the girl's long skirt? They walked towards Katie, towards the edge of the globe. They pressed against the curve of the glass and looked up. Katie was startled as their eyes met hers. They could see her. Their tiny hands were against the clear glass and Katie could distinguish the pattern of their palms.

'What the . . . Mary, Mother of Jesus,' Dolores gasped, just over Katie's shoulder. But Katie barely heard her. Slowly and gently, she placed the snow globe on the coffee table, and learning forward, careful not to fog the glass, she rested the tips of her index fingers against the glass – touching their tiny hands with her own large ones. The girl in the globe looked up. Her pupils dilated and her grey eyes turned to black. A voice called. Not the girl's voice. It was alluring, with a soft low hiss. It called her name 'Katie . . . Katie . . . the time has come to play your part.' She leaned forward, drawn to the voice.

Katie could hear Dolores, shouting behind her, but it was too late. Someone was yanking her forward, pulling her into a world that was inky, dark and wild. Something wrapped around her, cloaking her with energy both enslaving and empowering. An intoxicating pulse ran through her veins. 'Katie,' the voice demanded.

Katie gave a fierce shout in return, as strange wild impulses pounded through her. This was a new world – deep, evil and exciting. And then Katie came to a juddering halt. She could feel hands wrapped around her ankles, pulling her back. A completely different sensation surged up her legs. Snatches of sound came to Katie: the murmur of women together, the click of knitting needles and voices raised in song.

Steal away . . . steal away . . .
Steal away from evil
Don' take that hand of sin
'be buried in my grave
'for I become a slave
Steal away . . . steal away . . .

Hadn't she heard this song before? Some kind of Baptist spiritual that Dolores sang while she was ironing? The clicking of needles, the harmless gossip of a group of women, the soft wail of a hymn: these were the sounds of Dolores's life. They were prosaic and gentle, but as powerful in their own way as the vaulting shriek of blackness that threatened to engulf her.

'It hurts,' she thought, 'it hurts.' She was being pulled and pushed; her body would break in two. The walking stick juddered in her hand, banging against her head. The scarf around her neck tightened. Something rasped against her skin, scraping her badly. Friction turned to heat; she was burning – that strange, scorched, electrical smell filled her nostrils. 'It's like a space capsule, re-entering the atmosphere,' she thought, gasping. 'But I'm the capsule, moving through time and space. And I've got no protection. It's going to kill me.' She could feel her body beginning to splinter. She couldn't breathe. And then nothing – blackness – only the burning raging inside.

Chapter Five

Alice and James, 1861

The first thing Katie saw was the snow, through the window. Cool and white. Calm. For a long time she didn't move. Why should she? And then she turned her head gingerly to the side. She was lying on a bright, woven Indian carpet, next to a large tufted footstool. A fire glowed in the grate. Looking up she could see candles burning in their sconces. Her whole body ached. Was she bleeding? Katie closed her eyes.

She heard footsteps, running, a door banged open and two male voices argued as they crossed the room. One was obviously quite young, his voice cracking with anxiety. 'Dash it all,' he exclaimed. 'You could have told us that you had called her. And why has she landed here?'

'I haven't the slightest idea.' The other man was older, his world-weary voice tinged with a continental accent.

'You must have called her,' the young man insisted.

'I did not. And I certainly did not call the very unusual person lying in a heap next to her.'

A lighter step followed, and a girlish voice overrode them with a hint of hauteur. 'It doesn't matter who called Katie. She is our friend. We *do* need her. I do not know why you are standing here arguing. She might be hurt, and that person with her is decidedly so.'

At the sound of the girl's voice, Katie relaxed. She knew that voice: pretty, English, old-fashioned, surprisingly firm and just a bit grand. It was a voice she always kept locked away in her mind. She trusted it with all her heart. The voice belonged to Princess Alice. Katie opened her eyes.

All was clear. There was no point saying 'Where am I?' It was the place that lay hidden in Katie's memory, the cause of her scribbling, and the source of her visions. It was the reason Mimi looked frightened and the explanation for Katie's hours in a psychiatrist's office. How could she not have remembered it all – this vital and important part of her life? She was with her friends, not just Princess Alice, but also James O'Reilly. She was in the nineteenth century.

Then the pain came over her in waves. She felt as if an internal war had been waged through her body.

Princess Alice knelt down beside her. 'Where does it hurt, dear?' she asked.

'Everywhere,' Katie said. 'It's normally not this bad; I'm usually a pretty good traveller. Is someone here with me? Are they OK?' She turned her head to see James crouched over another person, a mass of rumpled and torn clothes. Gently he turned the body over. Katie gasped and tried to sit up. It was Dolores. 'Oh my God!' she cried. 'Is she breathing? Is she alive? You've got to save her, you've just got to . . .'

'What do you think I'm doing?' James snapped, loosening Dolores' collar and placing his fingers against her neck to check her pulse. 'She's breathing more steadily now and her pulse is beginning to slow, though she's still unconscious. She'll probably be fine. But Katie, do lie down. Try and do as you're told for once. Alice – make her . . .'

Alice pursed her lips and tried to look stern, but couldn't quite manage it. She was too happy at the sight of her friend. 'Please Katie, don't start by being so stubborn,' she lectured with a belying sweetness. 'We'll have lots of time to be stubborn together, but right now you have to rest.'

Katie had to admit, she felt much better lying down. James's father was the Royal Household physician and James was training to be a doctor. Alice, too, had excellent nursing skills. She'd best let them get on with the task at hand. Katie smiled at Alice. New York was a busy, exciting place to live and she attended one of the best progressive schools in the city. But she'd never really connected with the other kids. And Mimi didn't have a lot of time for her. Alice was the first person who'd really understood Katie, been truly interested in her and wanted to be her friend – Alice, a princess from another country and another time. Katie had missed her desperately. She just hadn't known it.

From the corner of her eye Katie could see the bottom tip of a walking stick; that final voice in the room had to be Bernardo DuQuelle. 'You didn't call me, DuQuelle,' she murmured. 'I heard you say you didn't call me.'

'We didn't call, yet you are here, quite the mystery . . .'

Katie glanced up. From where she lay, DuQuelle's long curved nose looked like an overhanging cliff. There was something ancient and monumental about him. He bowed low over Katie and, gently pulling back her fingers, removed the walking stick from her clenched hand. It had left a long red welt across her palm. Deftly, he untangled the scarf around her neck. Lifting it to his nose, he sniffed it and rolled his eyes. 'Travelling through time,' he snorted, 'this was more of a catapult. Something was urging you on, but the drag of this other . . . being . . . held you back.'

Katie closed her eyes again. She really was exhausted. 'Dolores,' she said. 'It's Dolores. She always looks after me.'

'But of course,' said DuQuelle, 'the nanny. Well, she almost killed you. You were lucky to avoid spontaneous combustion. You've been scorched. I can sense the struggle and smell the pain. The question is: why are you here? I don't like the smell of this.'

Katie was worried too. And even more unsettled than usual. That strong, dark thing that had moved through her. That strange calling voice. They had nothing to do with her friends.

'I for one am so very pleased to see you,' Princess Alice said, examining her friend's burnt hand. 'We do have troubles and we do need you. James must attend to that burn. And then, are you well enough to listen?'

Katie nodded. 'But Dolores first. Will she be OK?'

James scowled at Katie. He was struggling to get Dolores's bulk onto a sofa. 'She's just coming to. We should leave her alone for a few minutes.'

'Then tell me,' Katie said. 'Tell me all about it.'

'There is a war developing,' Princess Alice told her, 'a war with your country.'

'What year is it?' Katie asked. James had opened his bag, and was applying a salve to Katie's palm. He snorted. It always surprised him that Katie, the time traveller, had no concept of time.

'It's 1861,' Alice said, ignoring James.

Katie remembered the plaque on the snow globe. 'Is it Christmas, 1861?' she asked.

James rolled his eyes. 'If you didn't know the year, you certainly won't know the day. It's actually November. The 22nd of November, 1861.'

November 1861 and war was brewing. Katie ran through the timeline of all the awful wars America had fought. 1861 – way before Afghanistan, before Vietnam, before Korea, before WWII, before WWI . . . 'It's the American Civil War,' she decided, 'and it's a really, really bad one. North against South, Cotton is King, the Emancipation Proclamation, over 600,000 men killed, and then Lincoln is assassin . . .'

'Stop!' DuQuelle cried out. 'Don't you remember the damage you can do by revealing history? You have been chosen and you know what happens. As part of the Tempus Fugit, you must make certain historical events stay on course. To tell Princess Alice would be to change history, to . . .'

'I'm in a lot of pain,' Katie protested, waving her now bandaged hand. 'I forgot.'

'It's natural that she would,' Alice chimed in, defending her friend. 'She shouldn't be speaking at all. Now Katie, I will tell you what we know and you can listen quietly. America is at war, the Unionist North against the Confederacy South. It seems there will be a long and difficult war. I'm certain Katie is sorry for the damage done, but she has just confirmed this. The question is: does Britain enter the war?'

Bernardo DuQuelle caught Katie's eye and she remained silent.

'The South is prodding us to a declaration in their favour,' Alice continued. 'The Prime Minister thinks we will fight on the side of the South to protect our cotton interests. My father and mother are against this.'

'And they are right,' James added. 'The South depends on slaves and as a country we cannot support slavery, no matter what our financial interests.'

'My father is working so hard to keep us from war,' Princess Alice continued. 'This is taxing enough. But there have also been a series of events, strange and grue-some happenings. He is becoming suspicious . . .' Alice's voice tailed off. It was always embarrassing for her to dis-cuss the supernatural elements of their lives.

Bernardo DuQuelle felt no such qualms. 'Prince Albert is a man of intelligence. He begins to wonder and to doubt. He does not understand some of the occurrences. Why should he? They are not of his world. This has added greatly to his anxiety and fatigue.'

Katie thought about the snow globe. This might be November, but she'd had a peek at December. From what she'd seen, 1861 did not end on a high note

Princess Alice sighed. 'This additional worry is too much, particularly when added to his endless daily work.

I do not wish to be disloyal to my mother, but the Queen thinks my father is perfection and with this comes a burden. She believes he can solve any problem and complete any labour. Her faith in him is destroying his health.'

Katie looked at the strange trio. Princess Alice, James O'Reilly and Bernardo DuQuelle. She had lived through so much with these three: an assassination attempt on Queen Victoria, a duel on Hampstead Heath, the battle-fields of the Crimean War. She had met the Queen, THE Queen, Queen Victoria. Katie shook her head. How could she ever have forgotten . . . being presented at court . . . kissing the Queen's hand . . . working with Florence Nightingale at the Hospital in Scutari, sur-viving the Charge of the Light Brigade? She glanced at James and remembered, with a great pang that not everyone had survived. His brother Jack, that brave young soldier, had died. One of the noble 600 . . . She only hoped his sister Grace was still alive. She had been so ill. It was consumption . . .

All these people were so important to Katie. Yet in her own time, they were nothing but shadows. Katie couldn't take her eyes off Alice, so beautiful and serious; her time nursing in the Crimea had matured her. She turned to James. He had always been purposeful, even stubborn and occasionally rude. But she knew that his gruffness disguised a true heart and a fine brain. The years of hard work and study were now paying off. He was capable and confident and much more grown up. Alice and James were the same age as Katie, but she felt gawky and childish compared to her friends. Only DuQuelle remained unchanged. He had started old, and looked no older. He did not age. He was the one who held the answers.

'These strange happenings, do you think they are the work of the Malum?' she asked. Princess Alice moved closer to James. The Malum – potent and evil – fed off the brute force created by the worst type of man. 'They'll love this,' Katie added, 'I mean, a war. There's nothing the Malum likes more than a war. It will be a feast for them. This war could create the world they need to thrive and dominate. Can the Verus defeat them? Is the Verus even trying? Does Lucia continue the virtuous fight?'

DuQuelle lowered his eyes and examined the silver tip of his cane. He was not embarrassed by his own world and the battles of the Verus and the Malum. His relationship with them was complex though, particularly with Lucia. 'She fights the good fight, Lucia does,' he said rather drily. 'Good versus evil. It could almost be a pantomime, if it had less effect on your world. But you are correct, the Malum gains power. There is something afoot, something big – and it's gathering speed and force. We simply don't know enough about it.'

A frightened cry came from the sofa. Despite her pain, Katie was up, immediately, at Dolores' side. 'Don't worry,' she said. 'I'm here. I'll take care of you.'

Dolores took in the room. The overstuffed and fringed chairs, the ornate marble mantelpiece, the candlelit room. Her eyes became wider as she saw Princess Alice and James. When her gaze stopped at DuQuelle, they almost popped out of her head.

'I can't believe this,' Dolores muttered over and over. 'I CANNOT believe this.' She clutched Katie's hand. 'Child, either I've entered your mind, or gone out of my own.' Then she dropped from the sofa to her knees and began to pray, hard. 'Oh Lord, have mercy on me. I've seen the visions and I need your help.'

Bernardo DuQuelle tapped his walking stick impatiently on the floor. He did not find this helpful. An interloper – Tempus Stativus. Her presence here was awkward and he suspected it interferred with Katie's powers. He turned quite sternly to Dolores. 'Stop this caterwauling instantly or I shall send you back into the abyss.' Dolores hiccupped once and fell silent; Katie had never seen her so cowed.

'Leave her alone,' Katie said. 'What has she ever done to you?'

In answer, DuQuelle walked over to a nearby table laden with albums and books and, choosing one, handed it to Katie. 'The question is: what has she done to you? Let us examine the problem,' he said. 'Read this. Read any section of the book you wish.' Katie obediently opened the book and began.

Oh! But he was a tight-fisted hand at the grindstone,
Scrooge! A squeezing, wrenching, grasping, scraping,
clutching, covetous old sinner! Hard and sharp as flint,
from which no steel had ever struck out generous fire;
secret, and self-contained, and solitary as an oyster. The
cold within him froze his features, nipped his pointed
nose, shrivelled his cheek . . .'

'Nothing,' DuQuelle said. 'It is as I thought.'

'She read beautifully,' Alice interjected. 'Mr Dickens's work, *A Christmas Carol*, splendidly declaimed.'

'I begin to understand the problem,' James interrupted. 'Katie, did anything out of the ordinary happen while you were reading?'

Katie shook her head. 'Nothing. I get it too. The words were great – great to read, but I saw nothing and felt nothing. My power of the visions – the endless visions created by the written word – they are gone.'

DuQuelle took out a handkerchief and wiped his forehead. The paleness of his skin made the cloth look grey. 'Something *has* weakened your powers. I can only assume it is the pull of another, from your own time.' He cast a distrustful glance towards Dolores and she glared back with a mixture of fear and hostility. 'We must separate the two of you,' he decided. 'I will send for Florence. She has a knack for this type of thing . . .'

'I'm not going anywhere with that man,' Dolores protested, 'and I'm not leaving this here child with him neither.' Her face contracted with pain and she fainted.

'That's enough, DuQuelle,' Katie exclaimed. 'What are you trying to do? Kill Dolores? I don't think she's the problem.' The dark power that had emerged while she was hurtling through time, perhaps that was the problem. But for some reason she didn't tell her friends about it. Instead, she crouched by the sofa and wrapped her arms around the large woman. Dolores had looked after Katie for so many years. Now it was Katie's turn to look after Dolores. Bernardo DuQuelle watched them both with an impassive face. What was human so often did not touch him. 'I still believe this woman is the cause. You must be separated. I will call my carriage,' was all he said, leaving them without a backwards glance.

James prised Katie from Dolores and laid his ear against her ample chest. 'She has taken a turn for the worse,' he muttered, 'her pulse runs and races. Her heart rate has not synchronized to our time. She is in a state of apoplexy.'

'Apoplexy is common and normally very treatable,' Alice added, giving Katie a comforting look.

'Normally, yes,' James replied. 'But neither of us can truly help. It's the time travel. We do not understand the added components of time and space.'

Alice and James looked at each other. They seemed to be able to communicate, even in their silence.

'Yes, I agree,' Alice said, as if in reply. 'DuQuelle is right. Miss Nightingale is our best hope.'

James turned to his medical kit and began to mix something in a glass beaker.

'Warm this,' he ordered Alice, 'as close to the fire as possible.' When the liquid had heated he spooned it into Dolores's mouth. 'Quinine, camphor, capsicum, calomel and laudanum,' he explained. 'This will calm her for the time being, but truly, Katie, I cannot treat her. We must send her to Miss Nightingale.'

Katie nodded. She trusted James.

James's medicines began to take effect. As Dolores opened her eyes, Princess Alice spoke to her. 'Miss Dolores, I have heard so much about you,' she said. 'Katie is a true friend to us. She has come to visit before.' Dolores nodded, and then shook her head. 'You need medical attention,' Princess Alice continued. 'We are sending you to the leading expert on your illness. She will help you. But Katie will have to stay here with us. It's for her own safety.'

Dolores tried to stand up in protest, but she was too weak. Princess Alice sat down next to her on the sofa and fixed her with those serious grey eyes. Dolores calmed down immediately. Her face softened, her agitation vanished. Princess Alice had this effect.

'You need to convalesce,' Alice continued in her sweet, calm voice. 'But you won't be alone. Miss Nightingale has many interesting visitors. You will enjoy meeting some of them. Miss Mary Seacole is visiting from Jamaica. She is kind-hearted and most entertaining.'

'Alice is right Dolores,' Katie encouraged her. 'I promise you, I'll be fine here. And Florence Nightingale is the best, the greatest.' Katie couldn't help speculating. Dolores had bossed her, mothered her and nursed her for years and years. What would the mighty Dolores make of the mightier Florence Nightingale?

James helped Dolores to her feet as DuQuelle returned. 'I'm not going with that man,' she protested again.

'No, you are not,' DuQuelle replied crisply. 'James, my carriage can be found at St George's Gateway. Please escort this . . . person . . . to London – South Street, Mayfair, to be exact. There you will find Miss Florence Nightingale and her friend from the Crimea, Miss Mary Seacole. Give Miss Nightingale this letter, it tells all. She will receive you. '

'You'll be safe with James,' Katie reassured Dolores. 'He's, well, he really is a good friend.' James shot Katie a look – rather startled – but she felt he was not displeased. James might be gruff, but he valued friendship. Dolores was too weak for further protest. Katie kissed her gently on the cheek and James half led, half carried her from the room. Katie hated to see her go.

'I've had enough of hysterics, fainting and fits,' DuQuelle announced. 'These displays of emotion are most unsettling.' He looked decidedly unruffled. Couldn't he care for anyone? At that moment, Katie truly hated him.

'I have some understanding of your feelings, Katie,' he added. 'If I were capable if it, I'd probably dislike you as well. For now, though, we have work to do.' His uncanny ability to read her mind irritated Katie even more.

'Question number one,' he said. 'Who called Katie, and what were their motives? For once I am baffled. Perhaps Katie has re-entered our lives as a figure of malevolence.'

Princess Alice tossed her head and put out a hand to silence DuQuelle. 'James, Katie and I have a bond beyond your suspicions. We have been through much together, and I expect we will go through much more.'

Katie looked at Alice with admiration. She really could be quite regal at times. And yes, they had been through a lot – wars, and anarchists, duels and demons. But there had also been much laughter – midnight feasts, whispered secrets and good times. A wave of affection washed over Katie.

DuQuelle bowed slightly. He actually seemed to like being bossed about by Princess Alice. 'I believe Katie can do little harm if we guard her carefully. We will keep Katie here, at Windsor Castle. And while she rests, I will revive her alias, Miss Katherine Tappan, so that Katie can move freely at court. My forgery skills are quite useful in a case like this. There are letters to be written. Mr Lewis Tappan is sending his daughter to England, again.'

DuQuelle picked up the debris around Katie, handing her the walking stick and the ancient book. 'What is this?' he asked. It was the glass snow globe. He examined it carefully.

'That thing, that's the culprit!' Katie cried. 'You know perfectly well that's what started all this trouble.'

Bernardo DuQuelle ignored her, and rolled the globe in his slender white fingers. 'Now, what could this be?' he murmured to himself.

'Really, DuQuelle,' Katie protested, 'you might not have called me, but you did send this gift. It came with your calling card. The writing was yours.'

Alice came forward to look at the object. DuQuelle shook his head. 'I sent no gift.' He held up his pince-nez and examined the globe carefully. 'I have never seen this – not in your time, or any time.' He turned it upside down and then shook the globe. 'It carries no message,' DuQuelle said. 'It tells no tale.'

Katie tried to take it from him. 'But it's very clear,' she said. 'Let me show you.' Reaching for the glass ball she gave a startled cry. There was no snow. The snow globe was empty. The Victorian family was gone.

Chapter Six

The War in America

Katie should have had more faith in Dolores. The shock had been huge, of course. Dolores was no traveller, and now to be hurtled through time and space . . . But Dolores was a robust woman with her own equally strong beliefs. She had no intention of dying. Her health flourished in the care of Miss Nightingale. She was up and about within a week. 'Thank God for tough, capable women,' Katie thought as she walked along the London streets with James and Alice. At that moment, though, Katie didn't feel very tough. She feared she might collapse, right there on the pavement. Would she ever get used to these clothes?

DuQuelle's forgery skills had come in handy and Katie had a new identity, one more acceptable to the Palace.

She reappeared as Miss Katherine Tappan, daughter of Lewis Tappan – businessman and abolitionist from New York. Her identity had been a savvy choice by DuQuelle. Prince Albert, as the President of the Society for the Extinction of the Slave Trade, admired the anti-slavery work of Lewis Tappan, but did not know him personally. Katie had taken this role in her last plunge through time. She had been presented at Court and was now free to socialize in royal circles.

This freedom, however, did not extend to her body. With a Victorian identity came Victorian clothes. She wore a dark green silk-and-wool challis gown with double layered bell sleeves. The bodice hooked in front with hundreds of tiny buttons. To fend off the December cold, she was wrapped in a matching velvet mantle, wonderfully fringed and braided. She almost sank to her knees each morning when she put them on. Katie had to admit the clothes were beautiful. But this beauty came at a price. Underneath the soft woollens was a corset with whalebone stays, and that morning Princess Alice had laced it for her – very tight.

'Hold on, you guys,' Katie complained. 'I've got whalebone digging into my side, I really can't breathe.' She leaned against a lamp post, gasping.

'It's your own fault,' James snapped. 'You call yourself modern, yet you're trussed up in a corset. Don't you know how what a corset does to you? It will weaken your muscles, rearrange your internal organs, affect your respiratory system, and damage your health for life.' As a doctor in training, James felt he had the right to lecture women on their health, and their vanity.

'There was no other way to fit into this dress,' Katie protested. 'I'm so big – Alice filched it from the wardrobe of some courtier, a tubby middle-aged woman who's been eating ten-course meals for three decades.'

Katie pushed off from the lamp post, but came to an abrupt halt. The spring steel hoops of her crinoline had become entangled with the lamp post. James was scowling and even loyal Alice looked slightly disconcerted. Katie gave the thing a sharp tug and it sprang back into place, her skirt swinging madly like a tolling bell. Other people in the street stopped to stare. She was showing much too much ankle and leg.

Princess Alice turned slightly pink; but in truth she was used to James's direct way of speaking, and Katie's blunt manners. She'd even grown to like their quirky behaviour. It made life more exciting.

'First of all, I did not "filch" the dress, as you put it. I borrowed it,' Alice said rather primly. 'Secondly, you'll have to admit that the new steel hoops are ever so much lighter than the endless petticoats we used to wear, even if they are rather difficult to manage at the beginning. And finally, Katie dear, you are not big. It's simply that women are larger framed in your time. I think you look lovely.'

It was a kind compliment even though Alice was the pretty one. Now that she was older, Alice chose her own clothes, of a simpler, more elegant style than the rest of the Royal Family. Her dark blue velvet dress suited her slender frame. And when she walked, her crinoline skirt swayed gracefully.

'You're the only person in the world who thinks so,' Katie replied. 'Me? Lovely? I think we all remember my nickname at Court – the giraffe. And I'm even taller now. I'll have to leave Court life and join the circus if I keep growing.'

James spoke up, rather dourly, 'You look like Katie, that's good enough for us. And Jack so liked that lively funny look of yours . . .' He stumped along after that and all three were silent. Jack was James's older brother, killed in the Charge of the Light Brigade. After some time, James spoke again. 'I don't mean to spoil our day out,' he said. 'It's such a treat for Alice.'

Princess Alice hated her life of privilege and seclusion, and today she'd had a tiny victory, a minor escape. She had travelled by train from Windsor to London. Not in the Royal Carriage, attended by governesses, servants and a military escort, not even in a first-class carriage. She had travelled second class, in a carriage filled with normal people – her people, the public.

Princess Alice's eyes gleamed. She had found the speed and the crowds quite intoxicating. As they crossed

Piccadilly, James reached out to take her elbow.

Even studious James had noticed the glow in her cheeks and the toss of her head. Turning the corner to South Audley Street, they came upon a long trench in the centre of the road. Dozens of men were hard at work. James stopped staring at Princess Alice, and looked with even more admiration at the building site before them. 'It is the new sewage system, the most modern in Europe,' he explained. 'They have finally broken ground.'

Alice stepped closer to peer into the deep hole. 'How wonderful!' she exclaimed. 'Dr Snow says this system of waste disposal is vital. I've read his treatise on the spread of cholera. It is not air-borne after all, but comes from unclean water. But then you attended his lecture at the Royal Society. Oh! I wish I could have gone. I have so many questions, James. I am certain you will understand it better than I ever will.'

The din around them increased as a steam-powered digger began to fling up piles of earth. Katie couldn't hear a thing. She could only watch a mute show of affection, as James moved Alice away from the dirt and din. Shouting in her ear, he gestured to the piles of bricks and drew diagrams with his finger in the air. Alice nodded and smiled, looking decidedly enthusiastic about all this talk of effluence and disease.

Katie wanted to laugh. They were so suited to each other, so happy. 'They are falling in love,' she thought, 'and they don't even know it.' The laughter was quickly replaced by a pang of sadness. James and Alice came from different worlds. They could be friends, study partners, medical pioneers, but not the thing they might like most. Katie sighed, and they turned up Park Lane towards South Street, and the home of Florence Nightingale.

'I am so pleased Miss Nightingale has taken in Miss Seacole. I find it criminal, the way she has been neglected since the end of the Crimean War,' Alice said.

James nodded. 'She did much good for our soldiers and gave her all: her knowledge of natural medicines, her extensive experience nursing and all her wealth besides. And what did she get in return? A trip to the bankruptcy courts.' They both shook their heads over the unfairness.

'*The Times* has set up a subscription to aid her,' Alice said more brightly. 'My brother Bertie has agreed to give funds. There is a festive ball at Windsor Castle tonight; a large celebration with courtiers, clergy, diplomats and artists. This would be the perfect time to announce the subscription for Mary Seacole. Perhaps, James, you would draft a message. Bertie could read it to the guests.'

The streets became crowded once they'd turned into Park Lane – carriages filled with ladies out for a winter ride, hansom cabs hurrying to appointments. A military guard trooped out from their barracks, towards Buckingham Palace, and pedestrians stopped to watch. Despite the people all around her, Katie suddenly felt lonely. James and Alice had their talk of science, their shared life at court and their endless do-gooding. They'd grown closer and left Katie a little bit behind. She felt a tiny pang of bitterness. This would not do. She thought of Dolores and picked up her pace. Dolores's health might be improving, but she was still in a strange nation, and an even stranger time. Best get to South Street as quickly as possible.

James and Alice, wrapped up in their own conversation, had moved ahead and were soon lost amongst the many bobbing heads. Katie hurried after them, but then something pulled her back. 'Damn this crinoline,' she thought, and turning to unhook it again, came face to face with an unknown man. His clothes were rough and his face even more so. Dark lines fell from the ridge of his nose to the bottom of his chin. The man needed a shave and probably a wash. Katie's annoyance turned to panic when she realized that he was deliberately stepping on the back of her skirt.

'Going somewhere?' he jeered, 'I think not.' And pinning Katie's arms roughly behind her back, he hustled her along Park Lane. 'Any noise from you and I'll break your arm,' he hissed into her ear. A sharp tug showed Katie that he meant it. Alice and James turned the corner and disappeared from view.

Katie tried to attract the attention of the people on the street, mouthing the word 'Help', her eyes wide with pleading. But everyone seemed interested in their own lives. The nannies complacently pushed their babies in prams. Servant girls swung their baskets as they went about their shopping. Young ladies hurried into carriages with their lists of social calls. No one had time for Katie. Park Lane flashed before her, and then she was shoved down a flight of steps, into the basement area of a grand house. As Katie cried out, a coarse hand clasped over her mouth, and with a final painful twist of her arm, she was pushed through a door.

The basement was dark, and as she struggled, Katie couldn't see much. She only knew that there were others around her now. She fought hard, kicking and scratching, but they were too much for her. The corset, the skirts and the sheer volume of clothing did not help. She felt as if she might suffocate, but still she fought on. She had no choice. So few people knew who she was or even that she existed, and two of those few had moved on, talking together, unaware. She was on her own.

Katie was no match for the men. Quickly they tied her arms behind her, and balling a piece of cloth, forced it into her mouth.

'Is this really necessary? I'd hardly call it diplomacy,' called a young man's voice from the darkness.

'If she'd clawed you like a cat, you'd tie her up too,' came the gruff reply. 'She's dangerous, this one.' What was it about their voices? With a start, Katie realized they were Americans.

'Do stop struggling. Please sit down,' the younger voice said. A chair was pushed forward; a gentler hand guided her to it. 'We don't want to harm you,' he added, 'but we do need to talk with you. We need your help.' Someone struck a match, and in the brief glow Katie saw a face that startled her. The straight brown hair, the strong nose, the blue eyes that held a private joke – why did she know the face of this young man? He turned from her, and fiddling with the wick, finally got the oil lamp burning.

Her hands were tied, but Katie still had her feet. Rising, she made a dart for the door, but it was useless. 'Don't run,' he almost pleaded, 'don't make us tie you to the chair.' He held the lamp closer, and Katie again looked at the familiar face of a stranger. Gently he took the cloth from her mouth. 'Don't yell,' he said. 'Just listen.'

Katie's eyes began to adjust to the darkness, and the flame of the lamp grew stronger. There were quite a few of them in the basement – all men. They moved closer and, crouching on their heels, stared. Her thoughts changed abruptly. She now hoped Alice and James *wouldn't* find her. It would only place them in peril. With this dangerous band of men, who knew what would happen? It would be better if she didn't cry out. Clearing her throat to steady her nerves, and breathing deeply, she spoke quietly. 'Why am I here? What do you want?'

'We want the truth.' There was nothing gentle about the older man as he glared at Katie. 'We all know Lewis

Tappan, and you are not his daughter. You'll need to be telling us who you really are.' He appeared to be their leader, and he didn't like Katie at all.

Still, she tried to sidestep his demand. 'Why should I tell you anything?' she said stoutly. 'You're just a bunch of thugs. And I asked the first questions: who are you? And what do you want?' All this sounded very brave and tough, but it wasn't how Katie felt inside. She was sick with fear.

The older man stood up and Katie flinched. She wished she hadn't, it made her look such a coward. Her knees were shaking and her burnt hand pulsed with pain. She scanned the room, searching for the doorway. She had to get out of there.

The younger man sensed her desperation. 'You'll want to help once you understand,' he said encouragingly. 'I know this must seem terrifying to you – being abducted in the street, in broad daylight, and dragged into a basement – and we're sorry it has come to this. We did need to meet with you in secrecy.'

Katie tried to keep her guard up. 'Who are you?' she asked again.

The young man laughed. 'You are stubborn.' There was admiration in his voice. 'Our cause is just; I can assure you of that. We know you will sympathize once you hear our story.'

Katie peered into his face. He wasn't much older than

she was, but his face was etched with faint lines; a young face that had seen too much.

'OK,' she said. 'You talk. But it has to be you. I'll only listen to you.'

He pulled up a chair and sat directly opposite Katie. The others muttered in protest but kept their distance. 'We come from President Abraham Lincoln of the United States of America.'

Katie gave a start. She was used to Princess Alice and even Queen Victoria, but a figure like Abraham Lincoln – someone from her own country, her own history – that was a lot to take in. 'Abe— I mean, the President has sent you?' she asked.

'Yes,' the young man smiled at her reaction. 'We are abolitionists; our cause is to end slavery in the United States. President Lincoln is determined to free the slaves, but first the North must win our nation's civil war. We are here to influence Britain and convince this country to take up our cause.'

'Plead with this country is more like it,' the older man sounded bitter. 'The British, so high and mighty, they make us feel like beggars. This here is a country that condemns slavery, won't have it on their own shores, yet they aren't joining the Unionists in the North, and just might side with the Confederacy in the South. The Brits just ain't listening. They've got no sense.'

The younger man sighed and continued in his gentle

tone. 'My friends call me Sonny, I hope you will too.'

Katie smothered a smile – Sonny.

'You think it's a funny name,' he said, catching her look. 'It's quite typical of the South, for I am Southern born and raised. Our family lived in Virginia even before the birth of our nation. You will find my ancestors' signature on the Declaration of Independence. They see themselves as the finest folk in Virginia: cultured, enlightened Americans.'

The other men murmured dissent, and Sonny suddenly looked miserable. 'How could we be so blind?' he asked. 'We are plantation owners, and all of our wealth, our power, our influence, is based on slavery. My family believe they are morally superior, but this is absurd. All of our grandeur rests on the backs of men and women who came to us in chains.'

Katie could feel his sadness washing over her. 'There must be someone in your family who feels the way you do?' she said. Along with the sadness in his face there was now a touch of bewildered loneliness, like a child who finds himself lost in a crowd.

'No,' he replied, 'not one. I have seen my mother and sister, playing duets on the piano while a slave is whipped in the yard. And my father,' Sonny stopped and swallowed hard, several times, before he could go on, 'let's just say my father is worse, much worse.'

There was complete silence in the basement. If Katie's

hands hadn't been tied, she would have reached out to comfort him. 'I can't even imagine,' she said. 'It must have been . . . like . . . so hard . . .'

'I wanted to save the world,' he said, 'but in their world, I just seemed crazy.' Where had Katie heard that before?

'I had to leave,' Sonny explained. 'How could my family sit calmly taking tea, while hundreds of human beings around them were treated like animals? When war brewed, I knew I could never fight for the South. I left home and joined the underground movement against slavery. There I met this group of like-minded men – Jeb Lawson here, and Bill Patterson and Elias Finch.'

Katie wondered, would she have had the strength to leave home and fight for her cause? She was a Unionist of course. As a New Yorker, she was a Northerner through and through. But this was a war, well over a hundred years behind her. A low voice spoke in her head, 'don't get involved'. She didn't like this voice at all.

'I can't tell you how much I admire what you've done,' she finally said, 'but I can't think of any way to help.'

Jeb Lawson cut across her. 'There are lots of things you could do,' he said. 'You might already be acting – and not for the North, but for the South; for all we know, you might be some kind of Southern spy. Let's just take a look at you: an unknown girl, who shows up, all alone, in England. You're travelling under a false identity. Yet somehow you manage to worm your way into court life;

a complete stranger who is on friendly terms with the Queen's own daughter and has cosy chats with Prince Albert's Private Secretary, Bernardo DuQuelle. It seems a girl like you would be hearing many of the nation's secrets, maybe even the country's thoughts and plans on the war in America.'

Katie was horrified. She looked towards the door, calculating a means of escape. Sonny leaned forward in his chair, locking eyes. 'We want to trust you,' he said. 'I've told you my story, and every word of it is true. Now I think it's only fair if you tell us yours.'

He was so decent. And what he said made sense. But it was impossible for Katie to tell her story. She could just imagine the looks on their faces when she told them. 'I'm Katie Berger-Jones-Burg – my popstar mother gets divorced a lot – I live in New York City in the twenty-first century and I TRAVEL THROUGH TIME.' If she hadn't been so terrified, she would have laughed.

'I can't tell you who I am,' she said. 'It would put other people in danger. And even worse, I can't tell you why I'm here, because I don't know – I just don't know what I'm doing here.' She could hear her own voice and she sounded awful: defensive, frightened and really, really lame. Looking around the room, she saw suspicion and distrust. She sought out Sonny instinctively. 'The one thing I can tell you is that I am not a spy – not for anyone, but especially not for the South.'

Sonny smiled ever so slightly, the only friendly face in the room. 'You are about as far from a Southern Belle as they come. Somehow, I do believe you. So you are not a spy and you don't know why you are here. Then we can give you a reason to be here, a cause worth believing in. Help us to keep our country as one.'

Katie paused. She hated to give away anything about herself, but she was interested in this young man and she believed in him. When the dark voice rose in her, she batted it away. 'I support your cause,' finally she said. 'I admire President Lincoln. I mean, we all celebrate his life and mourn his—' she stopped abruptly, biting her tongue. She could not tell Sonny what every American in her time knew: that the North won the war and kept America together, that President Lincoln freed the slaves in 1863 and that the great man was assassinated in 1865.

Yet for Sonny she had said enough. 'I knew it,' he exulted. 'You had the look of a true patriot.' Katie smiled back at him, feeling like she had passed a test.

'So you say you support the North,' Jeb Lawson interrupted. 'Well then, prove it. Work with us. Use your position to talk up the North and pass us information.'

Katie wondered if she could really change the course of Lincoln's life. Could she stop the assassination? And then a dreadful thought occurred: could her actions actually make the North lose the war? And result in a world of slavery, which she, Katie, had created? Keeping history on track was one thing, but changing it was too dangerous. 'I can't. No matter how much I want to help, I can't become involved,' she said.

Sonny leaned forward and brushed a stray curl from her forehead. 'If you had seen what I've seen, you would not hesitate. You do not want to betray your friends, I understand that. Yet think of the burden of guilt, the blame that would befall the Royal Family should they choose to recognize the South as an independent nation. I have seen your friend, the lovely and gentle Princess Alice. How would she feel if Britain joined the South in battle and supported the enslavement of men?'

Katie's face showed her indecision and Jeb Lawson was quick to jump in. 'It is my belief that a girl, at court, who takes on a false identity, could be in big trouble. She could even be charged with high treason.'

Katie's heart had been thumping hard in her chest. Now it seemed to plummet to the ground. High treason. She knew the outcome of such a charge – hanging.

Sonny shot Jeb Lawson a furious look, and tried to reassure Katie. 'There's no need for such threats,' he said, 'as I know you will help us. All we need are trifles of information – anything you can learn of the Palace's opinions and the government's actions. And you can talk to the Princess; explain things to her that she otherwise might not understand.'

Katie tried to speak. There was a hint of betrayal in what Sonny was suggesting. He had misjudged two things: Princess Alice's intelligence and Katie's loyalty to her friend.

'Don't say anything,' Sonny continued. 'I don't need a reply. Just think about it.' He untied her arms. 'We're going to let you go,' he said.

'For now,' Jeb Lawson added. Right might be on his side, but Katie did not like that man.

Sonny simply ignored him. 'We will make contact again,' Sonny continued. 'You will come to make the right decision. I know you and I believe you know me. You will not let me down.'

Katie looked again at the straight brown hair, the strong nose, the blue eyes that had seen so much, yet still contained a hint of fun. She did know him, and this was baffling. She thought of her life – a life that spanned several centuries – and the people who filled it. How did this young abolitionist fit in?

Vivid scenes flitted and bubbled in the back of her mind. A doctor's office in New York City, a trivial funny conversation with a young man, and then abruptly she saw something that made her shut her eyes and press her hands against them: a stormy sky, the clatter and charge of horses, the cry of a young man, fallen in the battlefield. 'Oh, Katie,' he had said. 'Someone has blundered.' Jack O'Reilly – he seemed to be everywhere at times of duress.

She rubbed her palms hard across her eyes, trying to wipe this vision from her memory.

The men behind her were talking. 'I don't believe she is of any use,' one was saying. 'No girl is stable or steady enough to carry out such actions. There is that Lord, high up in the hierarchy, who sought us out. He's a strange man, but he says he has sympathy for our cause, influence at court and the money we need . . .' Sonny too heard these words. He turned to his comrades and, for the first time, Katie heard him lose his temper.

'Lord Belzen? You'd be insane to take him at his word. He is a dangerous man. I hear he is false. That he works with the South, burgling embassies and stealing dossiers of correspondence. Rumour has it that he is involved in the unrest in London. That gruesome murder, the body in the Thames – people say this is the work of Lord Belzen. Would you truly associate yourself with that man?'

Katie continued to rub her eyes, pretending that she wasn't listening. Belzen! To think that they were considering this, that the North would be in league with Belzen and the Malum. This war might be based on human freedom, but it could still be hijacked by pure evil. The low, soft voice in her head spoke again. 'This is not your concern.' Again, she pushed it away. Of course it was her concern; but could she help without endangering her friends, or herself?

Katie opened her eyes, ready with a hundred new

questions, but the men were gone. They had melted away, leaving her alone, in a dark basement, with some difficult choices to make.

Chapter Seven

South Street

It had seemed like hours – forever to Katie – but it must have been ten or twenty minutes at most. When she emerged from the basement, blinking at the cold winter sun, she could see James and Alice far ahead. James was consulting his pocket watch as Alice scanned the crowds. Spotting Katie, she waved and hurried towards her.

'I am so sorry we lost you,' Alice apologized. 'We thought you were with us, but when we turned you were gone.'

James loped over and, taking Katie by the arm, began to half-pull her towards South Street. 'We're going to be late now,' he complained. 'Besides, you've worried Princess Alice. What happened to you?' Katie opened her mouth to tell them everything. But that new dark speck of defiance stopped her.

'Everyone has a secret,' she reasoned with herself. 'Just look at James and Alice. They're not exactly opening up about their feelings for each other.'

'I just kind of got lost in the crowd,' she said, 'that's all that happened, OK? Now, what is Florence Nightingale's address? I'm dying to see Dolores.'

James and Alice nodded. They had complete confidence in her. Katie felt a pang; she was changing, and she didn't like it.

It wasn't a maid who answered the door to South Street, but Bernardo DuQuelle. His face, as always, was impassive, but his green eyes held a hint of frustration. 'I have been counting the minutes, awaiting your arrival,' he announced. 'Katie, perhaps you are the animal tamer we need. That . . . that . . . *nanny* of yours is an impossible house guest.'

'She's not exactly a nanny,' Katie explained. 'Dolores kind of does everything. Really, she runs our lives. Mimi calls her "our personal provider of domestic detox." You see, Mimi has problems with the concept of a master–servant relationship . . . but really she shouldn't, you know, Dolores has always been the master.'

DuQuelle shook his head. His usually coiffed and pomaded black curls were in disarray. 'Katie, don't babble. We need action. Your Dolores is trying to be the master in this house as well. And with a mistress such as Florence Nightingale, that is a mistake.'

At that moment Mary Seacole ran down the stairs. She was an unmistakable figure in her bright yellow dress and red calico scarf rising and falling on her bosom as she tried to catch her breath.

'I've no time for how-de-dos, my dears!' she cried. 'Get yourselves upstairs, or there'll be a bear fight in the sitting room!'

Florence Nightingale's elegant sitting room indeed had the air of a bear pit. Miss Nightingale and Dolores were circling each other, heads held high, tensed, as for battle.

'Katie!' Dolores cried. 'Thank the Lord, child, that you are safe and sound. We have got to get out of here – climb right back in that snow globe of yours. This woman here, she's crazy. I know she's fed me, and given me a comfy bed. But she says I'm in a whole other time, that it's a hundred years before I was born. She keeps sticking me in an ice-cold bath, and now she's trying to put mustard plasters on my feet.'

Miss Nightingale spoke with greater control, but there was tightness to her voice which conveyed her anger. 'I did not ask for your presence,' she retorted. 'I took you in as a personal favour to M. DuQuelle. Why you have come to us, I do not know. You are a guest, a visitant from another time. I suggest you listen to me and submit to your treatment. Do not irk me, for I am the only thing that stands between you and prison – or even worse, a lunatic asylum.'

'Now, Florence,' Mary Seacole interrupted, 'there's no

need to hit this lady with a stick, when there's a carrot that might tempt her.' Mary Seacole placed a sisterly hand on Dolores's shoulder. 'You know dear,' she wheedled, 'mustard plasters are very good for the figure. They bring the curves back to a woman, if you know what I mean.'

This was a step too far for Dolores. 'Mustard plasters,' she muttered with great contempt. 'Why don't you just give me powdered bat's wing, or a dead man's toe clippings? This is all a bunch of silly voodoo. The two of you might as well be witch doctors.'

Even Katie was shocked. Florence Nightingale was famous throughout the British Empire. In modern terms she was an international celebrity. Mary Seacole was the celebrated, big-hearted nurse of the Crimean War. To call them witch doctors! But Mary Seacole, as a foreigner of mixed race in London, was used to queer comments. She just laughed. Florence Nightingale was a different matter. In her anger, her face had blanched white. She was as eerily pale as Bernardo DuQuelle, and her eyes glittered in that same unearthly way.

Yet Dolores might be right about these two women. Katie eyed the amulet around Mary Seacole's neck. Her mind flew back to that terrible painful time, when Jack lay dying on the battlefield. Katie could remember now: something strange – really supernatural – had happened. The amulet, that golden vessel swinging around Mary Seacole's neck, had been used by her on the battlefield, in some mystical way. And there were so many questions about Florence Nightingale; the intense bond she shared with Bernardo DuQuelle was just one. Katie suspected Miss Nightingale knew a great deal about Bernardo DuQuelle's other, much more sensational life. Just how far did Florence Nightingale's involvement in this other world go?

Katie cleared her throat. It took a lot of courage to contradict Florence Nightingale. 'I'm not, you know, sure about mustard plasters,' she stuttered. 'I mean, wouldn't that just make things worse . . . and the cold baths . . . maybe Dolores just needs some rest, and less arguing . . . it kind of makes things worse when you're ill . . . all that shouting . . .' Katie's voice trailed off as Florence Nightingale fixed her with a terrifically chilly glare. She felt like she was dwindling away. 'Sorry . . .' she murmured lamely.

The room was silent. Finally Florence Nightingale spoke. 'But of course you know best, Katie Berger-Jone-Burg,' she said icily, 'with all your years of study and training. I am nothing compared to you. There will be no mustard plasters, or ice baths.'

Dolores had been saved from the more stringent forms of Victorian healthcare, but this still did not cheer her. 'If this is a dream, it's the worst I've ever had,' she said. 'I've pinched myself till I'm black and blue, but I just can't wake up.' For a big woman, she looked small and sad. A tear rolled down her cheek.

At this, Florence Nightingale melted ever so slightly.

'There, there,' she said with a hint of kindness. 'I do not see the need to cry. Let us try to make the best of the situation.' She walked over to the mantlepiece and, picking up a bell, rang it. 'Tea,' she said. 'I believe it is time for tea. Princess Alice, with your permission . . .'

Sitting next to Dolores, Katie gave her a hug. 'Wipe your eyes, Dolores, and we'll, you know, have some tea. The British – they really think tea fixes just about everything.' Dolores gave her a suspicious look. Had Katie gone native? But she settled down on the sofa. She'd already had tea at Florence Nightingale's home. There had been delicious buns . . . and some lovely little cakes.

Within moments a brisk and neat little maid began to bustle in and out of the room. A silver urn appeared, followed by a silver teapot, coffee pot, cream ewer and sugar bowl. The tea cups were of thin, almost transparent china, and wonderfully decorated with blue dragons. Tray after tray followed. There was dry toast, buttered toast, crumpets and muffins, white sandwiches, brown sandwiches, jellies, pastries, currant cake, sponge cake and lemon curd cake. 'Wow,' said Katie, 'high tea.'

Miss Nightingale hit her with another reproachful glance. 'This is afternoon tea, not high tea.' Alice looked at her with great sympathy, but Katie only shrugged. She'd obviously made some blunder, but the food looked great. Mary Seacole also eyed the trays with pleasure.

'Call it what you wish,' she said, 'but it's a jolly lot of

good things to eat. Makes you think back, Florence. We used to bargain for hours in the Crimea, spend half the day haggling with a young Turk to obtain a goat to cook.'

As Miss Nightingale began to pour the tea, Katie whispered to Dolores. 'She really did, you know. She's a very tough negotiator.'

Dolores accepted her cup of tea with the air of a warrior, defeated by a worthy combatant. 'So you nursed in a war?' she asked Mary Seacole. 'Well, my daughter Sonia is a nurse, one of the best.'

'Our people come to it naturally,' Mary Seacole replied. 'We've seen so much suffering, it's opened our hearts.' She smiled at Dolores and Dolores smiled back.

Florence Nightingale sniffed. '*Our people*,' she retorted. 'I don't see that the two of you have much in common.'

Mary Seacole patted Florence Nightingale's hand, a move that would terrify most people, and said, 'Florence, you might perhaps be colour blind, but that's not the way of the world. Dolores and I have a tie that binds, and that's the colour of our skin.'

Hearing Mary Seacole talk gave Katie an idea. She thought about Sonny and his story. Maybe she could help after all. 'Dolores, did you know the American Civil War is going on?' Katie asked. Dolores dropped her scone. She still couldn't take it all in. 'It's just beginning,' Katie continued. 'And Britain is thinking they might side with the Southern States.'

Princess Alice started to protest, but Bernardo Du-Quelle passed her a tray of sandwiches, with a warning look.

'Side with the South,' Dolores's tea cup came down with a bang. Florence Nightingale winced. 'This seems to be a pretty powerful country. If this England here fights with the South, the South just might win. Then we might, I mean, I'd be . . .'

'That is correct,' DuQuelle said, calmly stirring his tea. 'If we ever do manage to get you back to your own time, it is possible you will return a slave.'

'I've seen the Southerners,' Mary Seacole said, 'and the way they treat their coloured. It's not right. It's not even human.'

Here was reason enough to help Sonny and the abolitionists. Katie turned to her friends, sitting around a tea table, in an elegant house in Mayfair. 'There are a lot of brains in this room. And a bunch of people who count, who can change things. There has to be something we do.'

Bernardo DuQuelle continued calmly to drink his tea. 'We are already doing quite a bit. Miss Nightingale sits on an anti-slavery committee. In my position at Court, it is important that I am neutral.' Again Princess Alice tried to intervene, but he raised a hand. 'One can be impartial, but still have influence. I make certain that the more horrific facts of slavery are presented correctly to the government and throughout Whitehall. I encourage Prince Albert.'

Katie turned a piece of toast over in her hand. 'That's all fine,' she said. 'But it's the people on the street who really count; if they can be convinced of the horrors of slavery – if they make it clear that they don't want to support the Southern states in America and if they attend meetings and protests and make a lot of noise – then really the government will think more carefully.'

Bernardo DuQuelle looked at her with just a spark of admiration. 'At last, you begin to develop some kind of a mind,' he said. 'Politics are of importance and propaganda is a valid weapon.'

Katie was on a roll. 'I mean, who would people listen to? They'd listen to Miss Nightingale, she's a national hero.'

Florence Nightingale almost seemed gratified by the compliment. 'The public will listen to me on matters of health, on the topics of medicine, nursing and hygiene,' she replied. 'Though probably not on the American War. I have no connection to the United States. I'm a voice too far removed.' Everyone looked down, pondering, and then one by one, turned their eyes to Dolores.

'Of course,' James said. 'It's so plain to see. There is only one person in this room who would really know and understand the conflict and what the outcome can mean for her future.'

Princess Alice clapped her hands. 'Dolores, you are the perfect candidate for this,' she cried. 'Intelligent and warm-hearted – most able to explain the situation in America and the difference it would make to your people.'

'I don't know what you're all driving at,' Dolores said. 'Things here just keep getting weirder. Like Florence says, I wasn't born until almost a hundred years after that war.'

Katie took her hand. 'But think, Dolores, of the outcome, should the South win. You're always telling me to stand up, to believe in something – well, this is the time for you to take a stand.'

Dolores stroked Katie's hair. 'That crazy Bernie DuQuelle there is right. You've got quite a mind now, baby. This could be even better than Martin Luther King and the March on Washington. Can you believe it? Just think of me, changing the world. I'm gonna stop sitting around here wondering and being frightened. I'm gonna get to work!'

'Not changing the world, Dolores, just keeping it on course,' Katie replied. Everyone relaxed, just a little bit, and Katie cut herself a large slice of cake.

'You can take to the streets,' Mary Seacole said. 'Lecture to the public. Moncure Conway does it to great effect, and Clementia Taylor speaks out in her salon. I'll work with you. I can raise support.'

Florence Nightingale frowned slightly. She might be an innovator, but she was a lady-like one. 'Do you truly believe that would be appropriate?' she asked. 'I have doubts about women speaking in public, much less on the corner of the street.'

It was Princess Alice who answered. 'Nothing could be more appropriate,' she said. 'To speak out for the rights of our fellow human beings is what every man – and woman – should see as a commandment from God.' This was a truly radical line of thought, particularly coming from a woman, and one of Princess Alice's rank. James looked at her with admiration and Alice, eyes downcast, became busy with her tea.

'Well, that's settled,' Katie said, breaking an awkward silence. 'Dolores, do you think you could speak in public?'

Dolores snorted. 'Honey, I've watched that mother of yours prancing around on a stage for years now. I should think I'd have picked up some of her showmanship.' Everyone laughed, except Katie, who looked extremely uncomfortable. She tried to avoid discussing Mimi; she was far too wild for Victorian sensibilities.

Bernardo DuQuelle seemed amused by Dolores's new plans. 'So our rebellious patient has turned abolitionist, well, well, well. You must be pleased, Katie, one imagines you would feel a real closeness, a personal tie, to the abolitionist movement.'

Katie almost fell off her chair. Did DuQuelle know about Sonny? And was he about to expose her? She'd best try to get away from him. 'Good works certainly improve the appetite. I'll just check to see if there are more pastries,' Katie said, ignoring Florence Nightingale's remonstrations and walking right past the little maid.

Unfortunately, DuQuelle followed her into the hall. 'We've barely had time for a chat since you arrived,' he said.

'Well, Dolores was kicking up such a stink, there wasn't really time,' she replied vaguely.

'I meant since you arrived in this time, unbeknownst to me.' DuQuelle lifted his nose and sniffed the air. 'Dolores might be making a stink, as you so delicately put it, but there's a decided odour to you, something you picked up during your journey. It makes me most uneasy.'

It worried Katie too. Why was she there? Who had called her? She tried to shrug it off, questioning DuQuelle in return. 'Talk about uneasy. You've got a way of zinging me one. What's this about me and the abolitionist movement?'

Bernardo DuQuelle adjusted his cravat, a brilliant white against his strange chalky skin. 'To lose your friends in a crowd may be regarded as carelessness,' he said. 'To be kidnapped is a decided misfortune. But to tell no one of these adventures – that looks suspicious to me, Katie.' DuQuelle's green eyes rested on her, not in anger, but sharply, waiting.

Katie started to reply, to tell him everything, but that new unnerving feeling, dark and strong, flowed through her veins and stopped her. This new feeling wasn't a gift from the Tempus and had nothing to do with the power of words. She felt both rebellious and afraid.

DuQuelle knew, almost before Katie did, that she would give no answer. 'I too am familiar with the Unionists, the abolitionists,' he said. 'More talk and less violence would do their cause good. Already their impatient behaviour has created problems. They are being blamed for ships on fire and ransacked embassies, though I believe others are responsible. Their aggressive behaviour might push Britain into the arms of the Confederacy. I am trying to guide them, to keep them moving forward along diplomatic lines, but they are impetuous and unreasonable.'

'All but one,' Katie thought, remembering Sonny's calm persuasive voice and the way he'd protected her from the others.

'All but one,' DuQuelle continued. 'One in particular that I can think of. Did any of them catch your eye, Katie?' She started at this, and he laughed slightly. 'Just when I thought you were coming along, developing some mental acumen. Really, Katie, sometimes it is like playing cat and dead mouse.' His eyes glinted greenly. But Katie could tell, it had been a strain for him to read her mind.

Florence Nightingale stood in the doorway. How long had she been there? 'Our guests are leaving, I expect that means you as well, Katie Berger-Jones-Burg. Such an inappropriate name for a young woman; it is almost with relief that I turn to your alias, Miss Katherine Tappan.'

Katie for one was very glad of the interruption. 'We'd all better stick with Katherine Tappan from now on,' she replied. 'You can still call me Katie, just change the rest. No one wants to trip up.'

'No,' DuQuelle echoed, 'best to stay on our toes. When there's this much to hide, no one wants to get their story wrong.'

Katie moved away from DuQuelle as fast as she could. Princess Alice looked askance as she stood with James, but Katie avoided them too. Why did she not trust her friends? She hated this new feeling growing inside her.

'We do need to hurry,' Katie said. 'There's that big party at Windsor Castle tonight. I'm going, that is, Miss Katherine Tappan is going. Dolores, are you coming or staying?'

Dolores came down the stairs with Mary Seacole. One look and Katie could see – Dolores had made a friend.

'I'm staying,' Dolores said. 'Miss Mary Seacole and I have plans to make. We'll team up, use my knowledge and her celebrity. We're gonna take this town by storm and, God help me, we'll free the slaves!'

For Dolores, work was the core of life – and now she had something to do. This was better than any medicine Florence Nightingale could provide. She turned to Mary Seacole and gleefully they began to plot. 'We can begin with flyers,' she was saying to Mary Seacole. 'Pamphlets that explain our cause; we'll hand them out.'

Florence Nightingale was speaking in a low and quiet voice to Bernardo DuQuelle. James O'Reilly and Princess Alice, heads together, were sorting out the ills of the world. Everyone seemed to have a friend, an ally, a confidante. Everyone had a purpose, a reason for being. Only Katie stood alone – unable to share. That dark pin-prick of doubt and bitterness, the low voice that urged her to selfishness. She had tried to suppress it. But now it came sweeping through her, wave after wave of black fury, taking her by surprise.

Chapter Eight

The Ball at Windsor Castle

On 30 November Queen Victoria always held a ball to mark the start of the Christmas festivities. That night, as Katie dressed for the party, she felt weak and jittery. This temporal visitation wasn't like the other times. Something was very, very wrong. Even DuQuelle didn't know why she was there. Katie could swear that when she'd looked into the snow globe, Alice and James had called to her. Yet they denied this. Alice and James: there was another problem. She loved Alice and she admired James, yet here she was, jealous and bitter, keeping secrets from her friends.

Katie jumped at a soft rustling sound and swung round to find Princess Alice standing in the doorway.

'I didn't mean to spy on you, Katie,' Alice said. 'It's just you seem so sad. I am too. Tomorrow might be 1 December, but it doesn't feel like Christmas. Father is not well and this war . . .'

Guilt quickly replaced Katie's anger. Here was Alice, the best friend she'd ever had. No one was kinder. Alice was still willing to confide in her. Why was she holding back? After all, it wasn't Alice's fault that she was growing up and leaving the simpler friendships of childhood behind.

This new maturity was heightened by the finery Alice wore. Katie couldn't stop staring at her. 'Your dress is amazing,' she said. The sheerest white gauze draped across Alice's shoulders, intertwined with green vines of ivy. A white lace bodice came to a point at her tiny waist. The gauze skirt fell into three great flounces, looped with clusters of red roses. Alice had gathered the thick, shining waves of her hair into a Grecian knot at the nape of her neck, while a wreath of ivy and roses encircled her head.

Alice fiddled with a rose in her hair. 'Are you certain?' she asked. 'Don't I look just a tiny bit silly?'

'You look totally gorgeous,' Katie replied, 'kind of like a human snowflake, but a really pretty one.'

This did make Alice laugh, and she came to stand next to her friend. 'I don't care for such fussy, flounced clothing, but the Queen was adamant that I dress tonight. The party is a very large one, quite an assortment of guests. The Ambassadors will be here, the Court, of course, but also town mayors, people from the arts and sciences, even some men from the City. Can you imagine – bankers! James will be pleased, a true meeting of the classes. It won't be a total throng though. There will be some guests I know. I'm told Prince Louis of Hesse has just arrived. I haven't seen him since I was a tiny child.'

Alice turned in front of the mirror. She wasn't her usual calm, serious self as she twisted a strand of hair nervously and adjusted her flowers. She'd gone quite pink.

'You look wonderful in your dress, too,' Alice commented.

Katie was far from vain, but she had to agree. The rose tint of her Indian silk suited her complexion, and the endless corsetry did wonders for her figure. 'I do look pretty good,' she admitted, 'but I don't know how I'm going to get through the door in these skirts.' The crinoline for her evening dress was even wider than her street attire. As they stood together, the two girls' skirts seemed to fill the room.

'The crinoline cages, they are ridiculous,' Alice agreed, 'but so womanly, so becoming . . . we'll enjoy them, just this once.'

Katie wondered where the fiery feminist of this afternoon had gone. Princess Alice the reformer seemed now to be lost in a cloud of tulle and lace.

'This is a rather relaxed occasion,' Princess Alice added, 'the gentlemen are not in court uniform or dress.

Only formal wear, a simple cut-away dress coat.' With one final 'prink', Alice took Katie by the arm. 'Your gloves fit nicely,' she said running her eyes over Katie's costume. 'It was difficult to find that size. I've provided a second pair in case you spoil these. Please do not take them off during the evening. Now, do you have your fan? Your bouquet?'

'This is worse than my presentation,' Katie grumbled, but she had a final peek in the mirror too. She did look rather splendid. For a moment, the two of them were able to shrug off their worries. They were young after all, and they were girls, about to attend a very fancy party. With lighter hearts they made their way down the stairs.

James was waiting for them, shifting uncomfortably in his evening clothes. His brilliant white, starched shirtfront was in marked contrast to his dark scowling face. James's father was the Queen's doctor. Sir Brendan O'Reilly was a vain, handsome man, who owed his position to flattery rather than ability. Ever upwardly mobile, he had recently been ennobled from Doctor O'Reilly to *Sir* Brendan O'Reilly. He viewed this evening an excellent opportunity to promote his attractive family. He was particularly keen that James's sister, Grace, should catch the eye of an aristocrat.

The formal clothes, the tight dancing pumps and the pinching kid gloves had wrought havoc with James's temper. 'It's about time,' he said. 'Come on, let's get this over with.' Katie was used to James's curt way of speaking, but he usually spared Princess Alice. His admiration of Alice seemed to dissolve in the face of the flounced and feathered creature she'd become that night.

'You don't care for our dresses?' Alice asked before she could stop herself.

'I'd be more interested if you were a dessert. You look like a meringue. And Katie resembles nothing more than a large pink ice lolly. No, I do not *care* for your dresses.'

Princess Alice seemed to shrink, and then two red circles appeared on her cheeks. Underneath her serious demeanour, Alice hid a quick temper and a sharp tongue.

'Well, you look like a mannequin in a shop window!' she snapped back. 'I've never seen anyone less at ease in fine clothes.' The usually gentle Alice grasped Katie's arm with a pinch. 'We must arrive before the Queen does,' Alice said, 'some of us do appreciate court protocol. If you'd been born into this type of society, you'd know how to behave.'

'Ouch, Alice,' Katie muttered. 'You're making a big bruise, right above my long gloves. You must be really cross. I mean, you never pull rank and you've just hit James with eight hundred years of class superiority. That's not like you. James just doesn't like fuss and parties. But most of all, he doesn't want to share you. He really wants to sit you down in a corner and talk about sewage.'

Usually Princess Alice would have laughed at this. But she'd tried so hard that evening and wanted some acknowledgement, especially by James. Her wounded pride meant she would not relent.

'There is Grace O'Reilly, just coming up the Grand Staircase,' Alice said, changing the subject. 'I suggest you enter with her, as I must join my sisters now.'

Alice seemed in a hurry to get away and Katie was left standing alone. It was a large party, a real crush, and she couldn't possibly reach Grace on the other side of the staircase. Courtiers were hurrying from their rooms or ducking through the low doors leading from the many towers. Other guests had made the long walk from the Henry VIII Gateway, to the Middle Ward and then through the narrow Norman Gateway. Katie watched them throng up the Grand Staircase to the State Apartments. They were excited, but cold, and discreetly shook the melting snow from their coiffures onto the thick red carpets.

She fell into step with the crowd, and found herself in the Queen's Ballroom. Princess Alice might call it a 'relaxed' occasion, but to Katie this was the epitome of grandeur. The room was alight with hundreds of candles. The enormous glass chandeliers sparkled above, reflecting gilt and silver furnishings. The walls were swagged with evergreen garlands and abundant red ribbons – the first decorations of the Christmas season. Through the feathered heads and powdered shoulders Katie could just glimpse the ornate paintings of kings and queens past and their numerous children.

'The paintings, they are van Dycks,' a voice next to her said. 'Some of them are spectacularly good. There is a triple portrait of Charles I. Strange that; so many heads in a single painting, yet he couldn't keep even one on his shoulders. Ah, the transience, the mortality of kings. I will never forget the day of his execution. It was bitterly cold . . . the King wore two shirts to protect himself from the weather. He didn't want the waiting crowds to think he shivered from fear.' The dappled glitter of the chandeliers made DuQuelle look stranger than usual. His hair was so black, his skin so white; he looked more dead than alive. Only his eyes glowed with that unsettling, vibrant green. Had he really been there, at the beheading of Charles I?

Katie shivered. 'This really is a large crowd,' she said, trying to shake off the spell of DuQuelle.

'It's an absolute bun fight,' James O'Reilly said, joining them. 'I hate this kind of thing.'

'As do the Queen and Prince Albert,' DuQuelle replied. 'All they really want are charades and tableaux with the family. The Queen loved grand balls as a young woman. But Prince Albert has always hated them. So now she declares they are *as one* and she wishes only for the *gemütlich* – what is friendly, homely.

'Not exactly homely, this,' Katie muttered as someone in the crowd stabbed her instep with their heel. James's sister Grace had finally found them, and even in a room filled with beauty, her looks stood out. James was handsome, his father also, to the point of vanity, but Grace was extraordinary. It must be her hair, Katie thought. It was a deep dark red and curled wonderfully. Grace had no need for flowers and feathers; that hair, abundantly plaited and rolled, was ornament enough.

'This room is hot and very crowded, are you certain you are well enough to dance, Grace?' James asked. For years now Grace's health had faltered. But she was young, and still hopeful.

'Nonsense, James,' she said, tapping his nose with her fan. 'A party such as this is exactly what I need; a perfect tonic against the damp and cold. I have never felt better.' A slight cough belied this statement. Yet her eyes danced with a joy that comes from a love of life. James opened his mouth to object – her dress was too thin, the atmosphere too close, the excitement too high for an invalid like Grace – but at that moment the Lord Chamberlain stepped into the room.

'THE QUEEN,' he announced, and behind him stood a tiny plump woman. Victoria was in mourning for her mother, who had died in March. For the Christmas ball, though, she had consented to wear a bit of colour, a deep purple watered moiré silk draped over an enormous crinoline. The dress was ornamented with heavy gold tassels, which attached at the sleeves and fell down to her wrists. Her thin hair was pulled into a bun and circled at the back with a diadem of diamonds and emeralds, interwoven with live holly and carnations. Her round arms were covered in diamond bracelets and her dimpled fingers glistened with jewelled rings. On her bodice she wore half a dozen brooches and portrait miniatures. 'She's quite the show stopper,' Katie thought. 'She might say she prefers a simple home life, but she's not going for simplicity tonight.'

Queen Victoria might be a middle-aged, dumpy woman, made more so by her acres of silk and diamonds. Yet she held the room in her power. With great dignity, she turned to her husband and, resting her hand on his, skimmed through the crowd with a surprisingly light step. They bowed and curtsied as she made her way; wave after wave of respect for their monarch. Somewhere, an orchestra struck up. The crowds parted. The Queen and Prince Albert began to dance. A murmur went up. Many were surprised the Queen danced at all, and especially a waltz. This mainstay of the ballroom was still considered slightly racy. The Queen's rather ponderous cheeks grew pink and she looked up adoringly at Prince Albert. She would never pass up the opportunity to dance with him. After twenty-one years of marriage and nine children, she still loved her prince with the intensity of their wedding day.

At the end of the waltz, the Queen and Prince Albert left the dance floor and the orchestra struck up a spritely redowa. With amusement, Katie saw a trail of men all making a beeline for Grace O'Reilly. Her father, seizing his opportunity, stepped forward and made the selection for her, deciding who would be her most profitable dance partner.

James looked even gloomier. 'Poor Grace, it's like watching a cattle market, she deserves better,' he muttered as Grace was led to the dance floor by a young, chinless lord. 'You don't want to dance, Katie, do you?' Even for James, that was one insult too far.

'Really James, I mean, why not?' she began, getting ready to hit him with a barrage of abuse. But then someone coughed quietly behind her. When Katie turned around she was rendered speechless.

Chapter Nine

The Surprise Guests

Sonny stood before Katie, resplendent in full evening dress, complete with pristine kid gloves, his thick dark hair brushed back neatly. Of course she'd only ever seen him once before, that very afternoon in a dark cellar. Under the dazzling chandeliers she realized he was very handsome. She gawped and Bernardo DuQuelle almost smiled.

'Miss Katherine Tappan, Mr John Reillson. However, I believe you two have already met, though Miss Katherine here was most reticent to reveal anything . . . such becoming modesty . . .'

Katie was still staring, mouth open. Catching James's eye, she shut it and gulped. 'John?' she inquired. The young man smiled and bowed.

'My father was named John, as am I,' he said. 'Fond mothers, they will give their children pet names. So I was always called Sonny. Sonny-John or even Sonny-Jack. Silly, isn't it?'

'Very,' James said, still scowling. Didn't James see the resemblance? And then there was the name: Sonny, or Sonny-John, but also Sonny-*Jack*. He looked so much like James's brother, yet another Jack, killed in the Crimean War. Katie knew that James thought of his lost brother every day of his life, yet he seemed oblivious to the like-ness. He simply repeated. 'Very silly indeed.'

It turned out the American had finer manners than his British counterpart. 'Then you must call me John,' he said politely to James, 'as we have a mutual friend. Indeed, I am acquainted with Miss Katherine Tappan – through her father, the admirable Mr. Lewis Tappan.' Everyone in the tiny group knew this could not be true. Yet Bernardo DuQuelle nodded agreeably. 'But of course,' he said, 'I should have remembered. Mr John Reillson is a member of the Unionists delegation, attending the Queen on behalf of President Abraham Lincoln. He is here tonight with the American Ambassador, Mr Charles Francis Adams. Yes, you must have known Miss Tappan in New York City, or perhaps made her acquaintance in Boston . . . or was it Washington? In any case, you are certain to be very well acquainted. No need to make introductions here!'

James gave Katie a questioning look. She avoided his eye and fanned herself rather furiously.

'May I have this dance?' John Reillson asked her, as the spritely redowa gave way to a gentler waltz.

'No,' James interrupted, 'Katie doesn't dance. She'd be sure to stumble.'

'All she will have to do is follow my lead,' John Reillson said, ignoring James's bad temper. 'I have a feeling we are very well partnered. Come along, Miss Katherine Tappan. You were not meant to be a wallflower.'

'One dance,' James practically shouted after her, 'and then I will collect you.'

'That young man seems to think he's your father, or at least your brother,' John Reillson commented as he took Katie by the hand and led her through the revolving couples.

Katie thought for a moment about how this John had such a striking resemblance to James's older brother. Why was she the only person who could see this? John placed his hand around Katie's waist, and she was glad, for once, about the corset. At least he wasn't grabbing onto too much flesh.

'So where are your friends?' she asked. 'I'm a disaster in a ballroom, but Jeb Lawson would be even worse.'

John Reillson laughed. He was a great one for laughing. 'Your close friend Bernardo DuQuelle would agree. He gave explicit instructions on tonight's attendance.' Katie was silent. So DuQuelle was behind this, orchestrating the guest list. But to what purpose? Only he would know, forever the enigma. She stumbled in the swirling dance and John had to catch her.

'Whatever weighs upon your mind, put it aside tonight,' he said. 'At midnight the Christmas season begins, and we shall have some fun. I hear there's going to be a theatrical performance later. In a break from protocol, the finest acts from the West End music halls will be performing. Have you been to the music halls?'

'No . . .' Katie muttered. She wasn't really paying attention. The waltz was harder than it looked and she was bobbing and slipping like a moose on a frozen lake. People were beginning to stare.

John Reillson, in his enthusiasm for Katie and music halls, didn't notice. 'They are the most splendid entertainment,' he said. 'The best acts in Europe, in the world, can be seen in London. You should see Alex Kinch. They call him Little Kinch. Oh, but he's funny. He does this dance, in huge boots, twenty-five inches long. Picking up his top hat with his toes, shuffling and tripping and balancing on the points of those boots. He's the best paid performer in the West End. Worth every penny. He makes me roar with laughter.'

'Ummmm,' said Katie. She was busy with her own shuffling and tripping.

'And Harry Cheng. He must be the greatest magician

of our time! That man can make an entire horse and carriage disappear from the stage. But if it's pathos you're after,' John continued, 'no one can beat the Little Angel.'

Katie came to an abrupt halt, bumping sharply into another couple. 'The Little Angel!'

'Yes,' John Reillson tried to move her back into the dance. 'She's splendid. She sings at the Alhambra in Leicester Square. You should hear her rendition of "The Girl Time Forgot". There's not a dry eye in the house.'

Katie couldn't believe it. The Little Angel. The room swirled around her and it wasn't just the waltz. How could she have forgotten? The Little Angel was the closest link Katie had to the elite group of time travellers, the Tempus. She was joined to Katie through history and time. But the Little Angel had much more experience than Katie and far greater knowledge. She seemed to understand the Tempus Fugit. If anyone knew why Katie was there, it would be the Little Angel.

'You say the performers will be here tonight?' Katie asked.

'Some of them, I'm not sure which ones,' John replied. 'But if they're not here, I'd be honoured to take you to see them perform some other time. On Thursdays they have a ladies night when it's most respectable.'

The Little Angel had a lovely voice, Katie knew that. But she didn't need to hear her sing. She needed to talk with her, and soon. There were too many questions about

Katie's presence here, and those strange, unhappy feelings surging through her. She needed the Little Angel more than ever.

The waltz came to an end. Katie curtsied and John bowed. 'I'm embarrassed by this afternoon,' he said, his bright eyes growing serious. 'It was an unforgivable way to treat a lady. I cannot apologize enough. Jeb Lawson and I have had more than words on the topic. I've half a mind to inform our Ambassador, Charles Francis Adams. Though he is troubled enough, working night and day to keep Britain from declaring for the South.' He took Katie by the elbow. 'That's why we need you so desperately. Have you had time to think about what we discussed? Is there any chance that we can count upon your help?'

James appeared at her shoulder before she could answer. 'I believe this is my dance,' he announced stiffly. James was quick to lead Katie away, but slower on the uptake when it came to the actual dance. It was a quadrille, stately and complicated, and she had learned it for her presentation.

'Come on, James,' she finally snapped, leading him out. 'The dance has already begun.'

In the old-fashioned quadrille, the couples walked forwards and backwards, bowed and curtsied and circled each other. Katie had to concentrate on the dance, but eventually she noticed that James was paying no attention to her or his dancing. All of his focus was on a corner of the room, where Princess Alice stood, deep in conversation with a young man.

Katie had never seen him before. He was tall and slender, his figure accentuated by a cutaway evening jacket nipped in at the waist and tight-fitting trousers. He had wavy brown hair and ornate side whiskers. His moustache alone was a work of art. 'Who is that?' she asked. James's bad mood was becoming even worse.

'That is Louis of Hesse-Darmstadt.'

'Hesse what?'

'Darmstadt,' James replied through gritted teeth. 'The Langraviate of Hesse-Darmstadt. It's one of those tiny German states the Queen admires so.'

'Isn't Prince Albert from one of those *tiny German states* – from Saxe-Coburg-Gotha?'

'Exactly. Pathetic little countries overrun with royalty.' James was blunt, but rarely critical of the Royal Family, particularly Prince Albert, whom he admired. Katie thought he must be very annoyed by this Louis of Hesse-whatever.

'He's just talking to her,' Katie said. As she promenaded with James though the dancers, she watched Princess Alice too. Louis of Hesse bent protectively over her and she looked up at him, talking animatedly. He nodded again and again, all the while examining Alice, taking note of her dress, her bearing and her voice.

'He is kind of checking her out,' Katie admitted.

'I wouldn't worry though. Isn't he like, her cousin or something. I mean, you can't date – no wrong word – I mean, *court* your cousin.'

'Why not?' James asked. 'The Queen and Prince Albert are first cousins.'

Sometimes Katie forgot just how much they didn't know about medicine and science, even James.

'But to answer your question – no, they are not closely related. I have a feeling the Queen is hoping they might be, some day.'

Katie squinted at the young man with Alice. He was probably four, five or six years older than she was. And yes, he was handsome in that foreign old-fashioned German way, very like Prince Albert. To Katie, he looked like a stiff, coiffed man-doll. By the animated expression on Alice's face, Katie could guess their conversation. Alice wasn't flirting, but simply expounding her mission: food and care for the poor, hygienic living quarters and proper medical attention. Katie could also tell that this Louis wasn't listening to a word of it. He's just looking at a pretty girl whose serious grey eyes glowed with purpose, a slender girl in a becoming white dress, leaning forward to make a point.

'He doesn't look intelligent to me,' Katie said.

'He's an idiot,' James snapped. 'So stupid, he can't begin to imagine the intelligence of Princess Alice. All he knows about is drilling his military troops and combing his moustache. What can Alice see in him?'

'I don't think she sees anything, but, well, he is kind of gorgeous, if a bit bizarre – that moustache!' Katie conceded as she and James joined together, hand in hand for the final figure of the dance. He squeezed her hand so hard, it hurt.

As they re-formed the set with three other couples, James's sister Grace joined them. She was not happy. At her side was the debauched Lord Twisted. He held her gloved hand lightly. He looked as if he might devour her.

The ball had been a night of surprises. 'Lord Twisted!' Katie exclaimed. 'I thought he was locked up for treason. After his betrayals in Crimea, his spying for the Russians; how can he show his face in Britain, much less at Windsor Castle?'

James looked even more furious. 'It is the Queen,' he said. 'She could not believe that someone of Lord Twisted's rank and ancient pedigree could commit such a crime. The Queen pardoned him very publically and insisted he attend Court functions. She has been equally lenient on the failings of her military leaders . . . Lucan, Cardigan . . . all pardoned, and everything smoothed over. Young Felix has returned to Prussia, where he continues to make trouble. All that death and grief for nothing.' Katie gave James's hand a squeeze. She knew he was thinking of his brother Jack's death, and that is was in vain.

Thankfully the dance ended. With an abrupt bow, James was gone from Katie's side. With a look of challenge, he claimed the next dance with his sister. This was dangerous ground. Lord Twisted, on top of his other sins, had once fought James in a duel. Lord Twisted now began to protest and James looked ready to fight again.

Grace took her little brother by the arm and dragged him away, and was soon whirling across the floor with him. Thank goodness for Grace. Jack might have died, but James still had his loving older sister and his impish brother Riordan. Katie had thought a party like this would be decorous, but it was turning out to be dramatic.

There was a soft 'ahem' behind her. It was Bernardo DuQuelle. 'You are standing alone on the dance floor,' he said. 'Abandonment, that is more shameful than being a wallflower. You must be rescued immediately. May I have this dance?'

'Really? This just isn't my night, is it?' Katie said. But she put her arms out anyway.

DuQuelle shook his head. 'Not the most gracious of acceptances, but what I would expect of you.' And taking her in his arms, they began to waltz. Even Katie, who was clumsy and inexperienced, knew she was dancing with an expert. At times she feared him and dreaded being near him, but that tiny corner of female within her was pleased to have a good partner.

Bernardo DuQuelle glided and whirled across the floor, tails flying behind him. If Katie stumbled or tripped, he righted her immediately, making it look like a part of the dance.

'I can't believe how good you are,' she said.

DuQuelle actually laughed. 'The compliment is always backwards with you. Praise with a bit of poison attached. You have to realize, I have had more time than most to study the art of the dance. I worked with Lully on the composition of wonderful ballets for Louis XIV at Versailles. Who do you think made him the Sun King?' Bernardo DuQuelle gazed into a distant past. This always gave Katie the creeps. She was almost used to travelling back to the nineteenth century, but DuQuelle went even further and no one else could follow.

DuQuelle moved Katie into a reverse turn. Something was amusing him greatly. 'Is it my dancing?' she asked.

'That *is* entertaining,' DuQuelle conceded, 'but I am most amused by the youngest of the gentlemen in this room. They don't seem able to concentrate on their partners at all. Their eyes seek others.' He turned Katie so that she could see James, dancing with Grace but glaring at Alice, now dancing with Louis of Hesse. DuQuelle turned again, and over his shoulder she could see John Reillson staring straight at her. Suddenly she wanted to dance beautifully, to look graceful.

She should have remembered, DuQuelle could read her mind. He drummed his gloved fingers lightly on the back of her hand. 'Listen to the music,' he said. 'Look into my eyes.' She did so, and they glittered green. Suddenly her legs grew lighter, her feet less cumbersome, as she skimmed across the floor. Katie's shoulders went back and her head up. She twirled and whirled and dipped and spun. She could dance, and it was like flying. It was truly magical.

'Now John Reillson really does have something to look at,' DuQuelle commented. Katie scanned his face. Though he would smile and banter and sometimes laugh, there was always that waxwork quality to DuQuelle.

'You invited him here, tonight,' she said. 'Sonny, Sonny-Jack, John Reillson – whatever he's called. What are you up to, DuQuelle?'

His face stiffened and he slowed the dance. 'I was hoping he would take this opportunity to ingratiate himself to the Queen and Prince Albert. To put his best foot forward at a ball, so to speak. But instead he has concentrated all of his efforts on his old friend, Miss Katherine Tappan. Youth will be youth, and sometimes there is no guiding them to sense.'

Katie looked again at John Reillson. He had been approached by the Lord Chamberlain, who was speaking to him quite emphatically. It wasn't a conversation of festive pleasantries. Something was wrong.

DuQuelle twirled Katie to a stop directly beside them. 'Is there a problem?' DuQuelle asked. The Lord Chamberlain eyed him. Bernardo DuQuelle, his equal in stature as far as the Court went, but there was something about him . . . so many rumors . . .

'The young man is a part of the Unionist Delegation, I believe?' the Lord Chamberlain asked.

'Yes,' said DuQuelle, 'a very young member of the delegation, really too young and impressionable to be exposed to our daring English ladies.'

Even overlooking the slight on the beauties of his kingdom, the Lord Chamberlain was not amused. 'I am afraid the young man must leave immediately,' he stated with pomp.

DuQuelle stopped his teasing. 'Couldn't this wait?' he asked. 'The Christmas Ball at Windsor Castle – surely a social occasion such as this . . .'

The Lord Chamberlain was not interested in compromise. 'There has been a major breach in diplomatic relations between the United States and Great Britain; between the Unionists of the North and Britain to be more exact.'

'You must be mistaken,' DuQuelle said. 'Britain has not recognized the Southern Confederacy and has declared itself neutral in this civil war. The Americas' battles do not concern us.'

The Lord Chamberlain was not the kind of man to make a mistake. He became even stiffer as he addressed Bernardo DuQuelle. 'The Union of the North has violated Britain's declaration of neutrality,' he said. 'One of their warships has halted a British paddle steamer, the RMS *Trent*. The Union has fired shots, thereby taking our ship by force. Union soldiers have boarded the *Trent* and removed passengers. They have taken prisoner the two new commissioners the Southern Confederacy was sending to our country. The men and their secretaries are now incarcerated in Fort Warren, in Boston.'

Katie couldn't quite take it in. 'Is this serious?' she asked.

The Lord Chamberlain glanced at her with disapproval. He was a man who lived for propriety. He believed in rules and status quo. He'd attended Katie's court presentation and still cringed at the memory. Her upstart questions were true to form. He ignored her, turning to Bernardo DuQuelle and saying, 'The Prime Minister has been informed. He is furious. He views this as a major violation of maritime law.'

John Reillson explained it to Katie. 'This is serious,' he said, 'such a rash action. Who knows what the consequences will be? Our presence at the Queen's ball could cause further insult. If you will excuse me, I must find my Ambassador.' He bowed low – not to the Lord Chamberlain or Bernardo DuQuelle, but to Katie. 'We will meet again,' he whispered, 'I promise.'

The final quadrille of the evening began. For Katie, the ball was drained of gaiety, but DuQuelle bowed and took her hand. 'We must finish the dance,' he said, 'even if we are dancing on the precipice.'

The Queen and Prince Albert took their places at the head of the figure. The hour was late, but the Queen was still smiling up at her Prince. Despite her protestations, she really did love a party. And there was still the theatrical pantomime to come. Prince Albert was decidedly less animated. There were dark circles under his eyes. His once luxurious black hair was receding and streaked with grey. He was a man who longed for his bed, or at least to be back at his desk, working diligently at the endless red government boxes.

The rippling notes of 'Le Pantalon' rang out across the dance floor. Almost numbly Katie curtsied, rotating through the dance. At one point she moved forward, into a deep reverence before Prince Albert. He looked drawn and anxious, dancing automatically while glancing over Katie's shoulder towards some commotion at the other end of the dance figure.

She followed his glance. It was a cluster of men, not quite arguing, but in dispute. Lord Twisted was there. He seemed to be asking Sir Brendan to leave the dance, to give his place up to another dancer. At first Sir Brendan would not budge. But when the substitute dancer came forward, Sir Brendan blanched white and retired, not just from the dance, but from the ballroom. When Katie saw for herself, she almost dropped to the floor.

It had to be him. As always, he *looked* the gentleman: slender, of medium height and dressed with great elegance. His dancing partner was highly gratified by her catch. But Katie knew better. As he bowed, his neck arched and seemed to elongate. His head moved sideways in a strange, sly manner. His eyes darted in another direction. Though he danced with grace, there was something slinking and repulsive in his movement. It was the person, or thing, that Katie dreaded most. Lord Belzen.

The quadrille continued and the couples formed two lines. They advanced and retreated in stately formation. Then they turned and swirled and regrouped. Couple after couple advanced up the line, to bow to the Queen and her beloved Prince.

Katie watched Lord Belzen, so smiling, so evil, coming forward in his turn. What would happen when he reached the Queen? She feared it would be catastrophic. Katie must stop him. She tried to break out of the dance, but just then Lord Belzen lifted his head with the eerie swaying movement and looked at her. Something surged through Katie, leaping and black. She did not break the chain of the dance. She did not warn the Queen.

Midnight was near. The dancers smiled and nodded. The Christmas season would bring much cheer. And then, Lord Belzen danced forward, bowing before the Queen. Turning his head at that awkward angle he caught Prince Albert's eye and held his gaze. The Prince stared back, the colour draining from his face. Sweat broke out in cold white pearls on his forehead. His shaking hand went up, trying to loosen his collar as his breath came fast in pants. The Prince stepped backwards, trying to look away and break the link to Belzen, dragging the Queen with him.

The Queen looked up, a mixture of annoyance and concern on her face. She reached to her husband and turned his head, finally severing Belzen's connection. Albert would *not* take care of his health. He worked so hard that he couldn't even enjoy a party any more. *She* could have danced all night.

'You are fatigued and the room is too hot. All you need is a good night's rest,' she said reassuringly. 'We will cancel the theatrical performance and retire immediately.' With a reluctant glance at the revelries around her, the Queen took Prince Albert by the arm. As they passed, Katie could hear the Prince, gasping slightly and muttering in wonder.

'It was that man. Where have I seen him before? When he looked at me, it was as if a shard of ice did pierce my heart.'

The quadrille gave way to a rousing polka. As the bells chimed midnight, the couples romped and laughed, unaware of what had happened. The women were still beautiful and the men still dashing. The bright ballroom at Windsor still twinkled with chandeliers and Christmas lights. But for Katie, the world was far from merry and bright. James came quickly to her side, his grumpiness transformed to a more mature concern.

DuQuelle shook his head. 'The Queen is wrong. It will

take more than a good night's rest to repair this Prince. Belzen's damage has been done. Katie, find Princess Alice and bring her to her father's private rooms. James, gather your medical bag and come with me – perhaps your medicines can help Prince Albert, I do not know.'

Chapter Ten

Life or Death

The morning of 1 December arrived; a morning wiped of pre-Christmas joy. The night before had taken its toll. Everyone knew: Prince Albert was ill, again. Servants ran on tip-toe, clearing up after the ball, while keeping their voices down. Footmen stacked chairs and hauled away decorations as quietly as they could. The remains of the bountiful feast were dispatched to the poor.

The Queen persisted in believing it was nothing; just the usual cold. Her husband would be fine. At her insistence, Prince Albert was dressed and out of bed. He lay on the sofa in his study, eyes closed. The Queen veered between imploring him to 'buck up' and pleading with him to 'rest, mein Lieber'. She was a terrible nurse.

She did, however, bow to his request for quiet and privacy, though her idea of privacy meant keeping the children away. The courtiers, upon whom she was so reliant, still came and went. The Royal Physician, Sir Brendan O'Reilly, was in attendance, aided by his son James. The Queen's ladies-in-waiting clustered around, clutching their needlework. The Queen's Pekinese dog ran in and out of the room.

And Bernardo DuQuelle hovered, much to the annoyance of Prince Albert. DuQuelle's affectations irritated him in the best of times, and he had never felt worse. The strange events of the night before had disturbed Prince Albert's methodical mind. He needed solitude, so that he could dissect and analyse. What exactly had happened? But it was impossible to concentrate with DuQuelle watching him and practically reading his thoughts.

Banned from the sickroom, Katie and Alice had retired to the safety of the schoolroom. There would be no lessons for the younger children that day; the governesses and nursemaids were recovering from the jollities of the night before, and the Queen was too involved with her husband to think of her children. Alice had been ordered to help with the Christmas gifts for the Queen's innumerable servants. And though she longed to be with her father, she would carry out the duty assigned to her. They sat before a table, which was covered in trinkets. Alice, with a very long checklist, was wrapping and labelling each present painstakingly.

'Why doesn't the Queen just let him go to bed?' Katie asked. 'I mean, she loves your father so much. She even said he needs to rest.'

Alice took up a pretty work-basket and tied a bright tartan ribbon around its handle. 'The Queen has such robust health herself,' she explained. 'My mother doesn't understand illness. To be honest, she feels my father is slightly weak when it comes to his health. She is impatient and wishes he would *try harder*.'

Katie began to sort walnuts and oranges into little gauze bags. 'He looks pretty ill to me,' she said. 'And it's not just a cold. It's something much worse, because Belzen is involved. You didn't see what happened last night. Even Bernardo DuQuelle is worried.'

'I am aware that it is serious,' Alice said. 'I've known that for some time. But I had thought it had to do with us, our time, our own sickness and health. I'm terrified to think that Lord Belzen . . . Oh! I hate being stuck up here, making dainty things, when I could be of use.'

James came into the room and Princess Alice ran towards him. 'What news?' she asked. He bent protectively over her, as if to shield her from illness and distress. The misunderstandings of yesterday were gone. 'I know the Queen wishes to be alone with the Prince Consort, but I think you should come,' he said. 'Your understanding and persuasiveness are sorely missed downstairs. I need another good medical eye.'

They both looked embarrassed. James's father might be the Royal Household physician, but Sir Brendan was much more of a courtier than a doctor. He would flatter the Queen and echo her opinion. Prince Albert needed a better doctor; particularly at this moment, when Sir Brenden seemed so nervous.

Alice did not need to be persuaded. She ran from the room, followed by her friends. Through the long corridors and winding stairways of Windsor Castle they went, down stone steps that had been trodden on for hundreds of years, until they reached Prince Albert's study. Princess Alice brushed past Sir Brendan O'Reilly as he conferred in the hallway with a colleague.

Ignoring the warning looks of the Queen's ladies, she went directly to her father and knelt by his sofa. Katie did not enter; a glance from Bernardo DuQuelle kept her on the other side of the door, hidden in the shadows. The room had been cheerfully arranged, with a crackling fire and candles alight on the Christmas tree. A clock on the mantle gave a contented *tick-tock*. The Prince sat up to meet his daughter, but his face blanched. With a slight groan, he lay back down.

Turning from her ladies, the Queen came over to Albert, kneeling as well, her concern tinged with the slightest impatience. 'My dear Alice, you cannot be of any help. You will only tire your father.'

Prince Albert gave Alice a look that said 'don't go'.

Bending forward, Alice whispered to him. 'I will make you better. James and I, together . . .'

Outside the sky darkened, but the snow continued to fall, faster and faster. James came through the door and she sprang up to consult him. The two were soon deep in conversation, heads together, as they so often were. There was a deep worry line between Princess Alice's serious grey eyes.

The fire gave a sharp crack and the lights twinkled on the Christmas tree the Queen had requested to cheer up her husband. The clock on the mantle struck eleven and the dark red curtains framed the falling snow outside.

Katie gave a start. What was that expression Mimi liked to use? *Deja vu all over again*. This was the room in the snow globe. She had seen every one of these actions before in the snow globe, in New York City, in her own time. The snow in the window, the happy Victorian family turned mournful by the father's illness. The girl – of course, it had been Princess Alice – with worry lines etched between her eyes. And then those clear grey eyes had turned to black. Then the strange calling. The pull to this other time. It was all predestined, but by whom? And what would happen next? The uncertainty, with the underlying sense of dread, made Katie anxious and quite unreasonably angry.

'Can you describe his symptoms?' Alice was asking James.

'He is so weary and listless. Normally I would attribute it to the strain of his endless work – but he is shivering with cold, and suffers from bile. There are rheumatic aches in his legs and back. And he is terribly impatient. He will not lie still and mutters to himself,' James replied.

Bernardo DuQuelle shepherded them out of the study, into the corridor. 'Best keep your voices down,' he whispered. 'You know what the Queen is like when Prince Albert is ill.' He took James by one arm, and Katie by the other, to move them further down the hallway. 'This isn't a normal cold,' he said. 'Lord Belzen held the Prince's eye. He inflicted something – I am uncertain what – a curse, a malaise, upon that poor man in the study.'

James agreed. 'It is ill-health, but combined with a great depression. Something is weighing on his heart. And though he loves the Queen, he will never confide in her.'

They all turned to DuQuelle, the only one who could bridge the worlds of Queen Victoria and Lord Belzen. He stared into the distance, his green eyes dilating and darkening. Katie shivered. What did he see? He was still for so long that she thought he might have gone into some kind of trance. And then his gaze focused.

'I can't quite see,' DuQuelle confessed, looking at Katie. 'There's something out of kilter. I still can't understand. Katie, is there something you are choosing not to share? All I can do is return to the question: how did you arrive . . . and why?'

Alice began to protest, but DuQuelle raised his hand. 'I am not saying it is necessarily wilful on Katie's part. I am saying, though, that it is suspicious. I need to keep an eye on her. And she mustn't get too close to the Prince.'

Katie felt that strange dark surge of resentment. Why was she always kept on the outside, forever the stranger?

DuQuelle, so preoccupied with the crisis at hand, didn't seem to notice her anger. 'James, on the other hand, must stay as close as possible,' he continued. 'His medical knowledge is the finest available in the Castle. I say this with regret, but it is true. Do not leave the Prince's side for a moment. Catch the Queen's ear. Your father is out of his depth, contradict him if you must.'

'And what of me?' Alice asked.

DuQuelle looked at Princess Alice, his sculpted face softening at the sight. She was the closest to a human connection he could make. 'You are the most important of all,' he said. 'your very goodness will perhaps counterbalance the evil of Lord Belzen. I am more certain with every moment that the Prince does not suffer from a cold, or influenza, or even a gastric fever. This is the battle of good against evil. And you, Princess, are the best weapon we have to offer.'

Silently they returned to the study. Katie sullenly remained outside. After their sobering consultation with

DuQuelle, the Queen's optimism grated. 'Prince Albert is a little rheumatic,' she was saying to Sir Brendan. 'It is very difficult not to have something or other of this kind in this season. And I must admit,' she whispered in a conspiratorial tone, 'his inability to fight such aches and pains does plague me at times.'

Sir Brendan would usually have been thrilled to share the Queen's confidence, but today he looked anxious. This did not stop him agreeing. 'But of course ma'am,' he replied nervously. 'A chill. You have it in one. Your comprehension is amazing. There is no reason to be alarmed. A short feverish indisposition, that is all.'

The Queen beamed and even ventured a little joke. 'Perhaps if I were not Queen, I would be appointed as the Royal Physician?' Her courtiers laughed appreciatively, Sir Brendan O'Reilly the loudest of all, with a top note of hysteria. James winced, witnessing his father's follies. Meanwhile Prince Albert groaned softly from the sofa.

Princess Alice had heard enough. She was really quite steely under her tranquil demeanour. 'Even a chill needs great care,' she intervened. 'No one could be more devoted to my father than my mother, so she will know that quiet and rest is the best of cures.' The Queen looked rather put out, but Alice turned to her diplomatically. 'You have had a restless night as well, Mama,' she added. 'The governing of the country never stops; the country cannot afford to have *you* ill as well.'

This placated the Queen to a good extent, and Alice pressed home her advantage. 'A brisk sleigh ride is what you need. Fresh air always does you good.' The Queen was fanatical about the healthful benefits of fresh air. There was nothing she liked better than the icy wind against her cheeks. 'Do not worry,' Alice said in more soothing tones. 'I will sit with Papa, and perhaps read to him. We had just started *Silas Marner*. It is of such interest.'

The Queen was convinced. And after many directives to Alice on the care of her *dear* husband, and many touching goodbyes to the wretched man, she left. Where the Queen went, the courtiers followed. Soon the room was almost empty. Only Alice's friends remained. She turned to Bernardo DuQuelle and James O'Reilly. 'Thank you,' she said, and nodded their dismissal. There was a hint of humor in DuQuelle's eyes. He might have superior knowledge, but she was of royal blood. As a courtier he was there to serve, and to obey. He took the protesting James by the arm and ushered him out. Only Katie, forgotten by her friends, remained in the hallway. The door to Prince Albert's study was slightly ajar. Intently, she watched a tableau of daughterly devotion and fatherly love.

Prince Albert lay with his eyes shut tight; he'd been trying to block out the noise and confusion around him – so irritating to an invalid. Gradually he realized the room was silent. Perhaps he was alone? Tentatively, he opened his eyes. 'They've gone now, Father,' Alice said. 'I have remained behind. We shall do as you please. I can read to you, or play the piano softly in the next room.'

The Prince reached up a languid hand and stroked his daughter's cheek. 'Let us sit quietly then. I am happy here, in your company. My gentle Alice, you always understand so well. Your mother, your dear mother . . .' he trailed off, sighing, not wishing to be disloyal.

'It is Mama's great love for you,' Alice said, 'and her tempestuous nature; she worries so. If anything should happen to you . . .' Like her father, Alice couldn't quite finish the sentence. The Prince sighed again, watching Alice tidy the room and close the curtains. She understood. 'Tell me,' she said gently, returning to his side. 'You can tell me what you cannot tell Mama. I will be strong.'

The Prince studied his daughter. His sharp agile mind was still intact. She was so young, just a slender sapling of a girl. Could her narrow shoulders really carry such a burden? He thought of the rest of his family: his passionate Queen was so easily derailed by pressure, his eldest son amiable but lacking in intellect, his beloved older daughter far away in Prussia with her husband and children. And the others were still so young. There was only Alice.

It had been dawning on him for several years; he had undervalued Alice. She wasn't brilliant, like her older sister. She wouldn't inherit the throne, like her older brother. Yet she had a steady will and growing ability. She had not been a promising child, rather dull and mouse-like. When had the change begun? He cast his mind back through time. Was it the Crimea? Yes, the Crimean War. Alice had been separated from the family. He nodded to himself. That's right, the Queen had been with child, and they thought Alice might have the measles. She'd been sent to Buckingham Palace while the Royal Family had gone on to Balmoral. But she hadn't stayed put. There'd been some strange goings on where they couldn't locate her.

He rubbed his head; it all seemed so long ago. They'd found her . . . was it in the Alps? Baroness Lehzen had been involved. Prince Albert smiled despite his pain and weariness. Meddling, sour Baroness Lehzen: she'd been such a problem. The Queen's childhood governess had disliked Victoria's husband. But after 'losing' her charge, Princess Alice, he'd finally been able to remove Lehzen from the Court. She'd been pensioned off and now lived in Hanover, surrounded by paintings, photographs, miniatures and memories of her beloved Queen Victoria.

The Prince shook his head, irritated with himself. He must not let his mind wander. What had happened then? Ah yes, Princess Alice had returned to Balmoral, but insisted that she wanted to *nurse*. Not simply caring for family members, but outside the home, at the small hospital near Deeside that Lord Aberdeen had set up. She'd worked among the poor and been trained by professional doctors. That was it. Prince Albert pinpointed it in his mind. It must have been the nursing. Alice was still quiet and seemed gentle; but there was a determination about her. A force.

Princess Alice checked the medicines laid out near her father. She knelt down and, taking his wrist, tested his pulse against her little pocket watch. Yes, she was an excellent nurse, and she was ambitious to use this knowledge. Prince Albert sighed, again. It would be of no use to his daughter. Her ability might even harm her prospects. Alice was not destined for a career, but for life as a wife in some minor royal court; raising her own brood of children to marry yet more obscure royals. Even her progressive father would not consider an alternative. For the moment, however, Prince Albert was extremely grateful for this grave, studious child. Alice was the only one who could possibly understand what was going on.

Pain shot through Prince Albert's back and legs. A spasm clutched his bowels. 'Ah, my daughter,' he groaned, 'Bin so sehr elend. I am so very wretched!'

Alice placed a firm pillow behind his back. 'It is partly in your mind,' she said, massaging his legs vigorously. 'You are so distressed. You must rest. We will do everything we can to make you comfortable and well. And the nation! The nation cannot survive a day without your counsel. Do you not see how precious you are to us all?'

The Prince gazed at his daughter fondly, yet the sadness in his eyes made Alice grow cold. 'My daughter,' he whispered, 'oh my daughter. I love my family and I have given everything to this nation, this Britain. But you must know the truth.'

Alice continued to rub her father's legs, refusing to meet his glance. For that one moment, her love of her father turned her to a coward. She was afraid of what she would hear.

The Prince became quieter, the pain for the moment, gone. 'Why is it that I do not cling to life?' he whispered to his child. 'I have no tenacity for it.'

Princess Alice sat back, kneeling beside her father on the floor. She took his hand and said softly, 'The doctors are saying it is just a chill.' She didn't believe this for a moment, and Prince Albert snorted slightly.

'This is no snuffling cold. I am chilled, to the heart. There is something else I fear . . .'

The truth was coming, she must be brave. Alice moved even closer and laid her head upon her father's chest. 'Tell me,' she said. 'I know something of what you fear, and I will understand.'

The Prince lay quietly, gazing up at the ceiling. 'You will think the fever has affected my mind, that I am insane . . .' He paused, considering, and then sat up, resolved to speak. 'For some time, I have felt that there is a world other than ours. And not the world of our precious Lord; something strange and alien to us. A world of a good, so bright it hurts, and an evil, so dark . . . so dark . . .' He began to shiver and Alice moved to bring him a blanket, but he wound his arms around her, holding her as tight as he could.

'Such strange things are happening,' said Prince Albert. 'Incidents beyond our powers. It is war.'

'War in America?' Alice asked.

He was silent, gathering together his fantastical thoughts. 'Yes and no,' he replied slowly. 'It is part of this war in America; almost as if *they* are using the American war for their own purposes.

Alice lifted her head to look at her father. 'Can you tell me about these people? Who are *they*?' She dreaded the answer.

Prince Albert stared into space. 'I cannot tell you much, but I feel a great deal. Sometimes I catch a glimpse, from the corner of my eye, and then I hear the sounds so very softly. As if I am on the other side of a wall, unable to reach them . . . And then that man, last night, the most tangible evidence. He looked into my eyes. I felt as if he were draining my soul. He has left a terrible cold behind. A helplessness. A hopelessness. With that one glance, he has wounded me deeply.'

It was worse than Alice had suspected. Yet she still hoped to cure him. 'Dear father, you must put aside these morbid thoughts. You must rest,' she pleaded.

Prince Albert stroked her soft brown hair. 'No,' he said, 'I will never rest again. The time has come. The battles are merging. The violence of the Americas feeds a much greater battle. It is no longer of another world, but of ours. It is not by accident that I fear what I fear, or I see what I see. These strange creatures and half-seen fancies; it is me they want. I have suspected for some time and now I know. Death entered Windsor Castle last night. He came, dressed for a ball – and danced with me!'

Chapter Eleven

The Real Sir Brendan

The days stretched out and Windsor Castle closed in upon itself. In the Grand Corridor the courtiers conversed in low worried tones. The Queen continued to deny that her beloved husband was seriously ill. 'It has only been a week,' she insisted. Even the finest doctors in the land would not contradict the Queen, and Sir Brendan O'Reilly was not among the finest. He agreed with her, giving her false hope. At worst, he said, 'The Prince would be in bed for quite some time. He might still be convalescing at Christmas . . . a pity . . .'

Princess Alice carried the burden of knowledge. During their long night together, when Prince Albert told her what he feared she had tried to reassure her father, but she knew he spoke the truth. Quickly she sought out James O'Reilly and, ignoring DuQuelle's suspicions, Katie too. DuQuelle, of course, was vital. He was their only guide to this other world which they must battle.

With its courtyards and crenellated walks, it was easy to find privacy at Windsor Castle. The four made their way to the lower ward, and met in the Dean's Cloister, away from the curious eyes of the Castle inmates and visitors.

Katie was shocked to see the change a week could make. Alice, always slender, was now stick-thin. Her large grey eyes were ringed with circles. James's hair stood on end and in his absent-mindedness he hadn't even put on a coat to ward off the cold. Only DuQuelle maintained a sense of normalcy. He was dressed, as usual, with great care – in a natty fur-lined overcoat with a deep cape.

Together they paced under the arches of the old cloister, their tapping feet echoing on the cold stone.

'Could we not have met in the Castle?' DuQuelle asked. 'Preferably near one of those roaring beach fires?' He had a particular dislike of the cold, but was this really the time for flippancy? Katie looked at him closely. If any man that white could grow even paler – that man was Bernardo DuQuelle. Could he possibly be as worried as the rest of them?

'I feel so helpless,' Alice said. 'If it were simply a fever, even an ailment as serious as typhoid – my father is still young, he lives a healthy life, he could fight and win and live! But Lord Belzen is involved. I do not know how we can fight the Malum.'

They all looked to Bernardo DuQuelle. His face gave away nothing. He offered no hope. Katie couldn't bear it. Seeing Alice like this helped her push away the dark bitterness that kept trying to take hold.

'We have to fight what we can,' Katie said, 'and that's his physical illness. If only Sir Brendan would admit that the Prince is truly ill. I mean, the Queen believes every word he says, thinks he's a great doctor, but . . .' She trailed off. It was always hard to discuss Sir Brendan O'Reilly, with his feeble abilities and his lax morals, in front of his talented, upright son.

James flushed red, but was firm in his reply. 'You are right, Katie, this cannot go on. The optimistic attitude of my father is killing the Prince. We must bring in a better doctor and we have to act now. Bernardo DuQuelle needs to speak to my father – and Princess Alice must convince the Queen. I suggest we cable Sir Henry Holland. He's of a finer cut than most society doctors and the Queen approves of him. I will also telegraph to Dr Thomas Watson. He's a sound physician who is grounded in the treatment of fever. And the Prime Minister must be informed. We need backing at the highest level.'

Not for the first time, Katie looked at James with admiration. He had the makings of a true doctor and put knowledge and ability before everything else. She expected great things of him. Princess Alice squeezed his hand in sympathy. 'I'm certain that is the best path,' she said. 'This does not, though, address the bigger problem. My father says it is a battle, a battle beyond our abilities.' Again they looked to DuQuelle and again he was silent.

Finally he spoke. 'To fight on two fronts is always a mistake, but we have no choice. Let us deal first with the here and now. James, cable the doctors and tell them they must come at once. When they reach the Castle, make certain they speak with you first – yours is certain to be the best diagnosis of the case. Princess Alice, Katie, follow me. I will have that much-needed discussion with Sir Brendan O'Reilly.'

They found Sir Brendan in the Grand Corridor, pacing outside the Blue Room. 'Ah, DuQuelle,' he said. 'Just the man I need.' But his eyes said otherwise. DuQuelle, who knew so much and understood all, was rarely the man a courtier wanted to see, and with him were Princess Alice and that gawky American friend of hers – even worse. A most unwelcome trio.

'How does the Prince?' DuQuelle asked, knowing full well the answer.

Sir Brendan tried to smile, but it was a weak attempt. 'He has had a poor night, I am afraid of his own making. The Prince would not settle, but moved from room to room, sitting up and lying down. He is finally resting in the Blue Room. At my urging, he has taken some orange jelly and a little raspberry vinegar in seltzer water. I assure you, he'll sleep now and begin to mend.'

Katie looked at Sir Brendan in amazement. How could he continue this policy of cheery optimism?

Meanwhile Princess Alice had some questions. 'I've discussed the case with James,' she began, 'and to us it seems a much more serious illness, bearing the characteristics of a gastric fever. Don't you fear...?'

Sir Brendan frowned. At heart, he had always disliked Princess Alice. Despite her gentle voice and large grey eyes, she was pushy, something he hated in a girl. And worse, she was determined to study medicine. It was all so unwomanly. Then there were her relations with his son, James – in his opinion the least promising of the O'Reilly children – who would never adapt to court life. The last thing Sir Brendan wanted was the opinion of Princess Alice. He still wished to play the courtier, but his patience was running thin.

'You talk of fear, Princess?' said Sir Brendan. 'Oh yes, I have a single, looming fear. I fear that every year for the next thirty years, I will be tending Prince Albert for these same symptoms. The Prince, as always, is over-sensitive about illness. He makes a great mountain of a trifling winter cold.'

Alice looked grave. 'I would hardly call this the time to jest,' she reproved Sir Brendan. 'You misdiagnose this illness. In my opinion . . .'

There it was again. The opinion of a girl. He knew he was in too deep, in ways they couldn't imagine. Something in Sir Brendan snapped and his usual charm, saved for the Royal Family, collapsed. 'Your opinion? I have warned the Queen, again and again, that nursing – semi-professional nursing – outside the home sphere, would be the ruin of you. And look what it was done. This attempt to interfere, to impose your own half-baked theories, to overrule the Queen's physician!'

Sir Brendan's voice lost its upper-class drawl and went up an octave. Other courtiers, further down the corridor, looked up from their whispers, sensing something more interesting to talk about. But Sir Brendan could not control himself. 'Your father has indulged all his daughters, treating them as scholars,' he practically spat the word *scholar* at the Princess. 'This has fed an immodest curiosity in you. I feel for that penniless Grand Duke, that young Louis – what a wife for him! If he had any understanding of your temperament . . . I doubt even he would be interested in such an advantageous marriage. I suggest you stop playing at medicine and prepare yourself for the life you were born to, as a Princess and as a woman.'

He'd had his say, with all his natural coarseness and ignorance coming to the forefront. Princess Alice turned red with embarrassment.

Katie could feel her cheeks flushing too, but with fury. 'How dare you!' she cried. 'I mean Alice, who tries so hard and knows so much. How could you? You're a terrible doctor. You're nothing but a phoney!'

Sir Brendan really was at the end of his tether. He was more anxious and exhausted than he let on. A threat hung over him, perhaps more powerful than the Royal Family; and now this interference. He turned on Katie with double the fury.

'And you! You are nothing but trouble, the strange friend of this unnatural Princess. Everything you touch is tainted. Your interference with my own daughter Grace has seriously damaged her matrimonial possibilities. You have encouraged in her a most unbecoming sense of independence. I do not understand why someone of your ilk would be presented at Court. I have my suspicions. Mr Lewis Tappan. The Lord Chamberlain tells me it was an introduction through M. DuQuelle, and we all know how dubious *that* is . . . Has anyone at court ever met Mr Lewis Tappan . . . or his daughter Katherine? As soon as the Prince is mending, and he will be mending soon, I will make my inquiries. M. DuQuelle, your position at court is in grave jeopardy.'

Katie's anger was now tinged with alarm. Alice shook from head to toe. Only Bernardo DuQuelle remained calm. But when he spoke, it was with great force of will. 'We have no time for your insults and abuse. The Prince must see a more qualified doctor.'

Sir Brendan's bravery began to collapse. 'You must not do so,' he cried. 'It would only distress the Queen and worry Prince Albert. I am unwilling to cause unnecessary alarm when no cause exists, by calling in a medical man that does not upon ordinary occasions attend at the Palace.'

DuQuelle examined the silver tip of his walking stick. He seemed displeased with what he saw. 'You speak a half truth,' he said. 'You are unwilling – yes, you are most unwilling. You are unwilling to endanger your position at court. You are unwilling to alert the Queen to the serious nature of her husband's illness. In short, you are unwilling to save the Prince Consort's life. I sometimes wonder at your actions, and most particularly, at your motives. For whom do you really act, Sir Brendan? Who is your real master? You distrust me? Well, I am exceedingly suspicious of you. I suspect I shall see you leave the Court long before my own exit.'

Sir Brendan blanched. Watching him turn pale, something occurred to Katie. Sir Brendan had always appeared such a buffoon, and yet at the Christmas Ball, only a few days ago, she had seen him give way in the dance to . . . he'd definitely recognized him . . . could he be involved with—

'Lord Belzen'.

She'd said it aloud before she could stop herself. Sir Brendan's hands went up, over his head, as if to shield himself.

Bernardo DuQuelle smiled. It was a strange thing to do. 'Do not worry Sir Brendan,' DuQuelle spoke in a soothing voice, more frightening than his earlier anger.

'The responsibility has been lifted from your bowing, scraping shoulders. Your own son, an excellent physician by the way, has contacted two of Britain's finest medical men. James O'Reilly believes this is a germ-related illness. The Prime Minister has been informed of the true nature of the Prince's malaise and the actions we have taken.'

Like many bullies, Sir Brendan preferred to pick on those weaker than himself. He was no match for Bernardo DuQuelle. And to lose his temper with Princess Alice had been a major mistake. But Katie . . . He turned to her, his rage reigniting. 'I know you have something to do with this. I shall get to the bottom of who you are and what you are. You will be exposed.'

The other courtiers were edging closer now, sniffing out a good old-fashioned Court feud. Sir Brendan seemed suddenly to come to his senses. With a stiff bow, he returned to the sickroom and an ailing Prince he could not cure.

DuQuelle took each girl lightly by the arm. 'I suggest we walk and talk,' he said. 'And I recommend we speak softly. The ladies-in-waiting, the Queen's dressers, the Prince's valets – how they would love to hear our conversation.' Slowly they promenaded down the Grand Corridor, out of earshot.

Princess Alice was still trembling and Katie had trouble breathing. 'I just don't believe it,' Katie said. 'He couldn't, I mean *couldn't* be working for Lord Belzen.'

'We have no absolute proof,' DuQuelle said. 'If guilty, it is the most serious charge.' He looked down at Katie. 'Though anyone can be trapped by Lord Belzen. Do you think evil is stupid? No. True evil, magnificent evil, is the cleverest of clever. Lord Belzen has ways. He twists and turns and ducks. One may be working for him and not understand. He can reach out. His call can be sweet. The victim will come to him, without even knowing.' DuQuelle caught Katie's eye, his own green ones growing dark, searching.

And then Katie realized, he's trying to read my mind . . . and he can't find what he wants; for once he doesn't understand. 'I am the mystery,' Katie thought. And then she was very frightened, because her heart leapt with an ugly, strong triumph.

Chapter Twelve

Snow Hill

In Windsor Great Park the ancient oaks stretched their frosted branches skyward. To Sir Brendan O'Reilly, they looked like the giants of old, raising their arms to heaven, beseeching him to turn back. But there was no turning back. His horse continued up the Long Walk, away from the warmth of the Castle, towards Snow Hill. To his right, the sun was setting, a ball of bright red, reflected in the snow, crimson as blood. Sir Brendan shivered, and his horse skidded on the icy road.

He dismounted, to lead his horse up the hill. Ahead he could see the statue of George III, dressed as a Roman Emperor, astride his own copper horse. It was an inconvenient meeting place, cold and remote at this time of year. But for such a meeting as this, it was perfect. Sir Brendan looked back at the stand of trees and couldn't agree with them more. Turn back.

He reached the top and tied his horse to the base of the statue. It really was a ridiculous monument, he thought. Mad old George III with bare legs and a toga. For a moment Sir Brendan fancied the statue shivered too. Then his attention turned to a figure emerging from the shadows. It was another man; another gentleman, he might even venture. Yet when Sir Brendan saw this man, his stomach turned with revulsion and dread. 'I was afraid you might not come,' was all Sir Brendan said.

The other man laughed slightly, wrapping himself tightly in his warm fur coat. 'You are right to be afraid,' he said, 'though not of what you say, Sir Brendan.'

Sir Brendan hesitated. He almost turned back. And then the man spoke again. 'I have upheld my side of the bargain. My bankers have put aside a large sum of money. This should clear your debts. Lord Twisted will marry your daughter, should that be your wish. You must be aware that he had other, less honourable designs on her. But the promise of a hefty dowry, from me, has transformed her into wife material. Miss Grace O' Reilly will have one of the oldest titles in the land.'

Sir Brendan, looked worried. New lines were etched on his handsome face. The Prince's illness and his own part to play, the problems with money, the worries about his daughter – all this had taken its toll. He was on the brink of disgrace. Yet here he was – saved from bankruptcy. And Grace O'Reilly would become Lady Twisted.

He was on the brink of disgrace. Yet here he was, saved from bankruptcy. And Grace O'Reilly would become Lady Twisted. Lord Twisted might be corrupt and debauched, a spy and a traitor, but his title was ancient, and his bloodlines very blue. Through the lineage of her husband, Grace would be celebrated in every circle of society and Sir Brendan would rise with her. So many of his troubles were now lifted from his shoulders. He should have felt relief, but doubts continued to creep in with the chill.

Lord Twisted's noble family might go back hundreds of years, but there was little money left behind the title. He had spent it all. Then his luck had turned. His wealth had increased considerably; where the fortune came from, *society* had no idea. Yet *society* now considered him a splendid catch for any woman . . . until one looked closely at the man himself. He was a known liar and cheat. His behaviour during the Crimean War had been scandalous. A less well-connected man would have swung for his deeds. And this new-found wealth . . . Sir Brendan could guess its source.

A copse of trees lay beyond the statue, catching the last light of the day. Sir Brendan stared into the thicket, absent mindedly. Then something caught his eye. A shadow, flitting between the bare branches, and a sound, soft and sniggering, as if he were being mocked. After a hesitation, he bowed. 'I am grateful for your intervention,' he said stiffly. 'There is no way I can repay you. I must take my leave now. As you are aware, there is illness, trouble at Windsor Castle. I must attend at once, Lord Belzen.'

Lord Belzen bowed in return, that strange writhing movement he gave in pleasure or anger. 'To be of service to you is repayment in itself,' he replied smoothly. Again, an odd shrill yapping came from the woods below. 'I am all sympathy, for the troubles in the Castle. Tell me, how does the Prince . . . truly . . . ?'

Sir Brendan looked closely at Lord Belzen. His pale blue eyes were almost rimless and unblinking. Sir Brendan was not a reflective man, but he had begun to wonder, and to doubt.

He had met Lord Belzen at a fete in London. The man seemed well connected, charming and obliging. And he was rich – and generous. Sir Brendan, as he borrowed more and more money, had become indiscreet. From the beginning Lord Belzen had shown great concern for him and his trials. His listened with sympathy to Sir Brendan's complaints about DuQuelle and the upstart American girl. He asked many questions about the health of Prince Albert.

Lord Belzen was also generous with his advice. Do not alarm the Queen, he said. Ignore the Prince's constant complaints. Treat his illness lightly. And most importantly, do not consult other physicians. The Queen must place all her trust in Sir Brendan. Great things would come of this. There was even the hint that Bernardo DuQuelle and Miss Katherine Tappan would be taken care of . . . the problem would be solved . . .

Thinking now of the ailing Prince and the conflict with DuQuelle, Sir Brendan knew he had made a poor choice in his confidante. 'Prince Albert's health is deteriorating,' he said slowly. 'There are those in the Castle who begin to question my diagnosis. I dislike yielding authority. But it is perhaps best to bring in other, more expert physicians.' The weird yapping in the forest had grown to a howl. He wondered what kind of animal could make such a noise?

Lord Belzen writhed, this time with annoyance.

'You must not follow your original course of action,' he replied, his voice taking on a soft hiss. 'You must insist that the Prince will mend. You must continue to take charge. Heed my advice. We need you there, in the Castle, at the side of the Prince.'

Sir Brendan's doubts and fears were now tinged with anger. He could see clearly where the bargain lay. In exchange for the money and the aristocratic connections, Sir Brendan must act for Lord Belzen, be his pawn in the Castle. He might be weak and desperate, but this was a step too far. Gathering up his final shreds of conscience, he spoke to Lord Belzen. 'Do not forget, my duty is to the Queen and to her country. I shall be unable to act as you desire.'

A spasm passed through Lord Belzen's body. But then he regained control. 'You will do as I ask. And I will show you why.'

The wind picked up, shaking the limbs of the bare trees. Sir Brendan could see a cluster of animals, leaping from branch to branch. They were baying, as if for blood. He ducked, as one swooped out of the thicket. And then it was in the air, followed by another. Suddenly there was a drove of them, shrieking and cackling. They moved so quickly, he could not see them clearly. In the long shadows of the end of day, he could pick out a wing here, a spike there, the face of a man and the snout of a pig. A grotesquely long limb reached out to pull his hair and tweak his nose.

Sir Brendan was paralysed with fear. It was too late to turn back. In front of him, Lord Belzen's body began to quiver, from the ankles up through his whole frame. It was a repulsive movement.

'We need to feed,' Lord Belzen said, his voice thick and sibilant. 'And we must feed on brute force. We will sup greatly from this war in America. The girl I have called from times forward, Miss Katherine Tappan . . . Miss Katie . . . call her what you like, but you are right to distrust her. She is angry and alone. She feels left behind and useless. As the seeds of duplicity grow within her, and I will enter her soul. She is already weakening

Bernardo DuQuelle. The time comes and soon. She will turn against her friends in the Castle, present to them the face of a friend, but act for me. She will even turn from her Northern sympathies and fan the flames of war.'

'But why Prince Albert?' Sir Brendan asked through trembling lips.

Lord Belzen's head rose up with a reptilian grace. 'The Prince stands in our way. He will act to stop Britain, and the world, from going to war. He believes in communication, knowledge, negotiation, peace. These princely gifts, they thwart and starve us. There must be world war. To achieve this, we will remove him.'

Sir Brendan was terrified. He had feared social ruin, but he now stood at the gates of Hell. There was one last remnant of loyalty within him. 'The Queen,' he said. 'You must not harm the Queen.'

Lord Belzen's tongue flickered strangely between his lips. 'We do not want the Queen herself,' he whispered. 'It is the power, the potential for chaos and brutality.' A great cunning spread over his long face. 'We want this power for you. The Prince will die, you know that, surely. But you must save the Queen.' Belzen raised his arm, pointing to the statue, silhouetted black against the sky. 'The Royal Family. So unstable. The Queen's very grandfather, George III, was locked up, a madman, in the castle before us. It is you who must protect the Queen, shield her, hide her . . .'

'You will be rewarded,' Lord Belzen continued. 'The wounded Queen, the feeble Queen. You will become her adviser, her companion, and much more than just her trusted servant. She is susceptible to love, and what more charming consort could she choose? Think of the power you will yield, the position you will take in society. I can see you always at the Queen's side. The most handsome, powerful, wealthy man in Britain – in the world . . .'

At the best of times, Sir Brendan's mind was not strong. The paralytic fear, the vaulting vanity, the essential weakness now took its toll. Ignoring the demons above him, he fixed his sights on the castle, and his future. He was ready to serve Lord Belzen. 'My debts must be settled immediately,' he said, 'though my daughter's marriage should wait. There is certain to be a grander match, perhaps into the Royal Family as well.' Having settled his fate, he began to take steps, make plans. 'The other doctors will come,' he said. 'There is no way to stop them. But I also feel it is too late for them to change the fate of this Prince.'

Lord Belzen bowed deep. 'As yet, I cannot address you as "my Prince", but I can reward you with a princely sum.' He took a velvet pouch from inside his coat.

The sun had set; the sky had darkened. Sir Brendan pocketed his spoils, far more than thirty pieces of silver, and, mounting his horse, road back to the Castle and his destiny. Above him swirled a raucous chorus of singing and laughter. Not of angels, but of demons.

Chapter Thirteen

The Call of Duty

The doctors came, but to no avail. Three more days passed, and the Prince grew weaker. Sir Brendan, fortified by new ambition, put his courtier face back in place, and stayed by the Prince's side. He avoided Princess Alice at all costs; he knew he'd overstepped the mark and must heed Belzen and be patient.

But Alice had other things on her mind. As Prince Albert's health declined, the Queen's hysteria rose. She was never good under pressure and this was the crisis of her life. At first the Queen tried to countermand the illness, telling the doctors, 'the Prince is the most precious and perfect of human beings, he cannot be seriously ill'.

But her commands were not enough and eventually she turned to pleading. Her high wailing voice could be heard from the Prince's chamber: 'You will save him, won't you? I know you can!' More doctors arrived, sent by the Prime Minister, by the Emperor of France and even by Florence Nightingale. The doctors consulted together, reached no agreement and shook their heads.

Katie noticed, with the smallest trace of satisfaction, that they ignored Sir Brendan and turned to James O'Reilly for advice. Though so young, almost a boy, James had a knowledge and seriousness of purpose beyond that of most grown men. She would often see the doctors leaving the sickroom, deep in conversation with him. The courtiers mobbed them, desperate for news. Indeed, the entire nation held its breath. Regular bulletins were issued in the newspapers. The media had suddenly woken up, and realized just how important Prince Albert was to Britain – and that he was in danger.

And the Prince himself? At first he did try to rally. But he was overcome by nerves. He could not rest, or even settle into bed. Throughout the dark hours he wandered from room to room, followed by his little, distressed Queen. One sad night of shivering and sleeplessness followed another. Some mornings he would rise and sit on his sofa, wrapped in his quilted dressing gown, admiring the views of the garden and the orangery. He would take some broth with bread and hold his wife's hand. But on others he would lie still, with his eyes shut, seemingly counting the moments until it was all over.

Princess Alice barely left his side, showing fortitude far beyond her age. Katie tried to beat down her resentment and shut out the bitter selfish voice. Alice needed her. When Alice did leave her father, Katie was there to make certain she had a cup of tea, or lay down to rest. One afternoon, as the Prince dozed, Katie walked on the East Terrace with her friend. Underneath her fur cloak, Alice's dress sagged and dragged through the snow.

'Alice, you've got a big family, can't the others take some of the stress?' Katie asked. 'You're worn out, absolutely exhausted, and so thin . . . You're going to get sick yourself.'

A cold wind swept across the terrace. Alice took Katie's arm, teetering slightly. 'I am tired,' Alice admitted, 'and I am so worried.'

Katie gave her arm a sympathetic squeeze. 'It must be awful. I can't imagine. And it is so like you, to give your all to your father.'

Princess Alice walked along in silence. Then she turned to her friend with a face filled with anxiety and guilt. 'It's not just my father. It should be. That is my duty. But there is something else. Oh— I am an unnatural child, Sir Brendan is right . . .'

They stopped walking and Katie turned to her.

'Alice, you couldn't do something bad if someone offered you a million dollars to do it. How could you listen to Sir Brendan? I wish we could get rid of him. I know he's up to something really awful.'

Princess Alice sat down on a stone bench. Fretfully she tunnelled into a mound of snow with her boot.

'It's . . . it's . . . marriage! It's what Sir Brendan said . . . about Louis of Darmstadt . . . he says I am going to be married to him . . . Oh Katie! Is this really all that life has for me? I so want . . . I want . . .'

For a moment, the secret black speck in Katie's heart leapt up. She knew what Alice wanted. And if she got it, Katie would be left out in the cold, all alone again. But then a streak of winter light fell across Alice's bowed head. Jealousy. Katie was jealous of her friend. The idea formed into words before her. Words had such power over her. Once Katie could see the words, she understood: she was being stupid. She must try harder and defeat this jealousy. She didn't know what had hold of her, but she must fight back, through the strength of her friendship. Katie sat down next to Alice and put her arms around her. 'Don't cry, don't cry over this. It would be a good thing, to talk it over I mean.'

Alice was completely silent. She turned so red it was painful to watch. 'This isn't something I should talk about,' she finally said.

Katie didn't laugh at her primness. She knew how hard

this must be for Alice, being who she was; and living when she did. She tried to speak lightly to her friend.

'You know Mimi, my mother? She pays someone two thousand dollars a month just to talk about this kind of stuff. And sometimes she wakes me up at 3 a.m. to have another crack at it. You're a serious person, Alice, and this is important to you. Go ahead. Talk.'

Princess Alice shivered in the cold. Katie was freezing, but she knew enough to wait. This kind of conversation took time. Finally Alice spoke. 'I didn't have any idea that I might feel this way about, well . . .'

'James,' Katie supplied helpfully, and then was sorry, as Alice turned that dull aching red again and mumbled.

'No, I didn't know. And now I am so ashamed. Such a lack of modesty and discipline.'

Katie frowned. 'But it's not like you've done anything. I mean, kissed or . . .'

Alice jumped up from the bench. For a moment Katie thought she was going to run back into the Castle. 'Of course not!' Alice cried. 'I would never behave in that manner. Nor would James O'Reilly. It has never entered his mind. These feelings are all of my own making and I bear the responsibility.'

If Katie hadn't felt so sad, she would have smiled. 'Never entered James's mind? Alice, it's all he thinks about. For him, it's always been you. I mean, I know you're a princess and everything, and I know how different your time is.

But James has been raised in the Royal Court. He's ever so nice and he's going to have a great career. Isn't there any way that could be enough?'

Hearing that James cared for her made Alice turn a different kind of red-rosy and happy for one moment. And then the colour drained from her face.

'You don't understand, Katie. It could never be. I had hoped to stay with my mother and father. I thought that James and I could continue on, as we always had; as friends, sharing notes on science and medicine . . .'

Katie looked at Alice. She lived a life of privilege and luxury, yet she wanted so little.

'Hesse-Darmstadt is so very far away,' Alice murmured, looked down at her hands.

Just then, James came out onto the terrace. He'd been talking with the doctors about hygiene in the sickroom and was wiping his hands with tar water. Peering down at the girls, he scowled. 'It's cold out here. Princess Alice is too frail for this weather.'

Alice kissed Katie on the cheek, and ran past James into Windsor Castle. Katie stopped to talk to him.

'James,' she said, 'with all my heart, I'm sorry.'

He looked surprised. 'You weren't outside very long,' he said. 'And it's easy to forget that Alice is delicate. She has such fortitude and strength of mind. But even you must be cold. Come inside. The Prince's pulse rate is more regular. He's sleeping now. Even I hope against hope.'

Yet, as the day turned to night, the Prince did not rally. And now the doctors feared for the Queen. For ten days her husband had been ill and she was numb with exhaustion. Towards midnight, after much cajoling, she agreed to rest on the sofa in her husband's dressing room; the doctors had assured her there would be no crisis that night. She would only go, though, once Alice had promised to stay awake, all the night, at his side. As the candle burnt low, Katie made her way to her own bed.

When Katie reached her tiny room in the visitor's apartments she didn't even undress, just took off her shoes and loosened her stays. Within moments she was in a deep slumber. But just as quickly, about two hours later, she was awake. Eyes wide open, staring into blackness, as if she would never sleep again. Everything raced through her brain. They wouldn't make Alice marry that handsome stranger. Sir Brendan must be wrong. She tossed and turned. Sir Brendan, a human mine field, an explosion waiting to happen. How dangerous was he? Would he really going to track down Sir Lewis Tappan?

Katie buried her head beneath her pillow. One of the biggest problems was . . . well . . . she was one of the biggest problems. Who had called her to this time? Were they responsible for her secrecy, her defensiveness, her anger? She could not fight off that strange, secret darkness – a tiny pinprick of evil – that leapt in the furthest reaches of her mind. The call of the Tempus had come before, and she'd grown to understand, she was a force for good. Alice believed in her and, grudgingly, so did James O'Reilly. Even Bernardo DuQuelle had been won over. But this time . . . Could she? Would she really harm her friends?

Katie swung her feet off the bed, and pulling her shoes on, laced them tightly. There was no point staying in bed. She was searching for her shawl when she heard a noise. Standing very still, she strained her ears; was Alice calling to her? No. The sound wasn't coming from outside her door, or from the sickroom. Below her window all was silent. It was the sound she had come to expect and dread. The call was low but clear, and it was coming from inside her own head. It was not to be ignored. She took up the walking stick, for protection; lighting her candle, she opened the door. The hallway was quiet. Down from her little flight of stairs she could see the flickering reflection of the huge lamps that were left to burn all night. Katie followed the light, but instead of turning right, towards the Royal Apartments, she found herself turning left.

Soon she was outside, in the bitter winter night, the snow crunching underneath her feet. 'I'll turn back,' she thought, but the voice within her head led her on. It wasn't quite human and it wasn't really a song. More of a rhythm she could not withstand. Katie could see a guard in the courtyard, so she slipped into the quadrangle and then struggled up the snow-covered hill to the monumental Round Tower of Windsor Castle. 'Why?' she asked herself. There was no answer, but her body had a strange confidence. This was where she must go.

The tower loomed above her, block after block of grey limestone, circling to a great height. She could just spy a small arched oak door on the far side. The voice inside told her: this door would not be guarded and it would not be locked. Entering, she could see a long, steep stairway. The entire passage was cave-like, as if carved through dense rock.

Slowly she climbed the stone steps, passing under squared and rounded arches, built for need rather than show. On and on she went, up the steps, worn deep in their centres by thousands of feet over hundreds of years. Her little candle flickered and sputtered but did not go out. The steps seemed endless, her remorseless tread echoing through the dark and empty tower. 'It's just one of those dreams,' she reassured herself, 'the kind where you are exploring the jungle, or being chased in a house. I'll wake up soon.' At the top of the stairs was another low wooden door. It swung open almost before she could touch it. Katie was hit by a blast of freezing winter air. Her candle went out. No dream was ever this cold.

She stood at the highest point of Windsor Castle, the battlements of the Round Tower. The winter wind was brutal and a simple shawl was no match for it. Katie crouched down, clutching the shawl, shivering. But her shivers were a mix of excitement and fear. Whatever it was, whatever had called her, it had to be here. There was nowhere else for her to go. Regaining her breath, she stood and staggered to the edge, clutching the large carved crenellations. It was a wild night, the clouds whipping across the sky. The snow below reflected the light of a full moon, giving, for a brief moment, the eerie sensation of full daylight.

The clouds raced across the moon, blotting out the light. All was darkness. Through the pitch black and the bitter wind she could sense something – another presence. Someone was there. She could hear it, the clear ring of a step against the frozen stone. Panic rose in her throat. Whatever this call to her had been, she should have resisted. Instinctively she edged towards the door, scraping her back against the castle parapets. She reached out her hand, making a grab for the door handle. Her foot slipped and a gust of wind propelled her backwards. She was between the gaps in the battlements, flailing, trying to regain her balance. With dread, she realized she was going over.

Chapter Fourteen

On the Battlements

Can you die in another time? Katie wondered, almost idly, in that split second between the battlements and thin air. Dolores flitted through her mind. How could she leave Dolores in another century? Even as she fought to regain her footing, Katie could see herself toppling backwards, headlong, arms splayed, into the snow below. It looked so soft, but it was certain to be a hard landing. Goodbye to James . . . goodbye to Alice. They must battle on alone to save Prince Albert.

And then a hand reached out. It grasped her firmly around the wrist and pulled her forward, back from the brink and onto her hands and knees. She struggled, hitting out with the walking stick, only for it to be torn from her grasp. She was still in grave danger. The wind lashed across the sky and the clouds were swept from the moon. She could see. Before her a figure loomed, cloak whipping, arm raised. A strange white face stared down at her. It was Bernardo DuQuelle.

'You!' she gasped. 'You almost killed me.'

DuQuelle bent forward and, retrieving her walking stick, handed it to her politely. 'On the contrary, I am trying to save you.' He tapped his own walking stick against his chin, absentmindedly, as Katie caught her breath and sat back, wrapping her shawl tight around her.

'I wonder why?' DuQuelle continued. 'Why should I save you? You are, of course, one of the Tempus Fugit, the three. The child who brings peace, the child who brings war – and you, Katie, the child who brings war and peace. Your great gift has always been that you can choose: war or peace, evil or good. Time and again, you have made that choice, the choice for good. But now, I have my doubts.'

Katie huddled on the floor, tapping the cane against the stones. She had her doubts too, and it was doubly worse hearing it from DuQuelle.

'There is a darkness that blocks your thoughts,' DuQuelle said. 'I can no longer read them, and this fills me with dismay.'

The dark leaping thing rose up in Katie. What business was it of his? Bernardo DuQuelle had no right to try and control her.

DuQuelle sat down on the stone floor, next to her. He tucked the shawl firmly around her, and raising her chin with a long white finger, looked her in the eye. 'Do you know, Katie? Why are you here?'

Katie opened her mouth, and then shut it. Part of her wanted to tell him, even the little she knew, but that terrible feeling stopped her. Pushing the dark thing to the back of her mind, she forced the words from her mouth.

'I was led. Something called to me; the same thing that pulled me into this time.'

DuQuelle took her hand and held tight. 'Who called you, Katie?' he asked.

And now the blackness fought back. 'It is still calling me,' she said dreamily, 'a strange dark joy, a thumping, a sliding, undulating dance within my head. It has such a lovely tempo, soft . . . throbbing . . .'

'You must fight it,' DuQuelle said.

Katie stood up, moving towards the sound. 'It is like waves on the beach, lapping against fine sand. It is the wind, coming in low from the sea, circling the dunes.'

DuQuelle heard it too, and it was not a welcome sound. 'You've been deceived,' he told her. 'It is the most horrible sound; sush-sush-sush – I cannot stand the rasp and slink of snakes.' The sound was louder now, a rhythmic sliding and hissing as hundreds of undulating forms heaved themselves up the stone steps. They slithered round and round, towards the top of the tower. DuQuelle rarely showed emotion, but he blanched so white he was almost translucent. Reading his face, Katie felt dread spread through her body.

'What have I done?' she asked.

'You have followed a most sinister siren's song,' Du-Quelle replied. 'But how could you not? Evil is so often more alluring than good.' He took his own walking stick and tapped her lightly on the ear, first one, then the other.

A terrible knowledge swept through Katie. 'I know who called me. I was fooled by the snow globe. I thought Princess Alice needed me. But it was Lord Belzen. I've been lured to this time. And now Lord Belzen has come to claim me.'

DuQuelle circled the tower, for once impervious to the cold. 'Trapped at a great height, with only one way down, and an enormous slithering serpent blocking the way. Unless we choose to leap from the battlements, I do not see an escape,' he murmured.

Katie dropped her head to her knees, covering her ears. Among the sliding snakes, a distinct footstep could be heard. 'I can't think! I can't think!' she cried.

DuQuelle stopped pacing. He lifted his head and seemed to confer with some unseen being. 'Perhaps you do not need to think. Perhaps this is the time to trust in faith and simply choose. Of all the Tempus, you are the one with options. You are, after all, the child of peace and war. But you must understand you choices. It must be fair.

There is no need to die. You can still go to Lord Belzen. He called you. He wants you. As long as you serve his purposes, your rewards would be far beyond anything I could bring you. It is your choice.'

She hadn't thought of this. DuQuelle was right – again. There was great power in evil. And Lord Belzen possessed power in spades. She had no real place in this time. Sure, she was friends with Alice and James: but they really just wanted to be with each other. She was in the way. And in her own time . . . Mimi? She knew Mimi did need her and love her; but how much love could a completely self-centred, celebrity-obsessed mother actually give? Her modern world would get along perfectly well without her. It was a world where she just didn't count. Why not go to Lord Belzen? For once she would be important. She could fly through time with him. And as long as she did what he asked . . .

Katie looked out over the battlements, to the town of Windsor below and the countryside in the distance, imagining a life of such power.

DuQuelle cleared his throat. 'You can see twelve counties from up here: Middlesex to Bedfordshire. Our friend James O'Reilly could probably recite them in order. He loves facts. And he always has gentle Alice to listen to them. She believes him to be almost perfect. Thank goodness he has a friend like you, Katie, to occasionally puncture his pomposity.'

Friends and friendship. It seemed a strange, bland thing to talk of at such a moment. But it cleared Katie's mind. What luck, to have such friends. There was James, with his sharp, clean intellect. At the beginning he had questioned Katie's story. But once he'd accepted it, he'd accepted her. Since then, their friendship had remained steadfast. He might be gruff, but he was truthful and loyal. On more than one occasion he had risked his life for Katie. How could she have resented his new affection for Alice, when their own friendship was stronger than ever?

And Princess Alice. From the beginning she had believed Katie. Alice had an entire kingdom of friends to choose from, yet she chose this awkward girl from another time. She had such a fine mind and natural kindness. No one gave Katie more confidence and happiness. In Alice, she had found that vital thing: a best friend, the sister she had always dreamed of. How could Katie have been bitter and jealous? Now her heart yearned to help her friend, as she knew the road ahead for Alice would be a rough one.

Even Bernardo DuQuelle began to make sense. He tried to divert the world with his banter and his flippant observations. He confused most people and many disliked him. They saw him as affected and distant; removed from life. But this was not the essence of DuQuelle. Life wasn't just *around* him – it was inside him. She'd almost forgotten that in learning about humanity, Bernardo DuQuelle had absorbed it. He might pretend otherwise, by making inappropriate jokes and hiding behind his endless learning, but he understood friendship and he believed in good. For the first time, she could see, just a tiny way, into his mind. And now she knew for certain: he could feel fear. She took his hand.

'You're scared,' she said. 'I'm scared too.'

He gave her hand the tiniest squeeze back. 'You see the choice, and very soon it must be made. Who knows how any of us would act in the face of such temptation? Let us both try to be brave.'

There was a soft thudding against the door, as if something were piling up on the other side. 'Knock, knock; who's there?' DuQuelle said in one of his feeble attempts at humour. ' Mustn't keep them waiting.'

As Katie began to protest, DuQuelle took the tip of his walking stick and gave her a slight tap on the head. 'I don't know, Katie, whether you will be the making of me, or the destruction of me. So much conflict, and so many questions; they do fill your world with adventure.' Flinging back his cloak, and raising his walking stick, he strode to the small wooden door and flung it open.

A cascade of snakes fell through the door. Thin and shiny, thick and spongy, small light green ones glowed in the night while the scaled diamond patterns of others reflected the moon. They writhed and slid to the top of the tower and began to mass against the buttresses. For Katie, this was a new horror. She hated snakes. If she wasn't killed by Belzen, she'd be smothered by snakes.

And then Lord Belzen was before them. After the attack on Prince Albert, the drama of the night and the snakes, the appearance of Lord Belzen seemed almost anti-climactic. One would have passed him unawares on the street; an elegant, slender man of medium height: far more 'normal' than Bernardo DuQuelle. It was his movement that always gave him away. There was a strange disjoint in his walk, as if it had been learned by reading a manual. His neck seemed too long and his head too small. An almost imperceptible wave moved through his body from his toes to the top of his head. And then his hands, beneath his gloves . . . Katie shuddered. Really, he was much worse than the snakes.

His voice too was a surprise – modulated and refined, until he became angry.

'Bernardo DuQuelle,' he said quietly, 'always in the way. You cannot wait to protect these . . . *beings*. Why is that, when they only ridicule you? Either be of use to me or step aside. It will take me no time to dispatch you.' Around the top of the tower, the snakes lifted their heads, unblinking and alert, their forked tongues flickering at the voice of their master.

Bernardo DuQuelle was both amused and repulsed. 'Snakes,' he said, 'the biblical symbol of evil. A banal choice, and yet effective . . .'

The snakes looped around Katie's ankles and began

to urge her towards Lord Belzen. Though unwilling, she moved with them. The alternative was falling backwards into a pile of overly excited snakes.

DuQuelle reached out and pulled Katie close. 'Why do you want her?'

Lord Belzen's eyes narrowed. Katie noticed they had the same unblinking alertness of the snakes beneath her feet. 'No one *wants* her,' he replied. 'Neither her father, nor her mother. The housekeeper is *paid* to care for her. Even here, her beloved friends have found each other and left her behind. That is what made her so deliciously vulnerable.'

Lord Belzen had found Katie's weakest point. It was the dark corner of her mind she had tried to avoid: no one wanted her. Her heart became cold and her body stiff. Looking up, for the first time she stared directly into Lord Belzen's eyes. There was no warmth or acceptance, but the promise of power: an ugly way to defeat them all. Katie struggled against it.

'She's not really a good person,' Belzen continued. 'Not talented or beautiful or brilliant. But power will bring her rewards beyond any of these gifts. She will come with me, and she will do my bidding, because there is nothing of greater value than power.' But Katie had made her choice. She knew what to do.

DuQuelle locked eyes with Lord Belzen. 'You understand humanity well,' he said. 'Power is to them an elixir.

Yet still, you overrate it. The people of this world – they understand friendship and love, charity and hope. They will sacrifice much for these things.' He took Katie by the shoulders and shook her slightly. 'Pay attention. The moment has come. If you intervene, it will be the end for all of us. You must not look, not one glance, at what is about to happen. You must run, as fast as you can, through the door, and back to the Castle.'

He held her close for a moment. Katie noted, with surprise, that his usual chill was gone. Something stirred within him. Could it be the warm pulse of human blood? Turning back to Lord Belzen, DuQuelle laid his walking stick at his feet. 'I can do no more. You cannot kill me. But if you want her you must destroy me, dismantle me, whatever it takes to be rid of me.' The wind picked up; it was now near to gale force. The clouds, in their eagerness to race across the sky, crashed into each other.

Lord Belzen looked at Bernardo DuQuelle with contempt. 'It was bound to happen. After thousands of years living amongst them, you have adopted their weaknesses.' For a moment, all was still. And then Lord Belzen began to change. The undulation of his body became rapid and pronounced; his neck became longer, his head streamlined.

DuQuelle pushed Katie towards the door. 'Do not make this a useless sacrifice, run!' The snakes around her feet began to climb up her legs, binding her. From behind she could hear DuQuelle struggling. The shout he gave filled the air with fury, fear and pain, a bellowing revolt that could only be human.

The clouds blotted out the moon. Near her, in the dark, the cries became louder and more desperate. DuQuelle had ordered her to flee, but she knew she could not leave him. Not with that agony ringing in her ears. DuQuelle might not be completely human, but he was her friend. If he planned to sacrifice himself for her, then she could turn the tables. She must battle with Lord Belzen. Steeling herself, she kicked hard, shaking the snakes from her legs, and raised her walking stick to attack. Her eyes adjusted to a dreadful sight. DuQuelle was on his knees, gasping and struggling. But what was that thing lashing out to attack him? Could the repulsive shape really be Lord Belzen, transformed through his evil? Katie ran towards them, swinging her walking stick to cut a path through the snakes.

And then the heavens opened. The rain spat down, needles of freezing steel, followed by hard, sharp pellets of ice. The snakes lifted their narrow heads and hissed in alarm. One by one they were struck down and beaten back. They retreated from the elements to the edge of the battlements, and then went over – hurtling through the air to be crushed against the icy snow below. The wind rose into a frenzy and the clouds clashed high in the sky, striking each other again and again, creating a lightning of great power. It looked as if the sky were on fire.

Above the clouds and deep in the skies an even brighter light shone. Rain, wind and fire pelted the earth – all of the elements bound together. It was Lucia, Katie realized. She contained within her all the elements: wind, fire, water and air. Katie could guess from what was happening in the skies above that Lucia was very angry. But who would bear the brunt of her fury? Lucia and the Verus believed in a particularly stringent type of good – disciplined and strong minded. With Katie's behaviour of the past ten days, she just might be the object of Lucia's wrath.

The light became brighter and brighter, joining the wind and rushing across the battlements of the Round Tower. It tore past Katie, knocking her over, and seemed to position itself as a barrier between Bernardo DuQuelle and Lord Belzen. Katie, cold, terrified and dizzy, could see that the two forces – the dark serpent and the bright light – were each weakened by the other. Lord Belzen finally slunk down and coiled in upon himself, a large black rubbery mass. When he rose again, he was a man. The light flickered and waived; a shape, also human, could now be seen within it. A woman, with brittle delicate features emerged: eyes the blue of a sharp winter sky, blonde hair streaming behind her, like the foam on the waves of a stormy sea.

Bernardo DuQuelle struggled to his feet and limped to Katie's side. 'Lucia,' he gasped. 'Do not harm the girl.'

Lucia laughed, shrill and high, 'Harm her? This girl? She proved herself at the Battle of Balaclava and destroyed evil at the Charge of the Light Brigade. She has freed herself from the Great Experiment. And tonight she has chosen friendship, protecting you, even at the risk of her own life. Most important of all, she has chosen peace. And some day, in another time, and another place, she will use her gift for words to convince others: they must choose peace as well. Harm her? I have come to save her. Something you, M. DuQuelle, are now too human to achieve.'

She was cut short by Lord Belzen. He might have returned to human form, but only just. His skin glistened and sparkled with scales, his nostrils lengthened across his lean face as black slits.

'You can halt me, Lucia, briefly, but you cannot stop me.' He caught Katie's eye and she could not look away. That strange unblinking serpent's eye. 'You, Lucia, might have the very elements to serve you, but I bring my own changelings.' His body swayed, a single strong thrust, and then he held back his cloak. At his feet were a cluster of eggs. They were larger than ostrich eggs, with a leathery wrinkled outer shell. Snakes' eggs. They began to vibrate slightly, and then crack. 'What shall hatch?' Lord Belzen asked.

The gap in one great egg grew wider, and a small wizened hand reached out to pull the shell apart. The form wriggled free. It was not a snake, but a child. A girl with large eyes set in a skeletal face, the skin burnished and taut across her cheekbones. The child's stomach was grotesquely swollen, sticking out from the rags bound around her and held up by thin spindly legs.

'But this child is starving!' Katie cried.

Lord Belzen smiled as the child mewled and cried, pushing her away with his beautifully polished shoe. 'Famine and need. What more could I want? A lovely start to war and greed.'

The next egg broke open. A boy emerged, this time his eyes were hard and mean, his nose snout-like. He began to shout and curse. Katie backed away from him. 'Ignorance,' Lord Belzen cooed.

The third egg was quite different; larger than the others, strong and white and beautiful to behold. Out of the egg came a golden-haired boy with fine white teeth and shining eyes. He smiled and laughed in the most appealing way. But when he saw the other children, he scowled and pushed them to the ground, riffling through their rags looking for something, anything, to take. 'He is attractive, yes?' Belzen said. 'He will dominate and win. Don't you recognize him? He is of your nations. He is the one that bullies his neighbours, enslaves other peoples and builds your empires. Surely you must recognize empire and power?'

As each egg hatched, Lucia grew weaker. Her light dimmed and the wind began to die down. Bernardo

DuQuelle inched towards Katie. 'Lucia cannot hold him,' he whispered. 'His offspring are too potent. She will produce what she can: prosperity, knowledge, tolerance, equality. They will be beautiful to see, but there is never quite enough good to go round in this world.'

Now DuQuelle took Katie by the hand and pulled her down through the low wooden door. 'We'd best be quick. They need to be alerted in the Prince's sick chamber.' Katie looked askance, but DuQuelle's face had reformed into an impersonal mask. 'Belzen has failed to gain your spirit,' he told her, 'but there is still much to play for. The war in America, Lord Belzen hopes it will spread throughout the world. For this, Lord Belzen seeks Prince Albert. The Prince is a pure man and cannot be corrupted. If Lord Belzen is unable to take the Prince's soul, he will settle for his body.'

Chapter Fifteen

The Brink of War

With a foot in both worlds, Bernardo DuQuelle understood, and spoke the truth. The Queen, her children, the courtiers and the doctors all watched and prayed and worked to save the life of Prince Albert. They could sense a struggle around them that they could not see. Lucia and Belzen on opposite poles: light and dark, peace and war, life and death. The Castle was their battleground and Prince Albert their prize. The tension and gloom lay thick in the Castle. Even on a bright winter morning, Katie felt as if she was walking through cobwebs.

The Queen paced the Grand Corridor, wringing her hands and talking to herself. 'His face has become a foreign face . . . what is happening . . . where has my dear Albert gone?' she cried. Behind her followed a stream of her ladies. They too wrung their hands and wailed.

Bernardo DuQuelle, entering the corridor, looked momentarily annoyed. 'This is a fine way to treat a sick man,' he muttered to Katie, as one of the Queen's Pekinese nipped at his heels. 'Where is James O'Reilly?'

Alice and James came out of the sickroom. 'The Queen does hinder progress,' James admitted. 'She runs into the sickroom, bursts into tears and demands "ein Kuss" a kiss from the Prince. One cannot banish the Queen from her own Castle, though at times I wish we could. Thank goodness for Princess Alice. She not only nurses her father tenderly, but finds ways to keep her mother occupied. She has suggested the Queen take a long walk in Windsor Great Park.'

Katie looked at her friends. Her mind free of Belzen's influence, she saw two caring, loving people working together to do good in the world. It was an impressive sight.

The Castle was in such disarray, that Katie could come and go as she pleased, unchallenged. All four entered the Prince Consort's dressing room. Prince Albert leaned back in a large upholstered chair, panting slightly. For once he was without his valets, the courtiers or the doctors. The morning light shone through the windows.

'I love this room,' he murmured. 'It is so very bright. I have been listening to the dawn chorus. Oh, the winter birds . . . they come to this day with so much joy.' His little speech had cost him much, and he closed his eyes, exhausted.

Alice knelt next to the chair and brushed back his hair gently. 'Father, wouldn't you like to lie down? The bed will be so much more comfortable.' The Prince did not respond and for a moment all thought he was asleep. A change came across his face, a trace of peace. James started to mix some medicines, but Prince Albert sat up and took his hand. 'Ernst,' he said in excited German, 'it is so crisp and cold. Do you think the swan pond has frozen over? We could skate today!'

'Why does he say Ernst?' Katie whispered to DuQuelle.

Prince Albert turned at her voice and smiled widely. 'Mutter,' he said, 'do let us skate. We will study tomorrow. You are so soft-hearted I know you will say yes!' Katie backed away, startled by his outburst. 'Mutter!' he cried, 'do not leave us, Father will forgive you. Ernst and I need you . . .' he fell back, eyes closed, his chest rising and falling rapidly.

'This is very bad indeed,' DuQuelle muttered. 'The decline is so rapid, and there is still much he needs to do.' James began to warm something over a spirit lamp, but DuQuelle stopped him. 'I am not a doctor, but I suggest you do not administer any further medicine for some hours. He is delirious as it is. Prince Albert believes he is back in the Schloss Rosenau, his childhood home. James, he thought you were his brother Ernst and you, Katie, his beloved mother.'

'Did his mother leave him?' Katie asked. DuQuelle seemed to go back through time too. He studied his walking stick, seeing something the rest of them could not. 'A mother had no part in my creation,' he admitted. 'But they do seem terribly important in your formation of life. So nourishing and damaging at the same time . . . Yes, his mother left him. Banished by his father, for behaviour *much* less outrageous than that of *your* mother, Katie. And Princess Alice, I do *not* admire that look of condemnation in your eyes. She was a good woman who loved her babies dearly, rather weak, but sweet-natured. God rest her soul, she is long gone, stricken down by a terrible cancer. I knew her well . . .'

The room was silent, as they thought of their own mothers. Prince Albert sat up and then tried to stand. 'The red boxes,' he demanded, 'pass me the red boxes.'

'What is it now?' Katie asked.

Bernardo DuQuelle shook his head with a mixture of anxiety and admiration. 'Here is a man who is true to himself,' he said. 'He wants to work. The red boxes, the government dispatches. The Prince has worked through them with the Queen, side by side, since early in their marriage.'

'Oh, but he shouldn't exert himself,' Alice admonished. 'It will kill him.'

DuQuelle smiled his strange, joyless smile. 'This toil has already killed him. But to work now will ease his pain.' Turning on his heel, he left the room, returning almost immediately with the red boxes. 'Ah,' he was heard to mutter, 'perhaps, even yet, it is not too late.'

Katie had a sneaking suspicion DuQuelle had been waiting for this moment. The boxes were placed on a side table, next to the Prince's chair. Prince Albert fussed, opening one and then the other. Knocking one to the floor, he rubbed his forehead and closed his eyes again. It looked as if he had given up. But Bernardo DuQuelle came forward, and bowing, spoke respectfully. 'Your Royal Highness, please do let me be of assistance.'

A look of great irritation settled on Prince Albert's face. Bernardo DuQuelle: Private Secretary to the Prince, keeper of the Queen's archives, curator of the Queen's collections . . . 'Aide extraordinaire, and pain in the ASS!' the Prince exploded.

'Father!' Alice cried out, but DuQuelle raised a silencing hand.

'You are quite right, sir. You are a man of dignity. You try to protect your privacy. Yet I have been here, since the day you arrived in Britain, poking and prying. I am sorry. Our time together will be over shortly. I wish you to know, I admire and respect you.' DuQuelle usually addressed the Royal Family in a bizarrely embellished and flowery manner, the speech patterns of a courtier. But today he spoke in a plain, almost bald manner.

The Prince Consort exchanged a long glance with DuQuelle. They had reached an understanding.

'There are papers here that relate to *both* wars, the one of our time and the one you sense, but cannot see,' DuQuelle informed him.

The Prince sat up that bit straighter. 'You know?'

'I know.' DuQuelle rifled through the box. 'I believe these are the papers you seek.'

Katie peeped over his shoulder. Across the top she could see the words RMS *Trent*, and at the bottom, a signature: the Prime Minister, Lord Palmerston. 'Under normal circumstance I would not bring this to your attention,' DuQuelle apologized, 'but we have reached the crisis. Britain is on the brink of war with America.' Everyone looked to him, startled.

'It's the *Trent*,' he explained. 'Our ship was to transport the Southern, Confederate envoys to Britain. The North fired their guns, boarded our ship, and took the men prisoner. There was a certain amount of agitation on this topic at the Christmas Ball. It has been festering for over a week. I would have brought it up sooner, but . . .'

Prince Albert's delirium vanished. For the first time in days, he looked like himself. Work might have weakened him, it might even be killing him, but it was what Prince Albert did best. 'And this is the Prime Minister's response?' he said, quickly flipping through the pages. 'It looks decidedly war-like to me.'

DuQuelle leaned over him, pointing out some particularly belligerent passages. 'The Prime Minister is calling the boarding of the *Trent* an act of aggression on the part of the North, and demanding a full, official apology from President Lincoln as well as the safe return of the Southern men to Britain. If the North refuses, the Prime Minister is indeed threatening war.'

Prince Albert shook his head. 'I have worked so hard to keep Britain out of this war, and now, a careless swipe of the Prime Minister's pen could lead us to disaster. The President of the United States of America will not apologize. Britain will enter the war; France, Russia, Austria might follow. What is that man thinking? The Prime Minister cannot expect me to sign this. '

DuQuelle cleared his throat. 'The Prime Minister is under the impression that you are too ill to sign anything. He had suggested that I simply bypass you, slip the memorandum to the Queen, and that she will sign.'

Anger gave Prince Albert strength. He sat up, demanding pen and paper. The winter sun shone in a blue sky as he worked, but gradually a shadow fell across the bright windows of the room. In the Grand Corridor all was silent. The fire in the fireplace lost its comfortable crackle, replaced by a strange, ominous hiss. As the room became darker, Prince Albert's writing became slower. His head tilted back. His eyes closed. 'Ah, the pen is so heavy,' he murmured. Perhaps I shall go to bed. I will look again . . . later . . . later.' Alice took the pen from him, and James sprang forward to help him to bed.

DuQuelle ran his fingers through his hair, so that it stood, jet black, on the top of his head. 'This is disastrous,' he said to Katie. 'If the Prince goes to bed, he will never rise again. Without his intervention, Britain will enter this war. ALL of Europe will enter this war. The greed and brute force will feed the Malum for centuries to come . . .' Katie thought of John Reillson and his plea against slavery. If only she could find a way to help.

And then the light slowly returned to the window. A bright, thin streak made its way inside the room, stopping to rest on Princess Alice's forehead. She blinked at the brightness, and then found herself returning the pen to her father's hand. 'Dear father,' she said gently. 'Do take up your pen, for just one moment longer. I know you will want to finish this piece of work.'

Prince Albert sighed, holding the pen listlessly between his fingers. 'It is so complicated,' he complained, 'and I am so tired.' The room became light then dark, as shadow followed sun. And finally, the sun streamed into the little dressing room, bathing them all in brightness.

A burst of inspiration flashed through Katie. 'I know what to do,' she cried. Prince Albert looked startled.

Between the delirium and his work, he hadn't noticed her before.

'Who is this?' he asked. Katie could have kicked herself. She might know everything about Prince Albert, but he knew very little about her. For a moment, there was an awkward silence, and then DuQuelle came to her rescue.

'This is Miss Katherine Tappan,' he said, 'the daughter of the eminent American Mr Lewis Tappan. As the crisis at hand involved her country, and she was in attendance at the Castle, I felt she might be of help . . . as a reference . . .' It was a feeble explanation, but the Prince was really too ill to question it. 'Please precede, Miss Tappan,' DuQuelle continued.

The Prince looked so weary. Katie talked, as fast as she could. 'You must be as you always are,' she said to the Prince Consort, 'the diplomat of the family. All men are proud – the Prime Minister, President Lincoln. The President will not apologize, and male pride is a silly reason to go to war.'

Princess Alice looked very shocked by what Katie was saying and James snorted in derision. Strangely, it was Prince Albert who treated her with respect. 'Please do proceed,' he encouraged her.

'You must give the Northerners a way to back down,' she continued. 'Write to President Lincoln. Say that you kind of assumed he didn't know anything about the boarding of the *Trent*. Tell him, you know, tell him that you *suppose* the captain of the Northern ship, the Union boat, didn't ask permission to board the *Trent*. And if the Union will just return the men they've taken to Britain, quietly, kind of on the sly – they don't even have to say they're sorry – everything will be OK with you . . . If you could all just kind of do the whole thing without having to say who's wrong . . .' she trailed off, feeling like an idiot. Even as an American, her knowledge of the American Civil War was sketchy. Yet here she was, suggesting a strategy that might affect the outcome of a major war. The bright light now flooded the room.

Prince Albert's keen mind picked through Katie's playground vocabulary and found her advice sound and practical. 'That just might work,' he murmured, his pen moving quickly over the paper. 'I will write directly to your President. If we take the pride out of our demands, and simply ask for the return of the prisoners.'

The fire crackled merrily again and the sunlight flickered through the room. Princess Alice took each paper as he wrote, blotted it neatly and handed it to Bernardo DuQuelle. For a very long time the pen scratched across sheet after sheet of paper. As the last was handed to DuQuelle, the Prince seemed to collapse. He smiled weakly at the group around him, then turned to DuQuelle.

'This will be the last of it,' he said. 'I can do no more.'

DuQuelle bowed very low, then taking the Prince's hand, kissed it, sincerely.

'You have done more than your duty,' DuQuelle said. 'And now you may rest.' Quietly, he ushered the three out of the room.

'You think that's enough?' Katie asked him.

DuQuelle looked at her with something akin to admiration. 'More than enough,' he said. 'Prince Albert has provided the Unionists of the North with a dignified climb-down. He will keep Britain from joining this war. Europe, too, will stand back. This act of the Prince has kept us from a World War, and thwarted the Malum . . . for now.'

He turned to Katie, 'Welcome back,' he said. 'I hadn't realized how much they . . . well . . . we . . . need you.' Katie felt a surge of gratitude and relief.

'And now we need you even more,' he continued. 'If you could deliver a message to John Reillson that the North is safe from war with Britain. The Unionists need to know.'

Katie blinked in confusion. 'John Reillson? I don't know how to find him.'

This was no time for smiling, but DuQuelle almost smiled. 'I wouldn't worry about that,' he said. 'Go to London. John Reillson will be very keen to find you. And now I suggest we call the doctors back in. Though they can do so little, this poor brave prince has need of them.'

Chapter Sixteen

Yankee Doodle

All of London was waiting for word of Prince Albert. As Katie walked the city streets, she could see the crowds scanning printed bulletins, delivered by the hour, with news of his health.

When she rang the bell to South Street, Florence Nightingale herself answered the door. Like everyone else, she was impatient for news. 'How does the Prince?' she asked.

'Not too great,' Katie replied. 'Not great at all. Much worse than the bulletins are saying.'

Florence Nightingale nodded grimly. 'I'd expect no less, with that buffoon Sir Brendan O'Reilly at his side. Do you bring me a message from Bernardo DuQuelle?'

'Well, no,' Katie said, and then found herself examining

a pattern in the rug. She did not want to discuss John Reillson with this brilliant, impatient woman. A loud tread on the stairs interrupted her silence. It was Dolores, with her new friend Mary Seacole. In a moment she was down the stairs, wrapping Katie in her arms.

'There's my baby girl,' she said. 'No matter what Mary's said, I've still been worrying about you.'

Katie felt the tears, hot on her cheeks. When she was with Dolores, she could stop making decisions, carrying burdens, being so grown up. It was a relief. She looked Dolores up and down and smiled; her first smile in a very long time. Dolores had adopted the style of the time. Her grey wool dress and paisley shawl suited her and the dove-coloured bonnet with red ribbons was very fine indeed

'You look beautiful, Dolores,' Katie said.

Dolores smoothed her skirts. 'I'm not wearing those corsets though,' she said. 'I'm a big, broad woman and that's that.'

Mary Seacole laughed, and tied the ribbons of Dolores's grey bonnet, explaining, 'I tried to get her into something more colourful but she wanted to look "proper".'

Florence Nightingale sniffed. 'Soon enough we'll all be in mourning black, so you'd best enjoy your crimson ribbons while you can.'

Dolores squeezed Katie tight and said, 'I've finally come round to believing what they say. Just think, I've never been out of New York, and here I am, in a whole other time and place. And I owe you an apology, honey.'

'Me?' Katie asked. 'All you've ever done is take care of me. Sure, you get mad sometimes, but who wouldn't? I'm surprised you even stay with us. I'm bad enough, but Mimi . . .'

Dolores slumped down on the chair in the hall and, fishing around for a handkerchief, wiped her eyes. 'Mary here explained everything to me. There I was, thinking you were just some rich, spoiled kid, lying around on the sofa all day. How was I to know that you were flying around, saving the world?'

Mary Seacole smiled broadly, but Florence Nightingale seemed nettled by this description of Katie.

'I'd hardly call myself the saviour of the world,' Katie said sheepishly. 'It's this thing, the Tempus. I can't help that I'm part of it. I've got this power of words. I'm supposed to kind of keep history on course. I'm not doing a very good job of it . . .'

Florence Nightingale gave a soft 'harrumph', and busied herself with a tray of calling cards.

But Dolores would not be suppressed. 'Mary says that this group, the Versus? The Verpers?'

'The Verus,' Mary Seacole corrected, ignoring Florence Nightingale's warning look.

'That's right,' Dolores continued, 'the Verus. They're a civilization from a whole different world, and they need words to communicate. They get the words from us, but they have to keep our world in balance.' She looked again to Mary, who nodded away in agreement.

'I always thought it was kind of hard-natured of them,' Mary Seacole said to Dolores. 'Sending your Katie back in time – what did they call it? The Great Experiment? Getting the children to do the work and keep this planet in good shape. Just a young girl, who doesn't know any better, to take on the Malum. And the Verus. They're supposed to be so good. That Lucia – all bright light. Seems harsh to me. She's no wordsmith. Just won't compromise . . . kind of like Florence here.' Mary Seacole was one of the few people in the world who would, and could, contradict Florence Nightingale. In this she was fearless.

Miss Nightingale let it pass with a loud sniff. 'That is enough cats out of bags for one day,' was all she said. 'And don't the two of you have an urgent appointment? You seem very willing to loll about and gossip when there is vital work to be done against slavery.'

Dolores clapped her hands together. 'My Lord but we'll be late. We've got to get those pamphlets out to Hyde Park. Katie, honey, you come with us. We could use every available hand.' Taking Katie by the arm, she turned her around and pushed her out of the door.

Florence Nightingale closed it behind them, looking relieved and rather grumpy. 'Save the world . . . really . . . and to criticize Lucia . . .' Katie thought she muttered as the door banged shut.

'Dolores, Mary, I'm here for a reason,' Katie protested as they swung up South Street and crossed Park Lane. 'I have something important to do.'

'It will wait, dearie. It will wait,' Mary Seacole replied merrily as they headed into Hyde Park. 'We have important things to do too.' She handed Katie a leaflet. On the front was an engraving. It was of a man, a slave, on his knees, his hands bound in chains. Above him the words proclaimed: AM I NOT A MAN, AND A BROTHER?

'I listened to you, Katie, and made good use of my time,' Dolores said. 'Mary and I have been writing up flyers and passing them out at anti-slavery rallies. That nice young woman, Grace O'Reilly, helped. She's got a way with words. We're getting a lot of support for our cause. We're working with the Quakers, and even some boys from the North in the USA.'

They walked rapidly, Dolores's skirts swinging like a church bell, until they reached a small gathering of people. Beyond them Katie could hear music, a violin and recorder, playing a mournful tune. Dolores and Mary Seacole moved to the front of the crowd and raised their voices to join the song:

'be buried in my grave
'fore I become a slave
Seal away . . . steal away . . .

Soaring above the other voices was that of a girl. She was a great beauty, whose dark shining eyes seemed to hold all the pain of the world. As she sang, the song took on an almost unbearable sadness. Katie knew her. They had an unbreakable tie. And they needed to speak. The crowd grew, wondering at the girl's gifts.

'She sings like an angel,' Katie murmured.

' . . . and that is what they call her,' a young man standing next to Katie added. 'I told you all about her. That night at Windsor Castle. She's called the Little Angel.'

'The Little Angel,' Katie repeated. 'We go way back. This is my day for chance meetings, Mr John Reillson.' DuQuelle had been right. John Reillson had found her. 'I have a message for you,' she said, taking Bernardo DuQuelle's note out of her little reticule and handing it to John Reillson. 'But I've just got to talk to the Little Angel.' John Reillson looked rather hurt and puzzled. 'I thought you'd want to speak to me. I know it's only been a week, ten days at most, yet the ball at Windsor Castle seems so long ago.'

The Little Angel had finished her song, and her guardian, the Countess Fidelia, was standing atop a soap box, waving a tambourine. She was as flamboyant and dishevelled as ever. Her familiar pea-green shooting jacket had been exchanged for a navy one, with gold buttons and braid, echoing the Northerners' army uniforms. In her haystack of hair she wore a tiny soldier's cap. Standing on tiptoe, she led the growing throng in a rousing chorus:

Yankee Doodle took it up
To whip the Southern traitors
Because they would refuse to live
With black men as their brothers.

Dolores and Mary Seacole began to distribute their pamphlets. Katie could see some of the other Northern men talking to people in the crowd, Elias Finch and Bill Patterson. She was glad not to see Jeb Lawson.

'I do want to talk with you,' she said to John Reillson, 'and we will. But I must speak with the Little Angel first.' The crowd had become more active with the lively song. Between all the heads and shoulders, Katie could just see the Little Angel, clapping along with the rest of them.

John Reillson, next to her, was reading DuQuelle's note. Katie began to push through the crowd. So many answers would lie with the Little Angel. Then someone took hold of her arm. Why was she always waylaid? It was a woman, unrecognizable in a cloak and heavy veil. But when she spoke, Katie recognized the voice: distinct, crisp and decidedly upper class – Florence Nightingale.

'I could not risk sending anyone else. My carriage is at the side of the park. The train for Windsor leaves in ten minutes. For once we have been fortunate in its scheduling.

My footman will make the travel arrangements. I see that you have delivered your message. You must leave immediately.'

The Little Angel had now mounted the soap box. She began to sing a sad ballad. John Reillson was coming to the end of DuQuelle's message. 'I can't go,' Katie protested, 'I have to, I've GOT to talk to . . .'

For a small woman, Florence Nightingale had a very firm grip. 'This is not the time to think of "I",' she rebuked Katie. 'I should think you would have learned by now to put others before yourself.' Pulling Katie through the crowd, Florence Nightingale thrust her into the waiting carriage. 'I do have some sympathy for you,' she admitted, 'but you must wait for your answers. The time has come more quickly than we'd imagined. You are needed by your friends at Windsor Castle.'

Chapter Seventeen

Into the Light

Prince Albert had kept Britain out of the American war but, as they had feared, it was the last act of a great Prince. His final journey had begun. It is rarely easy to leave this life, and even a man as saintly as Prince Albert would succumb to pain. He complained endlessly about the stomach cramps, the nausea, the chills; the sheer exhaustion of the act of dying. The Queen snatched at any possible sign of improvement and Sir Brendan insisted that, though gravely ill, the Prince could recover. This irritated Prince Albert more than he could say. Why couldn't they just accept that he was dying?

The only person he could really tolerate was Princess Alice. As the days passed, Alice took on even more responsibility. She soothed her mother, took charge of the staff and courtiers, aided the doctors and corresponded with her extensive family abroad. On top of this, she rarely left her father's side. The doctors marvelled at her nursing skills and all admired her, with the exception of Sir Brendan O'Reilly. James's eyes followed her everywhere. She was truly the angel in the house.

On good days, Prince Albert was calm and lucid. Now settled in the Blue Room, he lay in bed and talked quietly with Princess Alice. Looking into the distance, he spoke of his childhood, his lessons with his brother Ernst and the harmless pranks they would play on their tutor. Alice would often read to him: a poem by Tennyson or a chapter from Sir Walter Scott. After a time, he said, 'the words confuse me, but music is still clear. I should like to hear a fine chorale, played at a distance.' So Alice retired to the next room and played the songs he loved the most: 'Nun Danket Alle Gott' and 'Rock of Ages Cleft for Me'. As she pressed the keys quietly, she looked back to where her father lay in bed, as quiet as an effigy in a church.

He had been ill for two weeks. One evening he asked to be left by the doctors.

'Do not worry,' he said. 'Faithful Alice will stay with me.'

'Shall I play, Father, or read?' Princess Alice asked.

The Prince looked at her with weary eyes. 'This is the last of my energies, I can feel it. I need to speak with you alone.'

Princess Alice took her place, kneeling next to his bed, and held his burning hand in hers. 'Anything, Father,' she said.

Prince Albert sighed. When had she grown so thin? Her face had become pinched, her eyes hollow . . . She had given so much, nursing him. And now he was going to ask for more. 'My dear Alice, I am leaving you,' he murmured.

She stroked his hand and smiled up at him. 'I know, Father, and I accept it. You go to a better place,' she answered.

The Prince smiled back, weakly. 'Alice, I am leaving, but I must make a final attempt to protect you, to be your father.' She started to reassure him, but he shook his head. 'It is hard to say, but I must shield you from your mother.'

For a moment, Alice thought he was delirious, but he continued on, with more firmness in his voice.

'Your mother, she has no gift for isolation. Her lonely childhood has led her to dread solitude. It is because of this that I have been so much to her, a friend, a husband, an adviser. I lived my life *with* her and *for* her.'

'You have done your duty,' Alice replied softly.

'I have done my duty,' Prince Albert repeated dully. 'Sometimes I think, I have been killed by doing my duty . . .' He closed his eyes and began to breathe deeply. Alice started to rise and call one of the doctors, but he tightened the grip on her hand. He had more to say to her.

'When I am gone, your mother, the Queen, she must have *someone* who will sacrifice everything to her. They will need to be at her side, carry out her correspondence, aid her in her political policies, her social duties, her family decisions. This person will never have a moment's rest, and certainly no life of their own. They will become, as I have, an adjunct to the Queen.'

Princess Alice willed herself not to pull away. Was he going to ask her to make this pledge? Though she tried to hide it, her father knew her thoughts.

'This is not the life for you,' he said. 'Already your ambitions cause you pain. Though you are dutiful in the extreme, sweet Alice, you see a life beyond royal duty.' Alice had willed herself not to cry for so many days, but now the tears fell. Her dear father had been thinking of her, protecting her even at this time. 'You must marry,' Prince Albert said abruptly.

Alice recoiled. 'I am too young,' she said.

'Too young to marry, but not too young for an engagement,' her father answered. 'If an engagement were approved, a marriage could take place in three or four years.' Prince Albert tried to sit up, to convince his daughter. 'I had hoped that you would care for Prince Louis of Hesse. He is a sincere young man, if not a brilliant one. He came to the Christmas Ball specifically to meet you again – how long ago that seems! Immediately Prince Louis wrote to me with the proposal. In normal times, I would have written back, said "she is young, let us wait and see . . ." but these are not normal times. Time has run out. I have told the Queen, it is my *final* wish . . . this engagement.'

'No!' Alice burst out, before she could prevent herself. 'It is too soon. I have met him only a few times – as a small child, and then recently at the ball. You would be promising me, practically selling me, to a stranger. Please, there must be others, someone else . . .' She faltered. The *someone else* she had in mind was impossible. She knew that.

Her father looked pained. 'I know Hesse-Darmstadt is a small kingdom, and you will not be as rich and powerful as your sister Vicky. His family, however, is grateful for such an important match. They will be kind to you. You will be left much to your own devices, to study and learn. It is the best I can do for you. It could be worse.'

Alice could tell, her father's lucid moment was fading fast. She had to make things clear to him. 'If we could just wait,' she pleaded.

Prince Albert became fretful, picking at his quilted robe, trying to arrange his hair. 'There is not time,' he said. 'Do you really wish to be a pinch-faced spinster, your mother's shadow, taking her notes and plumping her pillows? Chasing up her every whim? I love my wife, and honour my Queen, but I do not wish that life for you. You will marry, snatch this tiny freedom, and then find a way to be yourself, with a new title and a new country.'

Coughing and wheezing now overtook the Prince. 'I cannot breathe,' he gasped, 'my chest . . .' Princess Alice called out for the doctors. She knew the conversation was over. The fate of her father was sealed. And so was her own. The end was coming. The doctors began to dose the Prince with brandy, hoping to strengthen his pulse. James O'Reilly helped them, trying to convince them to use more modern treatments. Though several of them knew he was right, they didn't dare experiment on someone as important as Prince Albert. Katie, watching from a distance, saw hopelessness on almost every face.

Alice had sent a telegram to Bertie. It had to be done; he was the eldest child and the heir to the throne. He arrived from Cambridge, and spent most of his time peeking at his father from the doorway and getting in the way of the doctors. His mother glared at him, as if somehow it was Bertie's fault his father was ill. Princess Alice stayed by Prince Albert's side, praying as fervently as any of them. But now, she knew, there was something very selfish in her prayers. If only her father could recover, she would gain time, perhaps she could change his mind about her marriage.

The Grand Corridor became crowded: courtiers, servants, doctors, equerries and clergymen all wanted to be of help, or at least to hear the news. Katie, standing among the milling crowd, wondered for the hundredth time at the lives of royalty. So much seemed to take place in the public eye, even births. Alice had once told her that the Home Secretary had to be present when Bertie was born just to make certain there really *was* a male heir to the throne. And now, the most important man in Britain was dying, and they had to be here too, peeping into the very death chamber. There was one good thing about the crowds: Katie was able to see Alice and James without arousing too much suspicion. And goodness knows, they needed her help.

Katie was particularly worried about Alice. She never seemed to sleep and barely left her father's side. She kept her emotions firmly in check. As she read her father the psalms, her voice was clear, without a waiver. It was only when James praised Alice for her devotion and medical skills that tears sprang up in her eyes. 'Do not admire me,' she said. 'It is more difficult than you know to do my duty.'

The Queen and Sir Brendan O'Reilly continued their pantomime of optimism. At one point they passed Katie in the corridor. 'The Prince is so nice and warm,' the Queen was telling Sir Brendan. 'His skin is so soft. That is a very good sign, I think?' Sir Brendan nodded, he would agree with anything. More than ever, Katie thought him a very dangerous fool.

To the end, Prince Albert was kind to his Queen. He held her hand, and called her 'gutes Fräuchen'. At one point he rallied slightly, and teased her that her hair was in disarray. Day turned to night and the candles burned low in their sockets. A change crept over Prince Albert. His eyes became bright and gazed into the distance, as it were, on unseen objects. Only the Queen could see this as a good sign. 'But he is so beautiful!' she cried, 'so calm. I believe the crisis is over. He will definitely live.' And she ordered Princess Alice to telegraph her sister Vicky in Prussia. She must hear the good news immediately.

Princess Alice bowed assent and, kissing her mother softly on the forehead, left the room. But she did not send a telegram. She knew her father's calm beauty was the final stage. Moments later, Katie and James found her in a linen closet, crying wildly. Katie held Princess Alice in her arms, able to comfort her now that the dark bitter voice was gone.

James hugged himself, with that awkward sympathy boys have for weeping girls. He reached out and patted her on the shoulder. Alice became very still. 'I am afraid you have pulled away from childish things forever,' he said to her. 'You have become the person you were meant to be.'

Princess Alice kissed Katie on the cheek, and with great effort, regained her composure. 'Katie, I would never want to be without you.' Then she smiled at James. 'You speak some truth. I am becoming the person I was meant to be. Perhaps, though, that is the not the person I *wished* to be.'

They were interrupted by a call from the Blue Room. The Prince's pulse had dropped and his breath rasped in his chest.

Bernardo DuQuelle appeared in the doorway. 'This is your father's last earthly battle. If ever he needed you, Princess, it is now.'

James led her back to the bed, where Alice knelt and took her father's hand. DuQuelle stood in the corner of the room, next to Katie. She looked at him with surprise. His face was lined, deep furrows appeared in his chalk-white skin. There were waves of sympathy coming from him. She could feel it.

One by one, the royal children came to say goodbye: Helena tearful and Louise hysterical. Leopold was kept from the room, as the risk of infection was too great, but his bath chair was pushed into the doorway. Then overgrown Bertie came, sobbing, 'I will try to be the man you always wanted me to be.' At this, Prince Albert looked distressed and tried to push him away. Even now, he despaired of Bertie.

Prince Albert's skin grew dusky, his face dark. A grimace drew down his lips. The light was suddenly wiped from the room, as the candles, burning so long, went out. There was sudden confusion, as everyone scrambled to find a candle. The Prince Consort's voice rose above them. Just minutes before he had spoken gently to his wife, but now he seemed to argue with some great and threatening unknown. 'You shall not feed off me!' he cried. 'I have never relied on brutal ways. I have kept myself clean, as pure as I could. I will die in peace, for I have lived up to my purpose.'

Katie darted into the Grand Corridor. There the torches were still burning. Pulling one from the wall, she ran back to the Blue Room. As she stood, framed in the doorway, the Prince Consort sat up in bed. 'The light, the rock of ages,' he gasped, but not with fright. Everyone turned to stare. 'I see now,' the Prince exclaimed. 'What is *good* has come to claim me as its own.' The light pooled around Katie, so bright she could barely keep her eyes open. It couldn't possibly be the one torch. Turning around she shielded her eyes from an entirely different source of light, a blazing figure.

It was Lucia. Katie could see her clearly for once; she was truly beautiful, her features thin and fine, as if etched onto her face. Her blonde curls waved gently. The light, which so often consumed her, radiated from within.

Prince Albert opened his arms. 'It is the door to a new life.' Katie realized the Prince could see Lucia too. But what about the others? Candles had been found in the Blue Room. One by one they were lit, though they did not extinguish the light of Lucia. Katie looked from face to face. She saw tension, fear and sorrow, but she could tell, only three people in the room saw the supernatural.

Prince Albert fell back against his pillows. 'The light,' he murmured, 'the light.'

'What is it, Father?' Alice asked. 'Do the candles hurt your eyes? Shall I shade them?'

The Prince gave his daughter one last loving look, then turned to the light. His mind returned, just briefly, to forage among its harvest of knowledge.

How far that little the candle throws his beams!
So shines a good deed in a naughty world.

His eyes became brighter and brighter. Two or three long and perfectly gentle breaths were drawn. And then he closed his eyes. Forever.

All was silent in the Blue Room. Bertie turned to the wall, his head in his arms. The doctors stood, useless. Princess Alice sat in a heap on the floor, still holding her father's cold hand. The courtiers in the Grand Corridor stood as stone, frightened and still. 14 December, 1861. Would time freeze for ever, on this cold December night?

The answer came through one long piercing shriek. No one who heard it would ever forget the unbearable sound. The agony and fury of all mankind was contained in this one, drawn out, unforgettable wail. Katie shivered violently, chilled to the bone. It was the voice of a woman crazed with grief. It was the Queen.

Chapter Eighteen

Exeter Hall

All was grief. The country, which had often mocked the foreign Prince, realized too late how much he had done for his adopted nation. The people wept for their Queen. The Royal Family, that happy domestic circle, was broken forever. Newspapers were bordered in thick black edges, their pages filled with the heart-breaking story. All shops closed. There would be no buying and selling, no holiday entertainments and certainly no pubs would open. It was as if Christmas had been cancelled.

The Queen was in a state of shock. Bouts of her wailing echoed through the hallways of Windsor Castle. Christmas passed and then the New Year. There was no change in her grief. 'I have parted with my heart and soul,' she cried, and refused to look at any government papers, sign any documents or make any decisions. The country was coming to a standstill.

DuQuelle tried to rouse her to action, as gently as he could. 'It is a great trial you undergo,' he sympathized, 'but you must nerve yourself for it. You have governed the country once without him and you will do so again.'

The Queen would have none of it. 'Stop!' she cried. 'When you speak of such things, you are tearing the flesh from my bones. Why? Why must I suffer like this? I am one with Albert. I will do nothing without him.' She could not, *would not* be comforted. She must grieve, and she must share her grief. Princess Alice sat with her mother all day and slept in her mother's room at night. The Queen, in the great selfishness of her agony, did not give her daughter's health, or her own sorrow, one thought. But Alice was suffering.

The Queen also turned to Sir Brendan O'Reilly, a dangerous choice. He let her do as she wanted, to wallow in her grief. He pandered to her weakness. To Katie's frustration, she remained blocked out. Despite the heavy mourning, the Castle had returned to some semblance of order. There was no reason for Katie to be anywhere near the Queen, and she could not get to Alice. For weeks their only conversations were brief and whispered, as Alice hurried to *fetch this* and *do that* for her mother. The Queen showed no sign of improvement and Alice was wasting away. This made Katie worry all the more. She too, began to grow thin and was unable to sleep.

'We know now, I was called here by Lord Belzen,' Katie complained one day to Bernardo DuQuelle. 'I *think* I've managed to fight him off, but I'm still here, I can't help Alice, and I don't know how to go home.' DuQuelle always looked old, in a timeless sort of way, and tired. Katie didn't even know if he slept. She noticed, however, that his usually natty appearance had frayed around the edges. His cravat was limp and poorly tied; his finely coiffured hair unkempt.

'There is little certainty in this world of yours,' he said, 'but I am fairly certain there is more for you to do. If you cannot comfort Princess Alice, there is someone else who would take great pleasure in seeing you. In your crazy life, with your crazy mother, I believe Dolores is the one solid figure and helpmate.'

As he spoke, Katie realized how exhausted she was, and how she longed for the reassuring, straight-talking Dolores. 'Can I go and see Dolores?' she asked. 'I don't want to leave Alice, but . . .'

DuQuelle patted her on the shoulder, awkwardly. He had such trouble with these simple, human gestures. 'It would benefit you to see something other than grief and despair. Come with me to London. I need the rest and respite of my home on Half Moon Street, and you will be heartened by what you see.'

London was in mourning, as was all of Britain, but compared to Windsor Castle, it was a fairground. Life could not stop forever the metropolis. The government had to govern, the bankers to bank, the artists to paint. The flower-sellers had flowers to sell and the booksellers still provided books. A new kind of enterprise had emerged – the mourning emporium – and these shops were swamped as people bought ceremonial death clothes: black stockings, black shoes, black parasols, black bonnets, black-bordered handkerchiefs and yards and yards of black crepe to make into dresses, sashes and hatbands. They needed new black-edged paper to write letters on, and black ribbons for their hats. There was a brisk trade in mourning lockets, some carved from black jet, while others featured engravings of weeping willows or funereal urns. Every available photograph or engraving of Prince Albert had been sold within hours of his death.

But even as they mourned, the people of London still ate and drank, worshipped at church and attended events. Instead of being driven to his home off Piccadilly, Bernardo DuQuelle ordered his carriage to proceed past Trafalgar Square, turning onto the Strand. They stopped in front of a large impressive building, its doorway framed with high stone columns.

'I thought you'd go home and flake out,' Katie said.

DuQuelle shivered, pulling his cloak right around him.

'*Flake out*. What an odd turn of phrase you have, Katie. I'd like to *flake out*. Preferably in front of a warm fire. This is the type of raw grey day in which London excels. Instead we are visiting Exeter Hall. There is something important I'd like you to witness.'

They alighted from the carriage, and were immediately carried along by a large crowd. Men, women and children were queuing to go through the portico and double doors of Exeter Hall. They were talking animatedly and some held banners furled under their arms. Katie found herself swept up a flight of curved marble steps. When they reached the next floor, the crowd surged through double doors into a grand auditorium. Everyone scrambled for seats, but DuQuelle moved at a more leisurely pace. 'Do not worry,' he said to Katie. 'They are expecting us.' And he moved down the aisle to the front of the hall, directly before a large raised platform.

The room was abuzz with talk, and people began to unfurl their banners.

'This is really something,' Katie said. 'There must be over 4,000 people here.' She craned her head to see what the banners said:

***We are of One Blood Before God ***
Humanity Before Cotton
Unchain Our Brothers

'It is the abolitionists,' DuQuelle told her. 'They meet four to five times a week. And as Prince Albert was President of their society, today they come in tribute to him.'

Katie looked at people, rows and rows of them, leading high up to the tiers of galleries behind her. It was exhilarating. 'If the Queen could see this, I think she'd spend less time crying,' she said slowly. 'She'd see, kind of, how Prince Albert's actions made him great. She might stop weeping and start *doing* things.'

DuQuelle nodded. 'Terrible syntax, but an excellent sentiment. If only the Queen would listen.'

The day's speakers had now filed onto the platform. Katie started to ask another question, but DuQuelle shushed her. A sombre black-clad clergyman was standing behind the podium. He launched into a very long, very serious prayer, rolling his Rs. At the mention of *Prrrrrince Albert, the Prrrrrince Consort*, there were sniffles from those around Katie. When he had finished, a distinguished elderly man with enormous side whiskers stood up. He talked at length about mankind and freedom and God. His voice boomed and his language was ornate and sentimental. The audience nodded along, rather subdued.

This set the tone for the day, and Katie began to wonder, what did this have to do with her? Beside her DuQuelle was still as a statue. The wooden bench was extremely hard and she shifted uncomfortably and began to think about lunch, just like she did in calculus lessons when she didn't understand. After the fifth man finished, to a smattering of polite applause, a figure rose from the back of the platform. It was a woman, a black woman, whose face Katie had known since she was a baby. Dolores had taken centre-stage.

Clearing her throat and looking slightly nervous, Dolores began. She didn't sound anything like the men who had preceded her. She spoke naturally, using simple language, and from the heart.

'My people were taken from their homes and brought to America in chains,' she told the audience. 'America is supposed to be a land of freedom – we sure wanted to be free of you here in Britain. Even so, in America they made us slaves. I just don't understand. How could they do it? To treat us in this inhuman way. I mean, goodness, *we* knew we were human. Anyways, it makes sense that I'm here, saying *no* to slavery. I've got an awful lot to lose. It's pretty amazing though that you are here. I guess you're just really good people, who know a bad thing when they see it. And I testify before the Lord, that slavery is an evil sin.'

The crowds before her were slightly startled, then began to clap. Dolores relaxed.

'Amen!' she cried out. 'I have great faith in God, and God, with your help, will free the slaves. But we can only do this by defeating the South. As long as there's a Confederacy, there's slaves.' The audience looked askance. They wanted freedom for all, but they did not want to go to war. The boarding of the *Trent* had led them to the brink of war against the North, and now this woman was asking them to stand against the South.

Dolores looked down across the audience and then up into the galleries. 'I have a letter here,' she said, 'a letter from my President, Mr Abraham Lincoln.' The audience erupted into roars of approval as Dolores unfolded the letter. This woman held the voice of the President in her hands.

Katie, shocked and delighted, looked up at Bernardo DuQuelle. 'How did Dolores get that letter?' she asked.

'Your President has been writing to Florence Nightingale,' DuQuelle whispered. 'Everyone writes to Florence, she is so well-known. We needed a messenger to spread his word, and we couldn't think of a better one than your Dolores.'

As Dolores read out the words of the great man, Katie looked admiringly at her. She knew now, Dolores was the best education she could receive. Better than any museum or library in New York and certainly better than Neuman Hubris School. If there was any kindness in Katie, she must have learnt it from Dolores.

'. . . The peace and friendship which now exist between the two nations will be perpetual,' Dolores reads with a mixture of pride and humility. Her hands shook slightly as she looked down at the handwriting of this man who changed the lives of millions of people. 'We thank you for raising your voices against slavery. You have placed humanity above prosperity. God bless you, a people who understand freedom. We thank you.' Dolores finished reading the letter to thunderous applause. And looking straight at Katie, she smiled broadly and winked a little wink.

It was hard to reach Dolores after all the speeches. She was absolutely mobbed. But eventually Katie pushed her way through the throng and threw herself into Dolores's arms.

'Whoah baby, you're gonna knock me down, jumping on me like that,' Dolores laughed. But Katie could tell Dolores was just as pleased to see her. DuQuelle led them down the marble stairs to a small room on the lower floor. As they went, Katie noticed many people taking note of Dolores. Men doffed their hats and women bowed their heads in respect.

'Dolores, you were just so great!' Katie said, giving her another squeeze when they had left the crowds. 'I didn't know you could speak like that.'

Dolores grinned. 'I told you that I'd learned a lot from that shaking and singing of Mimi's, didn't I?'

Katie laughed too. It had been a long time since she had done so. 'You know Mimi mainly lip-syncs to a recording. And I've never seen her hold an audience like that.'

Dolores took Katie's hand, looking more serious.

'Well, she never had such an important message to give. You know how all this hocus-pocus works, Katie. Mary Seacole has tried to explain it a dozen times, the time travel and the Tempus children, but I think she's kind of confused too. I have the feeling that things can change in this time; that you and me could change the course of history. We've got to keep working. You know, the South could still win this war.'

This was a sobering thought. 'That would mean we could never go back to our own country, much less our own time,' Katie said. They were both silent for a minute, holding hands. In this strange place, each was to the other the only remnant of their real lives. 'Well, we'll just have to make sure the South doesn't win,' Katie added. 'Did you know Britain almost went to war against the North, just before Christmas? It was Prince Albert who put a stop to it. He wrote a memo, about the RMS *Trent*, right before he . . . well, it was a great letter.'

Everyone stopped to think about the Prince. Dolores sniffed a little and rummaged in her large bag. 'He might have been a foreigner,' she said, 'but he sure seemed to care about this country.'

Bernardo DuQuelle passed her a large immaculate handkerchief, bordered in black. 'This German Prince has governed our nation with more sense and intelligence than any English king ever managed,' he added, with great respect for his past master.

The gloom lifted as Mary Seacole burst into the room. She was usually dressed in the brightest hues, but the Prince's death had sent her into mourning. She was swathed, from head to toe, in the deepest, inkiest black crepe. Her vivid blue leghorn hat had been replaced with an equally large black one. It flapped backwards as she ran, its long black silk ribbons streaming behind her.

'Dolores, you are a one woman army, you are,' Mary Seacole exclaimed. DuQuelle observed them with some amusement. 'Florence sends her how-de-dos,' Mary Seacole told him. Dolores stiffened at her name. Her warm friendship with Mary Seacole obviously didn't extend to Miss Nightingale.

DuQuelle raised his hat and bowed slightly in recognition of the formidable Miss Nightingale. 'She would have been proud to see you today. She is a fierce abolitionist. You are making good use of your time.'

Dolores looked at him keenly. 'It's OK for you to cheer us on, but there is a problem, one that for some reason never troubles you.' DuQuelle raised his eyebrows.

'Money,' she continued. 'Mary here just doesn't have any. She spent every penny she had taking care of soldiers in that war you had over here.'

'The Crimea, the Crimean War,' Katie piped up helpfully.

'That's right, the Crimea. And everyone says she was a heroine, but being a heroine doesn't put a roof over her head and food on her plate. She can't stay with Miss

Nightingale forever, *no one* could stay with that woman forever.'

DuQuelle examined the silver top of his walking stick. He never thought about money. He had no need.

Katie watched him roll the cane through his fingers. It was engraved with fanciful letters and symbols that spun round as he turned it.

'The letters,' she exclaimed, out of the blue.

'A change of subject,' DuQuelle murmured. 'Quite right. One must never talk of money . . .'

'Of course *one must talk of money*,' Katie imitated his slightly foreign, disdainful accent. 'How else is Mary Seacole going to eat? The letters on your walking stick gave me the idea. She could write.'

Mary Seacole, usually enthusiastic about everything, looked doubtful. 'I can do a lot of things, but I've never seen myself as a writer,' she said. 'Besides, what do I have to write about?'

Katie grew quite excited, pushing back her own black bonnet and rubbing her head. 'Write about yourself. My mother, Mimi, is bringing out her autobiography and she's really kind of boring if you think about it. You've travelled the world, nursed on the battlefield and saved men's lives. You've probably met all the most famous people alive. Everyone would want to read your story. I can see it now: *Mary Seacole, Medicine Woman* . . . or maybe *The Wonderful Adventures of Mary Seacole* . . .'

'But I'm not a writer,' Mary Seacole protested. 'A letter to a cousin is one thing, but a whole book . . .'

Dolores shook her head at her friend. 'Now this is not like you, false modesty and self-doubting. Do you think Katie's mama is going to do one stitch of work on her book? She is not. You'll need a ghostwriter, just like Mimi has. We'll get someone in who's real good and I can help. You supported me when I stood up to address the crowds, and I can sure support you. I can run errands and get your thoughts in order. I'd say Florence could write it; she writes all night, letters and stuff, but it's pretty dry writing, kind of full of facts . . .'

'Grace O'Reilly will help you with your memoirs,' Bernardo DuQuelle said, without looking up from his walking stick. 'She has already assisted you with the pamphlets. And she is going through a difficult patch. Her father wants her to marry and encourages a string of idiotic suitors. There is even rumour that Lord Twisted is pursuing her again. This poor young woman is in need of refuge. Grace has a lively writing style and does not lack a sense of humour. I suggest she pays a visit to Miss Nightingale at the same moment that Mary Seacole and Dolores are there. Her father could not deny Florence's request. Together, the three of you might produce some-thing worth reading.'

Dolores practically bounced with enthusiasm. 'That's just the person, Bernie. She's a nice young lady with a good education. She can come help write and we can look out for her. Keep some of those sniffing hounds of men at bay.'

DuQuelle looked appalled at his new name, but for Katie, it was the joke of the century.

'That's right, Bernie,' Katie added, 'for someone who doesn't talk of money, you've come up with a pretty good plan.'

Studiously checking his pocket watch, Bernardo Du-Quelle ignored Katie. 'I find this hall extremely chilly. I suggest we retire to Half Moon Street for tea and cakes in front of the fire.'

Their good humour had given them an appetite and everyone bustled towards the door and the promise of a delicious tea. But as the carriage came round, the footman stepped from DuQuelle's vehicle, and bowing, handed him a note. 'It is from Princess Alice,' the footman said in a hushed, reverential tone. 'She said you must read it at once.'

Katie watched as DuQuelle tore open the message. As he read, he teetered slightly, leaning on his walking stick. Turning to the footman, he began to issue orders in a shaking voice.

'Please hail a hansom cab for these two ladies,' he said, gesturing towards Dolores and Mary Seacole. 'I wish you to accompany them to South Street, to the home of Miss Nightingale. Tell her I shall write shortly to explain. The train? No, we have missed it. Miss Katherine Tappan and I will return in the carriage to Windsor immediately.'

Something had gone very wrong. Both Mary Seacole and Dolores recognized this, and followed his instructions without protest. DuQuelle held out his hand and practically pulled Katie into the carriage. 'Drive on!' he cried and the carriage dashed off, leaving the others on the pavement.

For some time Katie didn't say anything. She watched DuQuelle, huddled in the corner, his cloak wrapped tightly around him, his top hat low on his forehead. He muttered slightly, resting his chin on the silver-tipped stick. His green eyes had dimmed.

Finally, she shuffled over on the carriage seat until she was next to him. 'Come on,' she said. 'Share and share alike. You've helped me through enough trouble. Now what can I do for you?'

DuQuelle sat up. He didn't smile, but he did look slightly less grim. Reaching inside his voluminous cloak, he took out the message from Princess Alice and silently handed it to Katie. As she unfolded the crinkled paper, she could see Alice's beautiful script, turned to a scrawl of distress.

Oh please do come – as quickly as you can – the Queen – she is gone!

Chapter Nineteen

Hiding the Queen

'I have been caught unawares. I did not foresee that the Queen was in danger,' Bernardo DuQuelle raged in the carriage. 'Since the Queen refuses to rule, I have been overwhelmed with paperwork, meetings, the day-to-day decisions of running an empire. The government's red boxes have defeated me. And this damned humanity welling up inside of me. It weakens me with each passing day.'

Katie watched London fly by – the beautiful stucco homes of Mayfair and Hyde Park, drab in the darkening winter sky, the villas and building sites in South Kensington – and then the market gardens and open countryside. She could not comfort DuQuelle, nor did she seem able to help him. He spent the trip talking to himself, trying to master the crisis.

Princess Alice had been watching for them. When they finally rode up the hill through the Henry VIII gate, she came running, followed by James O'Reilly. Katie's body ached. She could feel her muscles, tender and strained by two bumping, rolling carriage trips in one day. But looking at Princess Alice's face gave her that extra bit of toughness. Alice appeared haggard, she really seemed to have aged. The grief over her father and the unremitting care she'd given her mother had taken their toll. And now this.

'You must be tired,' Alice said, taking her hand. 'And cold, you're hands are freezing. Where are your gloves, Katie?'

'Never mind any of that,' Katie said. DuQuelle agreed, though Katie could tell he too was stiff with cold.

'Let us find a private place, and then you must tell us all.' They were up the steps and into the Castle in a moment. Its gloom and silence told the story of the months past.

Alice led them back to the Blue Room, where her father had died. 'I felt this would explain much of the Queen's state of mind,' she said.

The last time Katie had seen the room it had been chaos. Now it was tidy with the bed made, the windows washed, the curtains drawn back and draped. A marble bust of the Prince Consort stood on a column next to the bed. And on the bed a large floral wreath had been lovingly laid.

'My mother has turned this room into a shrine for my father,' Princess Alice explained. 'See, here is the glass from which he took his last medicines, and here is his pen, the one he laid down after writing the letter to President Lincoln.'

DuQuelle's eyebrows went up.

'You are right to question this behaviour,' James added. 'The Queen's mind is greatly troubled. Look here. These are Prince Albert's clothes. The Queen has ordered them laid out each day.' He picked up a jug, set in front of a mirror on a small table. 'This is water, brought in warm in the morning, as if the Prince were going to shave – again, on the orders of the Queen.'

Katie took in the room. It had a strange sense of antici- pation about it: as if Prince Albert might walk in any moment.

Princess Alice shook her head sorrowfully. 'The Queen has decided that my father is not gone. She says she will continue to rule with him, even if he has moved into another, better life. My mother believes he speaks to her from the dead. She made us hold a séance the other day.'

Katie choked back nervous laughter. Was the Queen of Great Britain really ruling the country through séances?

James gave her a grim look. 'It's not funny, Katie,

the Queen has been behaving in a very erratic manner. She talks to herself – or rather says she's talking to her husband. She won't eat much. She refuses to see any of the government – not even the Prime Minister. She sleeps very little, wrapped in Prince Albert's nightshirt. She says it still smells of him.'

Princess Alice became rather stiff at this last piece of information and eyed Bernardo DuQuelle under lowered lashes. 'James, there was no need to reveal that last bit of . . .'

'I am sorry,' James interrupted. 'But DuQuelle and Katie have to know just how serious the situation has become. The Queen is saying she will never appear in public again, and the country will stay in mourning forever. She has ordered all the rails in the parks throughout the country to be painted black. Her natural depression is turning to hysteria.'

DuQuelle looked serious. 'How are the doctors treating her?' he asked.

James was silent. It was his turn to be embarrassed. 'We had thought, with the misdiagnosis of my father; that perhaps Sir Brendan would leave the Royal Household. The Queen, for some reason, continues to hold him in high esteem. She has ordered the other doctors to withdraw. He is the only doctor she will see . . .'

As long as the other doctors had attended the Queen, they had felt safe. But they had been outwitted, by a man they had thought a fool. For Sir Brendan to have control of the Queen, in this weakened state, was disastrous.

'And what is Sir Brendan's *diagnosis*?' DuQuelle asked with much irony.

James had turned a dull, angry red. When Alice spoke, her voice shook. 'Early this morning I received a note from Sir Brendan. He said that, even if I am her eldest daughter living at home, my attendance at the Queen's side was hindering her recovery. He said she must be removed, not just from my presence, but from Windsor Castle.'

'Where has Sir Brendan taken the Queen?' Katie asked.

Alice was looking more and more distressed. 'James and I both thought he would take her to Osborne House, on the Isle of Wight. It's where we always had our seaside holidays. This did make some sense. It was still her home, but the scene of happier times. And we thought the sea air would do her good.'

'But . . . there's a but . . .' Katie said.

Princess Alice nodded. 'I assumed she would travel with her retinue, the ladies-in-waiting, her dresser, chambermaids, cooks. But when I conferred with Lady Augusta Stanley, the Queen's lady of the bedchamber, she had received an identical note from Sir Brendan. I telegraphed immediately to Osborne House. They have been informed of no such visit and the Queen has not arrived!' This was serious indeed.

'Shouldn't you do something like call the police?' Katie asked. 'I'm mean, that's what we'd do: the missing person's bureau.'

DuQuelle shook his head. 'We need to keep this quiet. The nation is already unsettled by the death of Prince Albert. There is great sympathy for the Queen, but unease about the future. If the people thought she would not, or could not rule, there would be rioting in the streets.' He looked at the three faces before him, and sighed. They were so young. 'We will find the Queen,' he said to reassure them, 'and we will bring her to her senses.'

'How do you hide the Queen?' Katie asked. 'I mean, it's not like people don't know what she looks like. Mimi would give half her life, or gain thirty pounds, to have Queen Victoria's kind of recognizable celebrity.'

DuQuelle took off his top hat and examined the rim. 'Perhaps it is a sleight of hand,' he said. 'The rabbit out of the hat. Smoke and mirrors. It could be that the Queen *wanted* to be hidden.' They all thought this over.

Then Alice gave a stifled gasp. 'He wouldn't . . .' she whispered. He wouldn't dare . . .'

'I hope we are not thinking the same thing,' James said.

Alice's eyes filled with tears. 'Poor Mama. She has fretted and cried that she cannot bear the grief, that she will lose her mind. Sir Brendan seemed to encourage this, to tell her that her mind had always the tendency to instability and now it was unsound, and she would not be well for months, even years. I heard him, relating to her the hereditary strain of . . . insanity . . . that runs in her family.'

Everyone's mind turned to George III, Queen Victoria's great-grandfather. He had spent the last ten years his life roaming the corridors of Windsor Castle, completely off his head.

'Why would he want to convince the Queen that she was insane?' Katie asked.

DuQuelle took out his handkerchief and brushed an imaginary spot from his hat. 'It may not be what he wants. For some time we have all suspected that Sir Brendan answers to another master.'

James thought carefully. 'His great pride has grown even worse since the Queen ennobled him. The title has gone to his head. He is desperate to make a match for my sister in the highest echelons of society. We've argued many times about this, and about money. He talks endlessly of keeping up appearances and spends far beyond his means. My father must be in terrible debt.'

Bernardo DuQuelle put his hat down at the foot of the bed and, taking off his cloak, smoothed its surface. 'I am reminded of Sir Lindsey Dimblock, that fool of a friend of Lord Twisted. Do you remember? He owed a great debt. His creditor urged him to turn spy and he refused. Sir Lindsey was found filleted and gutted – thrown into the Thames.'

Katie shuddered. 'I'd forgotten. That was just awful, but it was, wasn't he killed by . . . ?'

The three young people looked at each other, eyes widening. Alice instinctively reached for James. Even DuQuelle looked at him with sympathy. 'Our suspicions have come to fruition. I see all the hallmarks of Lord Belzen,' he told them. 'It is as we feared. James, this is dangerous indeed – for your father, and even more so for the Queen. Belzen will show no mercy.'

A great sense of shame seemed to weigh James down. 'I'm certain you are right. Lord Belzen feeds off the vanity and ambition of men like my father. He has fallen into Belzen's debt and now he is in his power.'

'Will he kill the Queen?' Katie asked before she could stop herself.

Alice blanched so white she could have been DuQuelle's daughter. But DuQuelle was quick to reassure her. 'He will not kill the Queen. Your brother Bertie would simply become King and order would be restored. Lord Belzen wishes to create the most upheaval possible. And a Queen whose sanity comes and goes creates much more unrest. She cannot truly rule and her son will not have power. This is the perfect storm: the best possible environment for upheaval and civil war. I have to give Lord Belzen his due, he certainly understands history.'

Each of them pondered the situation. Did the Queen

really believe she was insane? And if she did, where had she allowed Sir Brendan to take her?

Alice, though terrified herself, tried to comfort James. 'You are nothing like your father,' she said. 'We've joked about this many a day. Anyone who has made your acquaintance respects your abilities.' She stopped, turning slightly pink, fearing she had said too much.

DuQuelle, usually so insightful, did seem stumped. He paced the room, swinging his walking stick – a habit, Katie had learned, he adopted when he was anxious. And then he stopped suddenly. 'What is this?' he exclaimed, lifting the end of a pillow with his cane. It was the edge of a piece of paper.

Princess Alice ran forward and pulled it out. 'Mama has taken to writing my father notes,' she explained. 'She slips them under the pillow at night, as if his spirit will come back and read them.' The paper was neatly folded, but in places the surface was wrinkled, as if it had got wet, Katie suspected, with the Queen's tears. 'It would be terribly indelicate to read it,' Alice said.

Bernardo DuQuelle had a soft spot for Alice. He took the paper from her. 'If it will help us to find her,' he said gently, 'then reading it must be the proper thing to do.' Silently he read the Queen's words, shaking his head all the while. 'It says much,' he said, 'but nothing of her location. Katie, we know that Lord Belzen was responsible for the loss of your power with words. Perhaps, now that his hold on you has ceased, you will be able to help.'

He passed the note to Katie. She looked at the Queen's flamboyant handwriting, with her bold underlining:

I know you told me to be <u>strong</u> and not to give way to the passions of my <u>grief</u>. But I <u>cannot</u>. Life is <u>unbearable</u>. The world is <u>nothing</u> to me. I can see only <u>you</u>, hear only <u>you</u>. Good Sir Brendan is taking me somewhere I can truly <u>be with you</u>, without the <u>intolerable duties of ruling</u>. He assures me there will be quiet and solitude and that this will help me to <u>commune</u> the better with <u>you</u>. There we shall meet.

As Katie stared at the paper, she could hear the Queen's voice, silvery and sad, saying the words. Yet as the note ended, she heard the Queen's voice continue. Katie could see her, alone and heavily veiled, solitary in a dark, curtained room. She was lamenting – crying out for her husband.

'Don't cry,' Katie said. 'Wipe your tears.' DuQuelle's face took on a new eagerness. 'Katie, use your powers. Tell us, where is the Queen?'

Katie continued to stare at the small, lost woman, sitting in a heap on the floor. Then, in her mind's eye, she walked to the window and pulled back the heavy curtains. All around the house there were dark woods. With some difficulty a carriage rattled up the rutted drive.

The coachman hopped down and rang the bell.

'Brislington?' he asked at the door.

'Brislington,' Katie said in a low voice. 'She's at Bris-lington.'

DuQuelle took the letter from her and led Katie to a chair.

'Do you know what this is, this Brislington?' Princess Alice asked.

James O'Reilly looked furious. 'It is hard to believe, that he would do this. I can never forgive my father.'

Katie was coming out of her dream-like state. Princess Alice was weeping. DuQuelle handed her his handkerchief. He seemed to have a never-ending supply.

'You are right to weep,' he said. 'Brislington is a lunatic asylum. Near Bristol.'

Princess Alice twisted the handkerchief in her hands. 'Oh my poor mother! Oh the Queen! She must be so confused and distressed. We will leave at once for Bristol.'

DuQuelle put up a restraining hand. 'It is not that simple. We must save the Queen, but no one can know she has been in an asylum. Not her ladies-in-waiting or the rest of her family, and certainly not the people of Britain. How is this to be done?'

James paced the room, desperate to act. 'Brislington is very isolated,' he said. 'The buildings are set within acres of beautiful grounds. The Queen will probably be in a villa, separate from the institution, with her attendants acting as guards. But we cannot storm this place; that would draw the attention we fear. How can we rescue her?'

For a long time they were silent, mentally trying then rejecting one idea after another. Then it occurred to Katie. She was the key to this. She knew how to liberate the Queen.

'James, how many times have you told me I'm crazy?' she asked.

James looked annoyed. 'This is hardly the time . . . about a dozen I should say.'

Katie was frightened, but also a bit excited. 'Well this is your big chance to prove it,' she said.

Bernardo DuQuelle began to understand. 'That just might be effective,' he pondered. 'But how should we carry it out . . . ?'

Katie smiled at him. 'Bernardo DuQuelle, you are a much-respected courtier. James O'Reilly is acting as the household physician to the Royal Family in his father's absence. I am an eminent visitor from America, and under the care of the Royal Household. And now I've become the worst possible house guest and gone off my rocker. You can take me to Brislington and have me locked up. I will get to the Queen.'

She had thought it out in a flash. It would be quite easy. She'd simply blow her cover. All the things she knew, her life in New York City – aeroplanes, the internet, reality TV, atomic bombs, Mimi the pop star, space travel – to the Victorians, these would be the symptoms of insanity. And then there was that whole other world: Lucia, Belzen, the Verus and the Malum. The bizzare, magnificent world of the Tempus. 'I can't tell you how easy it will be,' she concluded. 'I'll be committed in a flash.' There was a slight twinkle in DuQuelle's eyes.

Alice looked even more anxious. 'I cannot let you do this,' she said. 'It is much too dangerous.'

But James too was excited by the idea. 'We can state that it's a temporary mental disturbance, and all Katie needs is some rest. That way we can take her out whenever we wish.'

For DuQuelle and James the matter was settled. Princess Alice was to stay at Windsor, and keep up the pretence that the Queen was in isolated mourning at Osborne House. DuQuelle prepared a series of letters from the Queen to her daughter and ladies-in-waiting as proof of this visit.

'You've got a knack for forgery,' Katie commented as the Queen's highly individual script came flooding from his pen.

'Your civilization's use of words, the reading and the writing – it was all so distant from what I knew, nothing came from within. So I can write as any person, in all languages,' he replied.

Sometimes Katie forgot just how strange DuQuelle was. But for now she had other things to ponder. She was about to become a lunatic.

Chapter Twenty

The Asylum

They had missed the last train to Bristol, so decided to travel through the night, by carriage. On the long journey, Katie practised looking crazy. She knew this was about as politically incorrect as she could get, but she had to make certain they would let her in. Taking off her black mourning bonnet, she unpinned her brown hair. It sprang around her face in its natural bushy, wiry mass. After several days of travelling by horse and carriage, her clothes were already wrinkled and soiled. She hated to think about how she smelled. Already Katie was losing her Victorian primness. She adopted a far away, vacant expression and repeated to herself, 'I don't know. I have no idea. Who am I? Where am I?'

James O'Reilly watched her. If he hadn't been so unhappy, it really would have been funny. 'My advice to you is *just to act natural* – you're strange enough as you are.'

'What symptoms do you look for, when you're declaring someone insane?' Katie asked.

James thought for a moment. 'Well in a woman, it's talking too loudly, too much laughing, discussing delicate matters with strangers – as I said, all the things you already do, Katie.' He smiled grimly to himself.

Katie decided not to be offended. It was such a tense time, and James had such heavy burdens to bear. Besides, she needed all the friends she had.

They stopped only to changes horses along the way. No one really wanted to talk, and Katie must have dozed off. Soon, it seemed, Bernardo DuQuelle was shaking her gently. 'We're almost there,' he said. 'I am aware of your mother's antics. That Mimi puts on quite a show. Now let's see what you've got, Katie. I'd pull out all the stops if I were you.'

It had snowed during the night and the ground was snapping crisp under the horses' hooves. Katie rubbed the frost off the carriage window and looked outside to the new day. She could see nothing for miles but trees.

'I told you it was isolated,' James said. 'Most doctors think it's best to house the insane in remote areas.'

'Yeah,' Katie replied. 'You wouldn't want to spook the

villagers or anything.' She was getting more nervous by the minute.

The woodland thinned as they went up a steep incline. At the top of the hill were two imposing coach houses. DuQuelle got out and spoke to the gatekeeper. Katie noticed an exchange of money. Finally the imposing iron gates swung open and the carriage swept up a long gravel drive. The grounds were extensive and beautiful. At the very end of the drive was a grand building with high stone pillars.

'Palladian,' DuQuelle remarked. 'Lovely, of course, but rather lonely in the snow – so much more suitable to the sunnier climes of Italy.'

Katie was no longer fooled by DuQuelle's clever asides. She knew he was nervous too. The coachman pulled on the reins and the horses came to a stop before the building, their breath hanging white in the winter air.

Bernardo DuQuelle scanned the gardens, his green eyes quick and sharp. 'Here is your cloak, Katie,' he said. 'Draw the hood over your face. Sir Brendan might still be in attendance. You do not want him to recognize you. Try and explore the house and grounds as soon as possible. We'll be nearby. When you have any information on the Queen leave a note in the small shrubbery next to the ornamental folly.' All three sat anxiously in the carriage, as a servant pulled down the carriage steps.

James O'Reilly leaned forward and took Katie's hand.

'You are the best sort of girl, Katie,' he said, as great a compliment as one could expect from James.

As she was handed out of the carriage, Bernardo DuQuelle murmured his assent. 'Good luck, Katie. Good luck to all of us.'

Yet as she looked up to thank him, his face had changed. The mask was back, with an edge of hauteur and a hint of disdain.

'Please call for the head of this institution. I have little time, and this young lady must be committed to his care,' DuQuelle said to the servant.

Katie turned to James, but he also had assumed a stern air. They were shown into a cosy sitting room. The fire blazed merrily and comfortable chairs were grouped throughout the room. 'Perhaps this won't be so bad,' she thought. Yet as she moved towards the fireplace, Katie realized the fire was caged in behind an enormous iron grate, and all of the furniture was bolted securely to the floor.

The doctor entered, grey-haired and seemingly gentle. And yet there was something about him. 'I am Dr Fox,' he said, coming towards Bernardo DuQuelle. 'It is a pleasure to meet you. I have read your work on the origins of language with admiration.' Katie didn't like him. He had a mild rather kittenish face but his sharp eyes were truly foxlike.

The doctor continued to smile, but his eyes darted at

her in distaste. 'Shall we have your young ward removed?' he asked.

'No!' said James, much too loudly, but DuQuelle appeared to be at his ease.

'Not just yet,' he said. 'I'd like to see you examine her. She is a very interesting case, Miss Katherine Tappan.' He lowered his voice. 'She is the daughter of a very important American and a guest of the Royal Family. The distressing circumstances of the past few months seem to have reopened some nervous strain in her. The young doctor here has diagnosed nerves. I really did not know what to do. One could certainly not turn to the Queen . . .'

Katie stared at Dr Fox to see his reaction. 'Our poor Queen,' he sighed. 'We all feel for her at this time of trial.' He obviously didn't know a thing about the woman holed up in his own institution. 'Now, young lady,' he said in his overly soothing voice. 'Tell me a bit about yourself.'

Katie held her cloak tight and wrapped the hood around her face until only her eyes showed. 'I am from New York City,' she said.

'Good, good,' answered the doctor, smiling.

'And I am from the twenty-first century.' The doctor stopped smiling. 'My mother has gotten divorced three times and has endless boyfriends. She's always in the gossip columns, all over the internet,' Katie continued.

By this time the doctor was frowning.

'I think we've heard enough.'

'She's a pop star, well, was – she really is too old to parade around with all that bare skin, and in those skimpy sequinned . . .'

'I said that is ENOUGH,' Dr Fox barked out. James was staring at the toe of his shoe as if the cure for consumption was on the tip of it. He was dying of embarrassment.

DuQuelle, on the other hand, was entirely composed. He handed Dr Fox an envelope. 'This should see to all her boarding costs,' he said calmly. 'Having heard the case, you will understand the need for confidentiality, bordering on secrecy.'

Dr Fox nodded his agreement. 'You have nothing to fear on that account,' he said. 'We have patients even I do not see.'

DuQuelle shot Katie a knowing look. 'I would let her roam the grounds a bit,' he continued. 'The exercise will do her good, and the landscaping here so eases a patient's mental strain.'

'That's right,' James agreed, 'you shouldn't lock her up. She's usually much better than, well, what you just heard. I mean, that wasn't acceptable, I know . . .'

James was obviously worried about Katie and DuQuelle had to pull him towards the door. Dr Fox was urging them on. Soon Katie would be alone. A wave of panic shot through her. She could hear the doctor, now in the hallway. ' . . . really, most indelicate conversation . . . in the female a sign of lunacy . . . delusional . . . complete rest and seclusion . . .'

Above his murmurs came the voice of DuQuelle. 'This patient must not be restrained in any way. She must be able to walk in the shrubberies at will . . . in the woods if needs be. Into the woods.' These last words from DuQuelle were practically shouted.

The front door shut and soon after she heard the carriage drive away. For Katie, it was a lonely sound. Only then did she realize, they had made no plans to contact her, or organize a possible escape. She ran to the windows, hoping to see the last of the carriage. It was a large window, set in the grand façade, but it was closely set with thick iron bars.

When Dr Fox returned, he was not alone. Two women flanked him. They were large, and of a certain age. They did not increase Katie's confidence.

'I think I'll go to my room now,' Katie announced. 'It's been a long carriage ride. I'm kind of achy. And do you think I could have something to eat?' Dr Fox stood in the doorway with his arms folded over his chest. 'Well, thanks, you know, for having me here,' she continued gamely. 'I mean, you're probably kind of full. Mimi, that's my mother, she says everyone's a little bit crazy. Especially Mimi, of course, she loves to see doctors. Used to date her therapist, Dr Fishberg, tried to run off with him . . .'

Katie was babbling. It's what she did when she was

nervous. And Dr Fox, with the two stout women, was certainly making her sweat.

'Extraordinary,' he finally said. 'The indecency quite takes my breath away. She has lost all sense of modesty.' He looked disgusted. The two women – Katie guessed they were orderlies – had perked up, as if they had a treat coming. 'Well, we know exactly what to do with this type of over-excited patient. Miss Grimm, Miss Barren, I leave her to you.'

The moment Dr Fox left the room, the two women took hold of Katie. She screamed out, but they did not try to stop her. Why should they? The only people who could hear her were the other occupants of this house, and they had probably been through the same thing. Katie struggled, and one of the women kicked her hard in the shin, sending her legs flying. They wrestled her arms behind her and began stuffing them into something. With horror, Katie realized, it was a straitjacket.

'How can you do that?' Katie cried out. 'Didn't you hear James? I am not to be restricted. What kind of a hospital is this?'

They had Katie flat on her back now. One of the orderlies picked her up by the ankles, while the other lifted her shoulders. 'You'd like to know what kind of a hospital this is?' The larger one sneered. 'It's the kind of hospital for girls who ask too many questions. But we'll get you calmed down. What you need is a nice bath.'

They dragged Katie up the stairs. She could hear voices, high-pitched and gibbering, coming from the hallways. Her plight had excited the other patients.

Bumping against the stairs and still protesting wildly, Katie was lugged to the very top of the house. It was freezing, and made more so by the large tin baths in the middle of the attic rooms. The orderlies unbuckled the straitjacket and, before she could fight back, had stripped Katie's clothes from her. It all happened in such a rush. One moment Katie was thinking about dinner and bed, the next she was sitting in an empty bathtub.

She'd started out cold and now she was freezing. Katie's teeth chattered and her limbs were goose-fleshed and blue. With sudden fierceness, one after the other, the women tipped buckets of ice-cold water over her head. It ran into her ears, eyes and nose. For a moment she thought she might be drowning. Then swiftly she was pulled from the bath, and a coarse linen gown yanked over her still wet body.

'If that doesn't calm you down, I don't know what will,' Miss Grimm commented with satisfaction.

'A bit of bromide in your supper and you'll be docile as a lamb,' Miss Barren added.

Katie shuddered with the cold. Furious, she realized: she had been their *treat*. She was about to scream and yell, but there was no point. She said nothing, and was led away to her room. It was small, with a single bed and a very high, barred window. Katie noted with alarm that there was a stout ring in the wall. Miss Grimm nodded in its direction. 'Sometimes we have to chain 'em to the wall, a socklet 'round the ankle. Would you like that?'

Katie ducked her head. Best not look her in the eye. 'No, ma'am' she said.

Miss Grimm took Katie by the chin and jerked her head upwards. Miss Barren giggled. 'What did you say?'

'No ma'am, thank you ma'am.' This seemed to be enough. The two orderlies left, taking the candle with them. Katie heard the door being locked from the outside. She was a prisoner.

The hours crept by, agonizingly slow. Katie had barely eaten in days, yet she hardly noticed. The cold over-whelmed everything. She wrapped her blanket around herself and curled-up tightly on the bed, but still she shuddered and shivered. There were curtains in her high little window. Katie thought about taking them down and wrapping them around herself. This, though, would certainly be viewed as an abuse of the hospital property, and she'd probably be punished. Strange sounds echoed through the building; murmurings rising into laments, scuffles and shouts that then subsided into silence. If you weren't crazy to start with, this place would drive you to it, Katie decided.

She watched the winter light move across her window. It must have been around late afternoon when the orderlies returned. Miss Barren had a bundle of clothes. Katie noted with relief that they were warm and serviceable.

'Put these on,' Miss Barren ordered.

Katie decided it was best to follow all orders – that was the only way she would be let out of this cell-like room. She quickly pulled the clothes on and even made an attempt to tidy her hair.

'You will take your meals with the other inmates,' Miss Grimm said. 'Let's see how you like your new friends.'

Katie wasn't at all keen on Miss Grimm's sense of humor. But she kept this to herself.

The dining room was a large room, well-proportioned and clean. It would have been an attractive room, except that there were no pictures on the walls and no ornaments whatsoever. Katie guessed this was to keep the inmates from throwing things if they became violent. She was seated at a table with seven other women. Several of them gave Katie a quick glance, sizing her up. A few others looked into space, completely unaware of their surroundings. One dark-eyed girl stared at her, long and angrily. When Katie smiled at her, she only shook her head and spat upon the floor.

Within seconds the orderlies were upon the dark-eyed girl. 'Halloo!' she cried, 'what's this? What's this? Do you expect me to dine with the devil, Miss Gimlet Simlet?' The girl was removed from the room, and she could be heard howling her protests as she was dragged down the hall. Some of the others moaned and giggled, but mostly there was silence.

Dr Fox entered in his dark frock coat and clerical collar. He was followed by his three sons, all doctors at the asylum, too. They bowed their heads and Dr Fox began a lengthy prayer. The women swayed or stared, picked their nails and bit their lips. Finally the food was brought – bread and cheese, stew and cold bacon. Katie's table was silent. Some of the women ate ravenously, while other pushed the food around their plates.

Dr Fox and his sons sat at a separate table, directly behind Katie. They talked about the girls around them – one's nonsense rhyming, the other's suicide bid – as if the girls had no feelings whatsoever. Then the conversation moved in a more interesting direction: privacy for the most exclusive clientele. 'Such a good idea,' Dr Fox was saying. 'The villas are perfect for the most refined of our patients, the most delicate situations. Why, in one villa, there is a woman of such a fine family, that even I cannot know her identity . . .'

'It must be the Queen,' Katie thought. Straining to hear more, she took a spoonful of stew.

Next to her, a sweet-faced girl of about her own age nudged her with a hurried whisper. 'Don't touch the stew.'

'What?' Katie asked.

The girl glanced around, making certain the orderlies were not watching.

'The stew on your plate. Don't eat it.'

'Why?'

'Bromide. It's in the stew. It's supposed to make you calm. Eat the bacon, or the cheese, but not the stew.'

Katie did as she was told. She turned to thank the girl, but found her looking up at the ceiling, singing quietly to herself.

Days passed and Katie heard nothing from either James O'Reilly or Bernardo DuQuelle. At night she began to wonder: had they actually decided she was insane? Were they going to leave her here? It was so easy for her to believe what Dr Fox was saying and to be undermined by the jeers and threats of the orderlies. It took every ounce of self-belief Katie had *not* to succumb. She followed her new regimen with due care, determined to win some simple liberties. Only then could she search for the Queen. And after her initial rebellion, Miss Grimm and Miss Barren found her a model patient.

Dr Fox was equally pleased, as DuQuelle had sent another packet of money. He was being paid double the normal amount to care for this submissive patient. He fancied the bromide was having an excellent effect. Within the week Katie was invited to play whist in the evening in the select patients' parlour. After two weeks she was given leave to walk within the gated grounds.

There was still the problem of Miss Grimm and Miss Barren. One or the other was always attached to her.

She could walk, with some liberty, but not alone. Katie discovered that, of the two, Miss Barren was the lesser evil. Poor woman, she wasn't cruel by nature, just big and ugly and not very bright, with no money and no future. Katie tried to sympathize with her, and listened to her complaints about the inmates, her long working hours, and her loneliness.

'It's me mum's birthday today,' Miss Barren announced one day as they walked on the grounds. 'She'll be home, with me sister, having an easy day of it.'

Katie had never thought of Miss Barren having a family. 'It's sad that you can't be with them,' she said. 'At least your sister is at home.'

'She's me twin,' Miss Barren added. Katie looked up at the large bulky figure, the lank hair and the spotty complexion: so there were two of them . . . 'I could be home,' Miss Barren continued. 'It's only a half day's walk. Only Dr Fox said I munent go. I mun be with you.'

Katie chose her next words carefully. 'I don't see why you need to be with me. I haven't been any trouble, and I'm certainly not going to start now. We're just going to wander around in the cold for hours, and then Miss Grimm takes over. Why don't you go home? I'll report to Miss Grimm at the right time. You're not working again until tomorrow morning. You could be back by then.'

Miss Barren hung her head, thinking things over. She had so little in life, really just her mum and sister. But you were never supposed to listen to the lunatics. And if she got caught . . .

'I bet there's a cake for your mother. A nice plummy cake for tea,' Katie added.

That decided it. With a list of warnings and threats to Katie, Miss Barren was over the high iron fence with surprising agility.

Katie calculated she had four hours before Miss Grimm came on duty. Where could Queen Victoria be? She reviewed the days, one melding into the other, that she'd spent at Brislington House. Every door led to yet another sad and hopeless woman. But there had been that snatch of conversation in the dining room. The Queen must be in an exclusive villa. Katie just needed to find it. So far she'd not been able to see anything from her small high window but endless woods.

'Into the woods.' Isn't that what DuQuelle had said, twice, and as loudly as he could, just when he and James were leaving. That's what she'd seen in her vision when she'd read the Queen's note, dark and endless woods. She scanned the building behind her. She could see one lone face, a sad old woman staring down at her, but no doctors or orderlies. Katie passed the ornamental folly and side-stepped the shrubberies, forgetting DuQuelle's instructions to leave a note. Wrapping her cloak tightly around her, she headed into the woods.

Chapter Twenty-One

The Secluded Villa

They were ancient woods, dating from the time of Henry VIII. The branches grew thick overhead, and even in leafless February blocked out the sun. The path was rutted and walking was difficult. Katie did not have proper outdoor boots. But she was heartened to see wheel tracks indented in the mud. Someone had come this way recently. After several wrong turns and dead ends, Katie saw something through the trees. As she came closer, the trees thinned out and a small house stood alone in the clearing. She stepped off the path and began to move through the trees. If the Queen was inside, she would not be alone. Katie had no wish to meet her guards.

The ground floor windows were closed and shuttered, but a dim light could be seen coming from the upper windows. Katie circled the house. On the back wall she found a wisteria vine spreading all the way to the roof. In the summer, the house must be covered in drooping purple flowers. For now it was bare, but the vine would serve its purpose. Planting a foot on its base, she began to climb. Katie had no fear of heights, but she'd never been any good with her arms. She'd been the only girl in gym class who couldn't do even one pull-up. Mimi was always going on about upper body strength and toned arms. For once Katie wished she'd listened to her mother. Panting, she pulled herself up the vine, holding on for dear life. Her arms began to ache.

When she reached the first floor, she hooked her foot around the vine and leaning hard to the right, peered into the window. The room was lit and a fire burned in the grate. But it was empty. Katie knew her arms weren't going to hold out much longer. She tried the window. It was closed, of course, but might not be locked. She caught hold of the sill, and gave the window a push, then a harder one. The wooden window frame was warped, and screeched as it gave way. Not exactly a sleuth-like entrance, she thought grimly, scrambling into the room and jamming the window back into place.

It was a bedroom, and someone had recently been in it. The lamp was lit on a small table, with a bit of crochet work under it. Katie looked around. The walls were hung with portraits and the tables covered in photographs. Drawings, pastels and engravings had been stuck up haphazardly, even pinned to the bed curtains. In every single one of them the subject was the same. He appeared in military uniforms, hunting attire, Scottish kilts, Roman togas and medieval armour: a tall slender man with silky brown hair and delicate mustachios. Everywhere Katie looked, Prince Albert stared back. The entire room was a shrine to him.

Katie whistled low. Maybe the Queen *was* crazy. But a sound in the next room sent her scurrying. She recognized the broken, querulous voice of the Queen. 'Never has death touched one so lightly. Did you see him lying in the bed? So beautiful! And that is because he is not really dead. He has simply *gone on before*. It is but a *physical* separation. Soon I shall be with him.'

'Yes ma'am,' was the reply and the voice filled Katie with dread. It was the fawning affected voice of Sir Brendan O'Reilly. They were drawing near the bedroom. Where could she hide? The bed was heavily curtained, piled with blankets and pillows. Katie dived in and, flattening herself, tried to smooth the blankets on top of her.

'I have decorated my room,' the Queen continued. 'Look! All the things I brought from Windsor. I know you voiced concern over the time it took, but what a lovely effect it has produced.'

'Yes, ma'am,' came the reply again. Katie felt Sir Brendan's voice had a nervous edge to it. Had he bitten off more than he could chew?

The Queen talked on, oblivious. 'How long do you think I shall stay here?'

This question must have panicked Sir Brendan. 'Ma'am, if you return, they will ask a hundred things of you. They will expect you to make decisions on everything – economic strategies, foreign affairs, domestic policies . . .'

Katie peeked from underneath the blanket. The Queen was wearing the heaviest of mourning clothes, right down to a sweeping black veil wrapped around her face. Underneath it she was trembling. She scooped up the little Pekinese dog at her feet, dropping her tears on his soft fur. 'I cannot!' she cried. 'How can I make these decisions? I would not, could not act without my husband. He has ruled Britain wisely. I was but his aide. I would not choose a dress or bonnet without his advice . . . I will not!' The veil swung from side to side as she shook her head stubbornly.

Sir Brendan murmured soothing words. There would be no need for her to act. If she would just stay here, with him, all would be well.

Immediately the Queen's tears dried. She dropped the dog back onto the floor and picked up one memento of Prince Albert after another, telling Sir Brendan of her husband's endless virtues. Katie suspected he had heard it all before. 'Have you seen this sketch?' the Queen asked, pulling forward the bed curtains. 'I've pinned it here, so that I can see it at night. It is by Edward Henry Corbould. I had requested that he draw the Prince on his deathbed. How beautiful he is, in death as well as in life!'

The little Pekinese began to sniff around the room. Katie watched in horror as his ears pricked up and his long tail began to wag. Sir Brendan might be oblivious, the Queen in her own world, but the dog could sniff it out – someone new was in the bedroom. He trotted over to the bed and began to growl gently.

'Looty!' called the Queen. 'Don't be naughty. Stay away from the bed. Why is it so rumpled? Have not the maids tidied this room?' Looty began bark loudly, pulling the edge of the blanket. The Queen dropped the sketch she'd been holding up for Sir Brendan to see and backed away, whispering. 'Someone has been in my bed, and they are still there!'

Katie tried to flatten herself against the mattress, but it was too late. Sir Brendan was beside the bed now too. 'Stay back,' he ordered the Queen. The blankets were whipped aside, and Katie was staring at Sir Brendan, standing over her with an upraised brass candlestick. His face changed from fright to fury. 'Do not worry,' he said to the Queen. 'It is an intruder, but a harmless one, I believe.' Reaching across to the night table, he rang a small bell, and an orderly appeared. 'Take our patient downstairs,' he ordered the nurse; and then in a softer voice, 'she needs her sedative, immediately.'

With the Queen gone, Katie was alone in the room with Sir Brendan. Eerily, he did not ask how she had arrived or why she was there. He went into the next room and came back with his medical bag. Snapping it open, he rummaged about inside, searching for something. Katie began to edge towards the foot of the bed. She scanned the room, looking first at the open door and then towards the window.

'It is no use,' Sir Brendan said coolly, 'there are two orderlies downstairs, blocking all hope of exit. I am standing between you and the window.' Katie opened her mouth. 'Screaming will be of little use,' he continued. 'The Queen has just been given a strong opiate. She'll be asleep – yes, that quickly. Medicine *can* be amazing. Ah, *here's* what I was looking for.'

'What are you going to do?' Katie asked. She wished she hadn't.

Sir Brendan spun around, his face tight with controlled wrath. He held a bottle in one hand, and a handkerchief in the other. She couldn't help noticing it had a black border. Even at his most corrupt, Sir Brendan followed protocol. 'You are a menace to society,' he said. 'I can only conclude that you have made your way here to kill the Queen.'

Katie gulped. She hadn't thought of this.

'I have always found you mentally unstable. Just think: the lunatic has found her own way to the asylum,' Sir Brendan continued, almost cheerfully. 'But there will be no rest cure for you. Sadly, I have no choice but to operate.'

Katie moved back towards the headboard. She could hear Looty trotting upstairs, barking warily. 'You can't operate on me. There's nothing wrong with me.'

Sir Brendan actually laughed. 'Ah, that is always the case. The more crazy they are, the more they deny it.' He pulled the cork from the bottle and clapped the handkerchief over it. 'You think my son James is the only one who reads. Well, I've been looking into medical research too. There is this amazing new form of surgery, recently performed by the Swiss. It is similar to trepanning, but more effective. You drill a small hole in the skull and insert an ice pick. You twist it. The cuts in the brain calm the patient to an amazing extent. Permanently.'

Katie was becoming hysterical. 'That's a lobotomy. It's against the law. You can't perform that surgery. You're a terrible doctor. You'll probably kill me.'

Sir Brendan shrugged his shoulders. 'You are not who you say you are, and you are not where you are supposed to be. Who will know if you are here, and who will care? I can only think of one: Lord Belzen. He thought you might turn up at Brislington. He welcomed it in fact, and has suggested you would be more useful with some mental modification. I for one am very inspired by this opportunity to experiment in my chosen profession. This could be an important medical breakthrough.'

'He's the one who's gone crazy,' Katie thought.

In a flash Sir Brendan had her by the shoulders, pinning back her head. The handkerchief was thrust over her nose and mouth. 'Chloroform,' he said. 'The Queen loves it. Used it for her last few childbirths. Not that we'll be going through that again.' Was he really laughing?

Katie thrashed her head from side to side. 'You don't know enough! You'll sever my brain nerves. If you don't kill me, I'll be little better than a vegetable.' She kicked against him, but in her panic breathed deeply, into the handkerchief. Her limbs began to grow heavy, her eyes to close.

'That's right, a good long sleep,' she heard Sir Brendan saying. He seemed so far away. She made one last supreme effort and lifted her head. Looty, barking madly, was trying to bite Sir Brendan, while he sorted through his medical bag again. The barking seemed to die away, and her head fell back as Sir Brendan turned around, a sharp metal object in his hand.

Blackness.

The pain was very bad. Her head throbbed and her mouth felt burnt and blistered. There was a terrible stinging ache in her left temple. The operation must be over. She kept her eyes closed. He'll still be here, she thought, I mustn't move. *At least she was able to think.* Something hot and wet trickled down the side of her face. Blood. A wave of nausea made her turn slightly and wretch. 'That will be the chloroform. He's applied much too much. Try and stay still, Katie, while I patch you up.' Relief flooded through her. That calm, rational, rather gruff voice: it belonged to James O'Reilly.

Katie sucked in her breath, as he gently swabbed and bound her head.

'Now get some rest,' James ordered. Instead she opened her eyes and tried to sit up. 'Well, we know your personality has not been altered,' James added. 'Here you are, immediately ignoring what you've been told.'

Katie felt dizzy, and her vision was blurred. She sank back on the pillows to rest for a moment and then tried again. The outlines of the room clarified. It was a mess. Chairs were overturned, pictures ripped from the walls, the bed curtains had been torn from their hooks. Sitting comfortably in the one upright chair, with the Pekinese on his lap, was Bernardo DuQuelle.

'He tried to save me,' Katie murmured through the pain in her head. 'Looty was a very brave little dog.'

'They call them lion dogs,' DuQuelle informed her. 'Looty is an excellent specimen. I knew his great, great, great-grandfather, Shizi. He belonged to the Emperor

Qianlong. I helped the Emperor collect the Siku Quanshu, perhaps the greatest library in the history of your world . . .'

'I don't understand what you're saying,' Katie whispered. 'My brain, he's damaged my brain.'

James O'Reilly sighed. 'There's nothing wrong with your brain. No one understands DuQuelle. Katie, lie back and close your eyes. I'd give you a sedative but you're full of chloroform already. Your brain is fine, at least as fine as it has ever been.'

Bernardo DuQuelle came over to the bed. Up close Katie could see strain etched on his face. 'James and I had not deserted you,' he said. 'We were nearby. The gatekeeper had been suitably bribed to tell us of any messages left in the shrubbery. But you forgot, Katie, a careless mistake that could have cost you your life. We only knew when the asylum reported you missing. Thank goodness Miss Grimm had turned up early for her shift. You had quite a head start on us,' he said. 'Young O'Reilly and I followed your footsteps in the mud, but with the twists and turns of the path, we lost you. Things had reached a crucial point by the time we forced our way into this secluded villa.'

Katie touched the bandage on her head. 'Don't worry,' DuQuelle added. 'Sir Brendan had only just started when we reached you.'

James actually smiled. 'He was having some problems

with the drill. Not surprisingly, you are very hard-headed, Katie.'

Was she really OK? Katie counted to ten, sang the 'Star-Spangled Banner' to herself and tried to list all of Mimi's top hits. 'Where has your father gone?' she asked.

James stopped smiling. 'Don't ever call him my father again. He fled, left you bleeding on the bed.'

The three of them were silent for a moment. Sir Brendan's vanity and ambition had led him to Lord Belzen and evil.

'Lord Belzen will be angered by his failure,' Katie said. 'I hate to think about his prospects.'

DuQuelle agreed. 'Sir Brendan backed himself into a corner. Once he had removed the Queen from Windsor Castle, there really was no future for him.'

'The Queen,' Katie cried trying to get out of bed. 'She's downstairs!'

DuQuelle stopped her. 'The Queen is fine,' he said, 'or at least as fine as possible, given her extreme sorrow. She is still sleeping; she has slept through the entire crisis.'

James poured Katie a glass of water. Looty jumped onto the bed and snuggled up next to her. The Queen had slept through everything. Sleep – that sounded good.

'I don't want Miss Barren to get into trouble . . .' Katie yawned and, holding Looty close, pulled the covers over both of them.

'I'll take care of that,' DuQuelle said. 'I advise you to

sleep when you can.' Katie knew she could. In fact, she could have slept for one hundred years.

'Sleep is a great restorative,' James added. And so Katie fell sound asleep in the Queen's bed.

Chapter Twenty-Two

Miss Nightingale

Under normal circumstances, a visit from Miss Florence Nightingale was an honour. But Miss Nightingale's appearance at Brislington House was, for Dr Fox, the stuff of nightmares. She had arrived that afternoon, having been secretly summoned by Bernardo DuQuelle.

She knew what she had to do. 'What kind of an institution did Dr Fox think he was running?' she asked in her refined but firm voice. The chaos, the crudity and the random cruelty of his establishment were beyond her comprehension. His ideas were more insane than the inmates of his asylum. Mysterious veiled women, brutal orderlies, experimental surgery – she was having NONE OF IT.

Dr Fox followed after her, explaining and apologizing – babbling in the manner of his own patients. To be condemned by Miss Nightingale, a national treasure, the heroine of the Crimea. This would be the end of his career. Miss Nightingale, grim-faced, laid out her demands. 'There must be reform in the care of mental patients,' she announced. 'I shall write, personally, to the Queen.'

To Katie, this was an amazingly bold move. How could Florence Nightingale write to the Queen? She was already here, recovering from her ordeal in the villa in the woods.

The Queen had woken from her sleep, but it would take much longer to rouse her from her sorrow. With Sir Brendan gone, however, there was a chance she would recover. Florence Nightingale was taken through the woods to the Queen.

It was a most unusual relationship. Katie was amazed to see the normally astringent Miss Nightingale bow to the will of another woman. The Queen was, after all, still the reigning monarch. And Miss Nightingale was a loyal subject. The Queen, for her part, was a little bit in awe of the internationally famous Miss Nightingale, a lady of rank who could still pitch a tent on a battlefield, and saw off a man's leg.

Florence Nightingale sat with the Queen in her villa, admiring image after image of Prince Albert. Together they walked in the woods, and finally, with the Queen heavily veiled, through the ornamental gardens. As they got to know each other, Miss Nightingale began gently to speak her mind.

'You are a strong woman and a passionate one,' she said to her monarch. 'You have taken your great will and put it at the service of your grief.' The Queen wept and wailed, insisting she could not rule alone. Florence Nightingale held her nerve and continued to argue her case. 'Unlike most women, you have a *must* in your life,' she told the Queen. 'You *must* rule your people. You *must* set aside your private griefs and attend to the public's affairs. It is a great thing to be a Queen.'

The Queen did not put aside her widow's weeds. Nor did she agree to end her mourning – not in a year, not in five years, not ever. She said she would never again open Parliament, nor 'show herself' to large crowds. She did, however, agree to return to Windsor Castle. The Queen would go to her large mahogany desk, sit down in the leather chair and open the red boxes, filled with the government's paperwork. She would begin the heavy burden of governing. The desk next to hers, equally imposing, would remain. But no longer would anyone sit in the adjacent chair. She would rule her country and she would rule alone. It *was* a great thing to be a Queen.

As Florence Nightingale put it to Bernardo DuQuelle, 'The Queen will behave like a heroine now, and knuckle down to business.' Florence was always that bit more crisp when among old friends. And her crispness turned acrid when confronted with Dr Fox. He continued to apologize profusely. Sir Brendan's reputation was so high. There had been no reason to question him. Everything had been in order. 'And all monies had been paid in advance,' Miss Nightingale added drily, 'really, when the Queen hears about this . . .'

February turned to March. The snow had melted and the winter sun took on a tinge of promised warmth. The orderlies bowed and curtsied endlessly to Florence Nightingale. After Katie's experiences, the staff were to be reorganized. Miss Barren would be retrained. Miss Grimm was fired. Workmen were installing a large new boiler. There would be no more cold-water baths. Miss Nightingale had also written to St Thomas's Hospital requesting nurses and doctors to assist at Brislington House. She insisted that Dr Fox be stripped of his position, but he would not be prosecuted, as long as he remained silent. And the mysterious veiled woman must remain a mystery.

One morning Katie sat with James and Miss Nightingale, enjoying the mild day with several of the female inmates. It was amazing how quickly the slightest changes in regime had benefited them.

Bernardo DuQuelle came up the hill to the house, holding a copy of *The Times*. He handed it to James. 'Read the editorial,' he said. 'They are questioning the Queen's isolation at Osborne House. We'll need to return as soon as possible. We can make the journey in a single day. We should be thankful Sir Brendan's hideaway was not even more remote.'

'There's something I don't understand,' Katie said. 'Why did Sir Brendan hide the Queen here? Wouldn't it have made better sense to simply declare the Queen insane and then have her committed?'

DuQuelle shook his head. 'It was a more cunning plan than that and Sir Brendan needed total control over the Queen. If she were declared insane, she would lose the Crown. The Prince of Wales would become King. The smooth succession would be complete. But if the Queen moved in and out of sanity, there would be a vacuum of power. Rumours would fly around, the country would be in disarray, and resentments would fester: the perfect breeding ground for revolution. Things are dangerous enough. We must return the Queen to some form of normalcy, and she must return to Windsor Castle.'

James turned to Florence Nightingale. 'Has the Queen recovered? Is it safe for her to travel?' Miss Nightingale looked towards the woods, where the Queen sat in her villa, looking at pictures of her beloved dead husband.

'She will never completely recover, but yes, she can travel, and she can rule.'

Katie jumped up. 'Well, I'm really glad to go. I'm worried about Alice and I miss Dolores. I'm packing my bags NOW.'

As they came out of Brislington House, Katie looked around her. Freedom. The sky had that sharp white and blue hue of a cold, cloudless early spring day. But there was something curious about the weather. On the horizon, past the woods, purple and black clouds were gathering. They clashed together, piling high, with sharp needles of lightning stabbing the ground. The storm did not spread, but stayed in one spot, growing darker and angrier by the minute. 'What could that be?' Katie wondered.

DuQuelle watched the lightning slash the ground. He took off his hat and bowed his head. 'It is Sir Brendan O'Reilly,' he said. 'I would say "rest his soul", but there will be no rest.'

'So Lord Belzen has found him,' Katie said.

'It is worse than that,' DuQuelle answered slowly. 'What you see is the fury of true good, when it has been thwarted. Sir Brendan's pain will know no bounds; for at the very end he will understand *what could have been*.'

Katie shuddered at the thought and instinctively reached for James's hand. It trembled slightly but his face was still, almost stern. DuQuelle turned to the young man. Again, Katie saw that passing flicker of human sympathy. And then he said the words, sincerely. 'I am so sorry, James. You father has been found. By Lucia.'

Chapter Twenty-Three

The Truth

Travelling with a Queen is never easy, but travelling incognito with Queen Victoria was very difficult indeed. They had booked a first-class carriage on the train, and the first thing she did was to fling open the windows. Steam, soot and icy air filled the carriage within seconds. Bernardo DuQuelle, who hated the cold, suffered cruelly. But the Queen was undisturbed. She reached eagerly for the hamper packed specially for the trip.

Queen Victoria, in spite of her great grief, had regained her appetite. Florence Nightingale watched in horror as she consumed compote, roast beef, cold potatoes and a whole boiled fowl. Afterwards she confided to Miss Nightingale, 'I suffer from such indigestion, it is a mystery to me.' Florence Nightingale sympathized but made no suggestions. She knew a hopeless case when she saw one.

They transferred to horse and carriage one stop before Windsor to avoid suspicion. As they pulled up at the top of Castle Hill, several of Victoria's ladies came running out. 'We have been so worried,' they cried to Bernardo DuQuelle. 'Why would you not let us come to her? We didn't know what to do, and we didn't want to alert the newspapers!'

'That would have been disastrous. I worried as well, so I travelled secretly to Osborne House to speak to the Queen. I do apologize for the delay. I took weeks to convince her. I brought my friend, Miss Florence Nightingale . . .' DuQuelle replied. The ladies had been fussing and curtsying to the Queen. They turned now, awestruck. The great Miss Nightingale.

Though grief-stricken, the Queen had no intention of being upstaged by a nurse, even if she was the heroine of the Crimean War. Throwing back her veil, for the first time in months, she strode over to Miss Nightingale. Queen Victoria was a tiny woman, but she still had royal stature. Florence Nightingale curtsied, very low. 'My little friend, Miss Nightingale, has been an invaluable aide,' the Queen said. 'She has helped me to see, again, my duty. I think I shall keep her with me for a time.'

Katie noticed that Miss Nightingale's demure smile tightened that little bit. Spending time with Queen

Victoria could be quite a challenge. She exchanged a long sideways glance with Bernardo DuQuelle. For the hundredth time, Katie wondered about their relationship.

DuQuelle came to her rescue. 'I quite agree, ma'am. Miss Nightingale will be very helpful to you. I am certain she will help you make decisions on the restrictions of diet, proper exercise and the occasional closing of a window.'

The Queen had no intention of following any dictates on these matters. She began to change her mind. Perhaps Miss Nightingale's visit should be a *short* one. 'I have much to do,' the Queen said, rather abruptly. 'The red boxes are certain to have piled up.' She sighed at the idea of her lonely study, where she would be working ceaselessly and alone. There would never be anyone now who would have the right to address her as 'Victoria'. That was gone forever. But she had begun to think again of other friendships – perhaps beyond her ladies-in-waiting.

The Queen lowered her eyes, and under her lashes, glanced at Bernardo DuQuelle. She had always liked him, so clever, in that way of certain foreigners. And she had a weakness for the exotic. Prince Albert might have questioned M. DuQuelle's motives, but to be fair, DuQuelle had always acted in the interest of the Crown. And he was so amusing . . . so well informed . . . so admiring and respectful . . .

The Queen cleared her throat. 'M. DuQuelle, you have long been my beloved husband's Private Secretary.

I wish you to assume that role for me. You are certain to be of great assistance in helping me carry out *his* wishes in *every* way.'

Several ladies-in-waiting stared and the Queen turned slightly pink.

DuQuelle showed no surprise, but then he never did. He bowed very low to the little, round woman, dressed entirely in black. 'Ma'am, I will serve you, to the best of my ability, to the end of our days.' And he did.

James and Katie found Princess Alice in the Blue Room. She had gone every day to lay flowers on her father's bed. She knew this is what the Queen would have wanted. The courtiers rarely came to this room. So it was a quiet place to think. For Katie and Alice there were hugs and tears, hundreds of questions and breathless explanations. But Katie could see, something was worrying Alice deeply. And from the way she greeted James, she suspected it had to do with him.

James seemed unaware of the trouble. 'I wish you could have seen Brislington,' he was telling Alice enthusiastically. 'It's the perfect specimen of how *not* to run a mental hospital. Within just a week, Miss Nightingale's makeshift reforms were proving helpful. I'd never been that interested in mental health before, but now . . .'

'James, Katie, I need to tell you something,' Alice interrupted. Alice was not an interrupter; her manners were always impeccable. This must be important. James looked at her, his face open, his mind still fixed on medical matters.

'Maybe I should just go . . .' Katie mumbled. 'I have some things I need to do.'

Princess Alice took hold of her wrist. Katie noticed her grip was tight and her fingers were ice-cold. 'No,' Alice said. 'You need to hear this too.' She took a deep breath. 'I am leaving, in a week. Sailing on the Royal Yacht *Victoria and Albert* from Gravesend across the Channel and then on to Hesse-Darmstadt.' At first James's face simply looked puzzled, and then Katie saw it darken. He'd put two and two together: the Christmas Ball – it seemed so long ago – the handsome young man with a dark mustachios in the style of her father. 'I am going to visit the family of the Grand Duke,' Princess Alice faltered on. 'My father arranged it, before he died.'

'You are going to visit the Grand Duke . . .' James said slowly, 'the Grand Duke and his son?' There was a long, painful silence.

'Yes, a visit to the Grand Duke . . . and his son.' Alice didn't have it in her to lie. Katie watched the struggle on both her friends' faces.

Then James bowed, very formally. 'Thank you for telling me . . . ma'am.'

Ma'am. That little formal address hurt Alice to the quick. She clutched Katie's hand for support. 'I promised my father, on his deathbed, that I would go. Whatever comes of this visit to Darmstadt, I will have to . . . accept. But I must speak with you now, James – and Katie too. It is immodest enough, what I wish to say, and certainly not for James to hear alone.'

James steadied himself. 'You don't need to say anything.'

'But I want to,' Alice replied with a hint of the regal. 'The friendship the three of us have shared is the greatest of my life. My affection for my brothers and sisters is strong; my respect for my mother is boundless. I love my father . . .' Her voice wavered at this last word, but she continued on. 'Yet it is the two of you, with whom I have shared the *most* of *me*. I did not have to be a sister or a daughter with either of you. In particular, I did not have to be a princess. You know more about my mind, and my heart, than any two people in the world.'

Poor Alice, Katie thought. Brislington was terrifying, but Alice had been left at Windsor all alone. She blinked hard. Alice was saying goodbye then, to both of them. While they'd been at Brislington, Alice had been wrestling with a future she did not want.

'I love Katie so dearly, but I knew she could never stay,' Alice continued. 'I know we will part soon, but I always have the hope we will see each other again. Don't cry, Katie. I'll cry then too, and I won't have the courage to say what I need to say.'

Katie did cry, though, and through her tears she saw Alice hold out her other hand to James.

'My parting with you is of a different sort. While Katie is so funny and unusual, she is a girl; our friendship might be questioned, but in the end it is accepted. But James, the deep friendship we have . . . it would be frowned upon.' James started to deny this, but Alice held up her hand and touched his lips with her fingers. 'Any bright spark within me, any flicker of knowledge – it has been coaxed out of me, James, by you. Our lives will no longer be together. It always had to be this way. But look what you have given me. James, you've made me into the person I will grow to be.'

James did not cry. Katie almost wished he would. He'd gone stone stiff with misery. He cleared his throat three, four times. 'There is one life we can have.'

Alice shook her head, but James, always less polite than she, interrupted. 'The life of the mind.'

'The life of the mind?' Alice questioned.

'No one can stop us from sharing that,' James continued with growing firmness. 'I couldn't go on – to learn, to strive, to achieve anything – unless I was able to tell you. We can still share our ideas. We can write.'

Princess Alice smiled. 'We can write,' she repeated. It was the saddest smile Katie had ever seen.

Bernardo DuQuelle came into the room and bowed slightly towards the bed with its wreath of flowers. 'A sad site for a reunion,' he said. 'No wonder you are crying.' But Katie sensed he already knew what had transpired.

'I have interesting news for you, James O'Reilly,' he announced. 'The Queen and I have had a *very* long discussion about your future.' DuQuelle was already enjoying his preferment at court. Katie suspected that soon he would become even more intolerable. 'She is very impressed by your early work on the germ theory of disease. In the lamentable case of her late husband, she accepts that you were above reproach. Indeed, if you own diagnosis had been followed, Prince Albert might be alive today. The Queen understands, now, the folly of taking Sir Brendan's advice.'

This praise from such high places did not cheer James. He looked even more miserable. At least Princess Alice could legitimately mourn her father. James could only despise his.

Katie flung a furious look at DuQuelle. 'What's all this leading to,' she asked, 'other than you showing off about your great relationship with the Queen?'

DuQuelle looked slightly offended. 'It is leading to an opportunity that will change James O'Reilly's life.'

'My life has already been changed,' James replied dully.

DuQuelle gave him a thoughtful, kind look. 'He must know,' Katie decided.

DuQuelle then passed James a folded note. 'This is a letter of introduction to M. Louis Pasteur at the École

Normale in Paris. The Queen has just sent him a personal message, outlining your abilities, with an added postscript from Miss Nightingale.'

James couldn't quite believe it. A moment ago he had thought his life was over. But now he felt the very faintest whisper of excitement. Pasteur! Why, he was at the forefront of disease. And even better, the French academies had accepted Pasteur's work and were funding it. Anything happening in the field of germ theory would happen at the École Normale. James looked less like a statue. Princess Alice actually clapped her hands.

Florence Nightingale entered just then. She looked at Alice with slight disapproval. 'This does seem an inappropriate place to romp,' she said, exchanging that long, communicative glance with Bernardo DuQuelle.

She obviously knew too. Everyone's relationships seemed to be unfurling. James and Alice would leave each other, but they had reached an understanding. And, in a way, they would never be parted. The Queen would go on, a powerful figure swathed in black, aided by Bernardo DuQuelle. He would play his part to perfection. But what was Miss Nightingale's role?

Katie decided she'd had enough of mystery for one day. 'Florence Nightingale, Bernardo DuQuelle, I think you should come clean,' she burst out. 'What *exactly* is your conection?'

Florence Nightingale looked disconcerted. Bernardo

DuQuelle was ever so slightly amused. 'You will never guess,' he said.

James O'Reilly and Princess Alice sat down, Katie noted, side by side. 'I would never dream of guessing,' Alice said, 'though we have always been curious.'

DuQuelle's face softened when he turned to Princess Alice. He had always found her admirable and though she'd clapped with joy at James's great prospects, her sweet face still looked so sad . . . Perhaps that is what decided him. 'I will tell you a tale of times gone by,' he said. 'By chance it might give you some heart's ease today.' Alice blushed, but nodded.

'Long ago, for you, but not so long for me, I made a friend,' DuQuelle continued. 'He was a fine man, a tremendous bibliophile – I believe it was our need of books that drew us together.' This made sense to Katie. DuQuelle needed words – in fact, it was this world's ability to communicate that had brought him here. DuQuelle smiled at Katie. 'Always the words,' he said, 'they lead us both on. I don't *do* friendship, as Katie might say, but this particular man was different. He spoke many languages, not anything like my range, but enough; and he understood the value of words. We formed a group, three or four of us. We worked together and published a learned work: *Curiosities of Literature*, it is still in print.'

'I've read it,' James said. 'Your friend must be Isaac D'Israeli.'

DuQuelle's eyes glittered green. 'It is Isaac D'Israeli I speak of. I was as fond of him, as, well, as one like me can be. His sister Devara was even more brilliant. Her Greek, Hebrew and Latin were perfection, her ear for languages pitch-perfect. I do not believe there is, or was, another woman like her in this world. I married her,' he said, enjoying the dumbfounded look on each face. 'We had a child.'

Princess Alice gasped, and then covered her mouth with her hand. Katie was astounded. How could this be? DuQuelle wasn't even human. She'd seen him cut himself and bleed – not blood, but words. And from this . . . a child?

DuQuelle seemed to enjoy their shock. 'You've always found me rather heartless,' he said. 'Will you accept this as proof of something akin to a heart?'

James opened his mouth, with a thousand medical questions, but Princess Alice gave him a discreet nudge. Her royal manners had kicked in. 'We congratulate you,' she said. 'I do apologize for our initial reaction. I will admit we are surprised.'

Bernardo DuQuelle bowed to her. 'I thank you for your rather belated felicitations. A surprise, yes. No one was more surprised than I. But Devara was delighted.' He paused, and then seemed to relive times past, in the way only DuQuelle could. His green eyes glowed. Katie watched him carefully. He'd lost his ominous, mysterious air. He seemed . . . almost . . . happy. And then his countenance grew cloudy. 'It was short-lived. As often happens in this world of yours, my wife died.'

The warm light in DuQuelle's eyes died. He didn't just look old. He looked ancient and so tired. He tried to speak, to finish his tale, but nothing came out. The words he had fought so hard to gather and use failed him. Katie noticed that Florence Nightingale had lost her usual competent demeanour. It wasn't sympathy washing through the room, it was something else.

Katie began to suspect the answer to her original question. 'What happened to the baby?' she asked.

Florence Nightingale drew a deep breath and continued the strange story. 'With such a father, no one knew how this child would develop. Isaac D'Israeli decided it would be best to place his sister's infant with a more *traditional* family. One of their literary friends had recently married. That man agreed to spirit the baby into his home, and raise it as his own. He loved letters and was known as W.E.N. He did the best he could with the child, though his wife was always resentful. It caused much disruption in their home.'

Alice stood up, wide-eyed. 'W.E.N!' she exclaimed.

'Yes,' Florence Nightingale said. 'You will know him, always called W.E.N. – an abbreviation of William Edward Nightingale.'

Bernardo DuQuelle came to stand next to Florence Nightingale. He did not embrace her, or kiss her, but he did look proud, and protective. 'Florence Nightingale is my daughter.' It took them all quite some time to absorb this strange fact. DuQuelle had been right about one thing: Alice and James and Katie forgot their own troubles in this new wonderment.

Finally Katie spoke. 'This explains so much,' she said. 'The way you can read each other's minds. Those things Florence did to me in the Crimea. Her understanding of the Little Angel, it all makes sense now.' Katie was getting more excited by the moment. 'It kind of seems to me that, with Florence and DuQuelle and Lucia, we really could defeat the Malum. We could find the Little Angel and . . .'

Florence Nightingale sighed and shook her head. 'You are not the first to think so, Katie. But it is not to be. My powers are more than yours, though less than M. DuQuelle's. It is the mixture of the two worlds – one might say the sublime and the ridiculous – that gives me such understanding. And I know, better than they know themselves, the Verus and the Malum will continue their battle.'

Katie started to protest, but Florence Nightingale raised a hand – small, white and commanding – for silence. 'Neither will win, because they are in balance. Good and evil. Peace and war. Benevolence and brute force. They will continue to coexist. But we must be vigilant. Lord Belzen has a more willing audience, and it is easier to swell the ranks of his armies. I believe you saw some of his children. Ignorance, want and fear are always with him, always on his side. That is why you are so important, Katie. Unlike the other Tempus, you *can* choose. And each time the challenge comes, you choose what is good.'

Alice linked her arm through Katie's and gave her a squeeze. 'I've always known, from the beginning,' she said.

Katie felt a wave of pride, quickly replaced by shame when she thought of the darkness she had hidden in her heart. 'I almost went the other way,' she said. 'This time, I got so jealous of Alice and James – I just felt lost. And then I got angry.'

Bernardo DuQuelle smiled. There might have been love in his life, but his smile was still a rather creepy, acquired expression. 'We know, Florence and I. We were very worried at one point. If, as we suspected, Lord Belzen had called you, then he had access to your thoughts and your heart. But on the top of the Round Tower I saw you choose. No matter how many times you are called, I believe you will make the same choice.'

Once again DuQuelle could see right into Katie's mind, and now she too could see, that tiny bit, into his. She liked what she saw: love for the daughter he longed to call his own, affection for Princess Alice, respect for James. And for her? She saw friendship, true and sincere.

There was change everywhere – for Alice, for James, and even for Katie. She realized with a start, they were all time travellers. Their journeys were just beginning, as they left childhood for ports unknown.

Katie knew it was time for her to go. She just didn't know how.

Chapter Twenty-Four

The Travellers

The three travelled to Gravesend. The *Victoria and Albert* had weighed anchor in the Thames Estuary, awaiting her royal passenger. The yacht's black and gold hull bobbed gently in the river. It was surrounded by tiny pleasure boats, waiting for the colourful standards to go up the masts: the Admiralty flag, the National flag and the Royal standard. The Queen did not accompany Alice. She didn't wish to be 'viewed' by the public. Nor did she want the inconvenience of travelling with a reluctant potential bride.

As a tiny recompense, she let Alice's American friend travel with her as far as the pier. Bernardo DuQuelle attended them, the senior Palace representative. He had recommended that James O'Reilly come as well, in case the Princess's nerves needed tending before the departure.

Katie could have told the Queen that Alice was too dignified to be sullen, and she would not succumb to nerves. She was calm, though very quiet, as they made their way down the Royal Terrace Pier. Behind them came the rustle of skirts, and a slight high cry, as the wind across the pier caught the ladies' crinolines and whipped them above their knees. These were Alice's new ladies-in-waiting – a rather chilling reminder of her life to come.

One of the ladies hurried forward to Princess Alice. 'Ma'am, may I suggest you wait in the carriage. You might find the wind too taxing.'

Princess Alice turned; her kind grave eyes had become distant and formal. 'I thank you, but I do not find the wind taxing. I find it invigorating. I would prefer to stay here, in the freedom of the fresh air. However, I suggest *you* retire to the carriage. I would not wish any of my ladies to catch a cold.'

The ladies could do little other than follow Alice's orders. Bernardo DuQuelle bowed his head to her. Princess Alice might not be happy, but she was in charge. She would rise to the occasion. She would be a Princess worthy of Great Britain.

'You should take note,' DuQuelle said to Katie. 'This is an excellent study of how to handle adversity with dignity.'

'I don't want to take notes,' Katie muttered. 'I want to sit down on the pier and blub. I don't think I can bear this parting.'

DuQuelle shook his head at her. 'There are partings and there are partings,' he said, 'and I predict a rather splendid reunion for you.'

Katie smiled weakly at Alice and handed her a knobby bundle. 'You'd left this behind,' she said. 'I know you're too old for it. You'd really already outgrown it when we first met. But, I thought, just as a memento . . .'

Princess Alice turned over the package and it emitted a plaintive 'Baa'. 'Woolie Baa Lamb!' Alice exclaimed. She gave Katie a long, affectionate look. 'He was my favorite childhood toy. I loved him dearly, and one never really outgrows those childhood loves.'

James was searching for something in his pockets. 'Katie, you and DuQuelle have always spoken of the force of words. That is all we shall have now. I hope they are as powerful as you say.' James found what he was looking for, and handed folded letters to both Katie and Alice. 'I for one believe in them. And I have already begun to write. Here is the first of my correspondence. It is not a letter of goodbye, but I hope a letter of welcome.'

Princess Alice turned pink, but with happiness. 'I have done the same,' she admitted. 'One for Katie, and one for you. Though if Katie leaves us, I don't know how the rest of my correspondence will reach her. Can the post fly through time?'

Katie watched Alice very carefully. She didn't know when they would see each other again, and each time she left, she forgot this rich life. She would have given anything not to forget. Katie took her two letters and opened them. Princess Alice's perfect penmanship and James O'Reilly's medical scrawl bounced up from the pages. The wind ruffled the letters as she read, and the words began to blend together. Katie could actually hear the voices of Alice and James, alternating back and forth, but never ceasing – not just their words to her, but all their words, particularly to each other.

In those few minutes, she heard the story of a lifetime. Within the letters lay James's medical research, Alice's reading on welfare, his theories on disease and her intelligent observations. James became a modern man of medicine and Alice a politically aware woman, with advanced beliefs on society and the poor. Interspersed with these were the mundane trivialities of life: a visit from a relative, a particularly boring lecture, toothache, a new pair of spectacles . . . Through their writing, Katie could actually see the two of them: Princess Alice as a mother, with her own growing family, and James increasingly important in the medical world.

Alice's voice did not grow old, at least when she wrote to James O'Reilly.

I could clap my hands, indeed I could! Your latest news is so heartening. I always knew you could do it. And the vaccinations you have developed are the final, irrefutable proof. All of Europe talks of your discoveries. The genius of James O'Reilly. I am so proud to be your friend . . .

In James's voice, Katie could hear warmth and devotion.

Grand Duchess of Hesse, Princess of Great Britain and Ireland. Yet for me you are always Alice, still a girl, the serious and intelligent companion of my childhood. I received your praise with such joy. Sometimes I think I strive so hard and do so much, simply to please you. I cannot recognize or believe in any of my achievements, until I have written of them to my dearest friend. No day of my life has been lived, until I tell you . . .'

Katie understood why James would never marry. Letter after letter, their voices rushed through her ears. And then James's tone became worried and urgent:

What a troubled time for you, Alice. Diphtheria is a serious illness and you must be very anxious about your children. It is highly contagious. You must not touch them. No matter how they cry for you, show self-restraint. The children need you, not just as a nurse, but as a mother, for many years to come . . .

And then Katie could see Alice as a grown woman, standing at the door of her children's sickroom, reading James's letter. But even as Alice read, her son cried out from within. 'Mama! Mama! I am so frightened . . . Please come to me . . .' The child held out his arms.

Princess Alice was shaking Katie affectionately by the shoulder. 'Where have you gone, Katie? You look terrified. It is your amazing link to words. I should have known better than to give you a letter!' Katie came back, with a jerk, to the Royal Terrace Pier. She watched as Princess Alice turned to James to say goodbye.

Bernardo DuQuelle took Katie's arm, and led her away. 'It would be kind to give them some privacy,' he said. Katie stared up at him.

'I don't like what I just read,' she said, 'what I saw and what it might lead to.'

DuQuelle sighed. 'It is your gift. I cannot remove it. Perhaps you see too much. Such a gift can be a curse.'

Katie wondered: had he known this all along – that this is how it might end? Was this the seed of his special affection, his softness towards Princess Alice?

DuQuelle answered, as he so often did, her unspoken questions. 'The Princess is worthy of great respect, no matter what lies in her future. I do not pity her, for she does find love, through her children. And she never abandons her early affections. She is true to the end.' He shook his head, as if clearing sorrowful thoughts. 'And the future can change, as well as the past. You can change it. And that is quite a gift,' he added more brightly.

Princess Alice called to them. 'The longboat has arrived, it will ferry me out to the Royal Yacht.'

The ladies-in-waiting tumbled from the carriage, the longboat bobbed below them as a ramp was steadied against the pier. There was a flurry of cried goodbyes and promises, of anguished parting looks. And then Princess Alice was gone, down the ramp and into the longboat. They watched her progress, and then strained their eyes to find her on board. The wind was high and the sails were raised. As the sun set, the *Victoria and Albert* was silhouetted against the light, every mast and spar highlighted.

And then they saw her: Princess Alice was learning against the rail, her face caught in the glow of the fading sun. She kissed her hands to them and Katie waved back enthusiastically. James held out his arms, his fingers taut, as if he could clasp Alice's hands in his, despite the tumbling water between them. The cannon fired a salute and the *Victoria and Albert* lifted anchor. People cheered from the quay as the sails rose and the yacht moved on. Alice had begun the most significant journey of her life, into her own future.

DuQuelle had been waving his black top hat. As the yacht moved to open sea, he bowed his head in respect.

'Goodbye, dear Princess,' he murmured. 'It is the greatness in you that brings adversity. Be true to yourself. You will find your own voice.'

For Katie, there were no words, just tears. She was unaware of anything, except the loss of her friend. James was as stone. Wisely, DuQuelle left them to their grief.

After some time, the chill wind reminded Katie where she was. The ship was long gone and the sun was setting. Turning from the sea, Katie realized they were not alone on the pier. Other ships were leaving that day, though none as grand as the Royal Yacht. Trying to pull herself together, Katie watched a colourful cluster of people on the pier. From their loud dramatic voices, and bright if tattered clothes, she guessed it was a theatrical troupe. She had never seen such a disorganized lot. Trunks popped open, spilling out sequinned capes and slashed velvet doublets; musical instruments lay in piles. No one seemed to be able to find their travel documents, or their money. Normally they would have been of great interest to Katie, but today she viewed their antics with listless incomprehension.

'I am really not much of an actor. But I can certainly help them in the role of manager,' a voice behind Katie said. 'Have you truly come to say goodbye?' She spun around. She recognized that voice. And so did Bernardo DuQuelle, who bowed low.

'I had heard that you left the American delegation,' DuQuelle said.

John Reillson took Katie's hand and kissed it.

'That's a very un-American move there,' she said, whisking her hand away.

John Reillson laughed, his bright blue eyes shining with excitement. 'But I'm a Bohemian now. I'm allowed a certain licence. Truly, I had to leave the Unionists. They had achieved their goal and kept Britain out of the war, yet they continued their own form of rough diplomacy. You saw them. They were bullies. I must say, Katie, I am amazed to see you here.'

Katie started to tell him, but it was too difficult. How could she explain the whole strange story, filled with danger, adventure, grief and friendship? She choked up and DuQuelle had to step in, with a few well-chosen phrases.

John Reillson gave her shoulder an understanding pat. 'It must be hard, to lose your best friend. But perhaps you will meet again. And there might even be new friends on the horizon. You never know which way the winds will take us.' The pat on her shoulder turned into a squeeze. She was grateful for the sympathy.

'But I still don't get it,' Katie said, trying to brush her own sadness aside. 'How did you end up with a theatrical troupe?'

John Reillson laughed again; despite his sad childhood, she'd never met anyone who enjoyed life more. 'I didn't have the money to get back to America. So I joined this troupe. I told you all about them at the Christmas Ball.

And we saw them together in Hyde Park. It's spectacular entertainment: Alex Kinch, Harry Cheng, the Countess Fidelia, the Little Angel.'

'The Little Angel!' Katie cried. And down the pier she could see her. A lovely girl, the child who brings peace – and, like Katie, the Tempus, one of the chosen.

The rowing boats were bobbing now at the pier's edge, the sailors within them calling urgently. The tide was high, and all must board or miss their passage. But John Reillson hesitated. As he looked at Katie, he thought he might just stay.

DuQuelle could guess what was happening. 'Why do you travel from Gravesend? You will not reach America from here,' he asked.

'What?' said John Reillson. 'Oh yes. So sorry. We travel through Europe, and then to America – or as the Countess Fidelia likes to call it, the New World.' Still laughing, he struck a pose and recited.

'O brave new world, that has such people in't.'

A cry came from the theatre troupe. Harry Cheng's trunk of magic tricks was missing. John Reillson dashed off, to make himself useful.

Then the Little Angel glided up the pier and put her arm around Katie. They rarely met, yet there was a mysterious bond between them. Together they looked at John Reillson, issuing orders to the company of performers. Perhaps it was the touch of the Little Angel that helped Katie to understand: Jack O'Reilly, Reilly O Jackson, John Reillson – all different people, but also, somehow, the same. Here was another triumvirate, another three who travelled through time. It quite took Katie's breath away. 'Will we be travelling together?' she asked the Little Angel. 'Am I to go with you?'

The Angel tidied Katie's flying hair and straightened her bonnet. 'Not this time,' she answered. 'John Reillson and I will sail, but you will stay on land.'

This was to be another loss. Katie peered at the Angel, perplexed. Long ago, when Katie had first encountered her, the Little Angel had been a small child; when they next met, she was a beautiful girl. But something had changed. Katie had grown but the Little Angel had not. 'It's my age, isn't it?' Katie asked.

The Little Angel nodded. 'It's so much easier for a child to understand that words can come to life, to believe what is fantastic and to brave that which is fearful.'

'So I am to grow up, and be left on my own,' Katie said. 'I am no longer part of the Tempus. I will not change time, or history. I will, again, become nothing.'

The Little Angel kissed Katie on the forehead. 'That is nonsense, and you know it. Nothing! You have fought on the battlefields of the Crimea and put a stop to the Great Experiment. You have saved the life of Queen Victoria

– more than once. Unlike the others of the Tempus, you were not instilled with good or evil. You have to choose. It is not as easy to choose good as one might think. Yet each time you have faced the challenge and chosen well.'

Bernardo DuQuelle came to stand with them. 'You have already changed history,' he said to Katie, 'your own history. And it is more important than you might think.'

Still Katie felt she was being abandoned. She shivered, and DuQuelle took off his own dark cloak and wrapped it around her. It smelled of him, of powder and musk and the particular electric scent of time travel. 'You will never leave the Tempus,' he assured her, 'but with age comes new responsibilities, in your own time.'

'But what can I do?' Katie practically wailed. 'My powers are in *this* time, I am *nothing* in my own time.'

DuQuelle raised an eyebrow. 'Really, Katie. Sometimes you see so clearly, and at others you are blind. Your power lies in the words. The very thing I seek in this world – you have it in abundance. The words, or at least your use of them: this is the true gift. Use them carefully and to some purpose. In your hands they are extremely powerful.'

'Like the rest of us, your journey is just beginning,' the Little Angel said. 'And Katie, don't be afraid of your future. I like what I see.'

'My future. You know what happens, of course,' Katie said. The Little Angel smiled at her. Katie looked up, that little bit angry, at DuQuelle. 'And you *always* know. Yet you never tell.'

The Countess Fidelia, celebrated in the great capitals of Europe, was calling frantically. The tide was high, the ship was in the river, the signal for sailing at her mast-head. The Little Angel must come, and Mr Reillson too. Alex Kinch had already been fished out of the water, and they feared Harry Cheng would be seasick. It was a hive of activity, as they were bundled over the pier into the rowing boats.

Something in Katie broke free. 'I want to go with you!' she cried, looking at the beautiful girl, and the young man, retreating from her now.

The Little Angel waved to her, calling, 'We will meet again, I promise.'

Katie ran along the pier, keeping pace with the little boat. 'But I'm trapped,' she shouted, 'I don't know how to get back.'

The Little Angel's sweet voice floated across the water: 'The way back lies through your own free will.' The rowing boat climbed a wave, and then tipped down the other side. They were out of sight.

Katie was left on the pier with Bernardo DuQuelle and James O'Reilly. DuQuelle looked at her with that strangely blank face of his. James hadn't even noticed. He had not been roused by the meeting with John Reillson or the voice of the Little Angel and was quite oblivious to the antics of the theatre troupe. He was still staring out to sea, and only now lowering the arms he'd held out to Princess Alice. 'I will write,' he said, yet again. Katie hoped the promise gave him some comfort.

Chapter Twenty-Five

Learning to Fly

The way back lies through your own free will. It had sounded lovely, as the Little Angel called out across the waves. But just what did it mean? Katie was sprawled on the sofa at South Street. She couldn't exactly live at Windsor Castle once Princess Alice had left, so DuQuelle had brought her to stay with Florence Nightingale. 'I am adrift,' she grumbled. 'Shipwrecked. Up a creek without a paddle. No better than a castaway.'

Dolores came through the door, and without thinking, began to tidy Miss Nightingale's sitting room with exactly the same vigour she applied to Apartment 11C. 'This pretty little house was neat as a pin before you arrived,' she said. 'My, but you are messy. And grumpy. And bored and cranky. You sure are missing your friends. Why don't you try and make yourself useful. Me and Mary Seacole, we're so busy we can't catch our breath.'

Katie flopped over, groaning. She was swinging her legs in the air and trying to scratch an unreachable part of her back, when a hand grasped her shoulder and jerked her into an upright position.

'This is unacceptable,' Florence Nightingale said in her clipped fashion. 'You are a visitor, in my home, and you lounge about and scratch yourself as if you were a chimpanzee at the zoo!'

Katie sat up straight and looked rather sheepish. Florence Nightingale had entered with Bernardo DuQuelle and Mary Seacole. She continued to glare at Katie, though her two companions seemed secretly amused.

'Dolores is right,' Mary Seacole said. 'You are grumpy. Now I know your Princess and young James O'Reilly have gone, but we're here. You'd better make the best of it until you figure out how to move on.'

Dolores bustled back in with a tray of tea things. Much to Miss Nightingale's annoyance, she insisted on shouldering such domestic chores. 'Now Mary,' Dolores said. 'You're been on the streets pamphleteering. That's cold work. You help yourself to a nice hot cup of tea. You too, Miss Nightingale – I know you've been shut up at Windsor with that bossy little Queen.'

'That is a very disrespectful way to speak of our Queen; and don't you find it rather rich, describing *others* as bossy,' Florence Nightingale reproached Dolores. But she did take the cup of tea.

Dolores grinned at her and poured some tea for DuQuelle. 'Here you go, Bernie. Nice and hot. Good enough to warm up a cadaver like you.'

Katie had to admit, it always cheered her when Dolores called the mysterious, gothic DuQuelle 'Bernie'. She helped herself to a biscuit. 'That's some bounce in your step, Dolores,' Katie said, nibbling the biscuit and sprinkling crumbs across her dress. 'What gives?'

Dolores sat down on the sofa and brushed the crumbs from Katie's lap. 'I'm glad everyone is here,' she said, 'because I have an announcement to make.'

Katie looked from face to face. Florence Nightingale was shooting DuQuelle the look – one of their secret, silent conversations. Mary Seacole was beaming benignly at her friend. Dolores herself seemed both excited and frightened. She took Katie's hand. 'You know baby, how worried you been, about getting us home?'

Katie nodded. 'I'm still trying,' she apologized. 'I'll figure it out somehow.'

Dolores squeezed Katie's hand so hard, she could feel the knuckles pop. 'Well, you don't have to worry anymore. I know what to do,' she announced triumphantly. 'We're just not going home. We're gonna STAY.'

Katie blinked hard; the breath wasn't quite getting to her lungs. Mary Seacole clapped her hands.

DuQuelle gave a low groan. 'I had feared this,' he murmured to Florence Nightingale. Miss Nightingale had the look of a hostess whose guests have outstayed their welcome. Her lips tightened into a thin line.

Katie was no longer bored and not even grumpy. Now she was frightened out of her mind. It was one thing to try and hurtle two willing people through time, but to try and budge the stubborn bulk of Dolores . . . 'Oy vey,' she groaned.

Miss Nightingale actually rapped her on the top of the head. 'In my home you must behave yourself,' she admonished Katie. 'Such language! You are not an East End barrow boy.'

Bernardo DuQuelle looked thoroughly entertained. He whispered to Miss Nightingale. 'Actually, my dear, the phrase is Yiddish. Whatever you inherited from your parents, it was certainly not an ear for languages.'

Katie tried to collect her thoughts. 'But Dolores, we have no choice. You and I, we have to leave.'

'Leave!' Dolores really was going to kick up a fuss. 'Why should I leave? I'm doing good work here. I have spoken and this nation has listened. I don't see no reason to silence my voice. I'm changing the world for the better. Back in New York, I don't think I'm much more than a slave. Do you really want me to go back there and spend my days ironing Mimi's silk undies?' Katie found herself nodding in agreement. Dolores had a point.

DuQuelle tried to reason with her. 'Dolores, you were never supposed to be here. It almost killed you. It turns out you were not responsible for Katie's diminished powers. That was the work of Lord Belzen. I have admired your work, both in the streets and the halls. You roused the people to stand up against slavery at the exact time we needed it. But the crisis point has passed. Britain will not enter the American Civil War. I do not believe the South can win, and I assure you, the slaves will be freed. But we must leave it at that. I sometimes fear we've done too much. You are still Tempus Stativus – not chosen, but thrust upon us. It is dangerous to tamper with history.'

Dolores eyed him up. 'Bernie, you've got a lot of nerve to talk danger with me. Now, if I was butting into someone else's world and *pretending* to be just like them, or if I was *harvesting* up words and exporting them to another world; maybe even if I had the idea to parachute children through time as an *experiment* – I think I'd be pretty dangerous then. But Bernie, *you* know a heck of a lot more about being a dangerous person – or *half person* – than I do.'

Bernardo DuQuelle's white skin went rather green. He turned to Katie for help.

'Come on, Dolores,' Katie said. 'You know we can't stay. I feel the same way, every time. Why do I want to go back to school and psychiatrists and reading endless stuff about Mimi? What's the point of living in a time and place where I feel unpopular and weird? Here I have friends, and I count.' She took Dolores's hand. 'It's not me and Mimi you have to go back to. It's Sonia and Tyrell. It's your children. Your life isn't, like, the most exciting thing in the world. Neither is mine. But the people back there need us.'

Mary Seacole had been listening carefully. 'I love you like a sister, Dolores,' she said, 'but your family is back in that other time. What would they do without you? If there's one thing you understand, Dolores, it's responsibility.'

For a long moment Dolores struggled. She'd always seen herself as one of the workers of this world. The one who did the grunt work, the one stuck in the background. For this single shining moment she'd been able to do good, and do it centre-stage. It was hard to give up.

Katie put her arm around Dolores. 'Think of how much you've seen and learned,' she encouraged her. 'This could change your life. Dolores, you don't have to work for Mimi and clean up after me. We all know Mimi will never really grow up. But I will, I mean, everyone keeps banging on about it. I'll look after Mimi. You can go ahead and look after yourself. Why not become a nurse? Or a teacher?'

'A missionary,' Dolores said rather shyly, 'as a girl I always wanted to be a missionary.' Her misty eyes sharpened when she glanced at Bernardo DuQuelle.

'Lord knows, I've have done some pretty tough missionary field work here; seems to me I've met with the devil and I've stood up to him.'

DuQuelle looked rather affronted. He'd been called many things, throughout many periods of history, but never the devil.

Days passed, then weeks. April came and with it the spring. Still Katie could not figure out how to leave. She spent much of her time with Mary Seacole and Grace O'Reilly, working on *The Wonderful Adventures of Mary Seacole*. Under the eye of Florence Nightingale, Grace's health had recovered. She was brilliant at organizing Mary Seacole's notes and writing it all down in her beautiful handwriting. But it was Katie who could take Mary Seacole's stories and turn them into a riveting adventure. The words were alive to her, as clear as reality. At the end of each day, Bernardo DuQuelle read what she wrote. 'I was right,' he said, 'as I so often am. You use the words as if they were magic.'

At Miss Nightingale's home she learned a new lesson from each inhabitant. Katie had always liked Mary Seacole, and now she grew to admire her. In their daily talks, she told her personal story: how, as a Jamaican creole, she rose above prejudice and came to the aid of a far off nation. Katie listened to Mary Seacole chatting with Dolores, and came to understand so much more about their lives.

She mulled all this over with Grace O'Reilly late into the night. Grace's life had changed forever. Her father, now in deep disgrace, had disappeared. His plans for her, as a beauty he could barter on the marriage market, would fortunately come to nothing. Katie found in Grace another person adrift in a strange world.

'What do you think you will do, Grace?' Katie asked one evening as they sorted through Mary Seacole's rather chaotic notes.

Grace smiled to herself, a bittersweet smile. 'At first I was frightened,' she admitted. 'But now I feel strangely liberated. I will try to have a life that does not depend on my face and figure.' Katie did wonder, with such a face, would this be possible? 'I've always lived on the fringe of the medical world, first with Father, and then James. As you know, Father disapproved of women in medicine. But I do think I've finally caught the bug.'

'Will you become a doctor?' Katie asked.

Grace O'Reilly turned as red as her hair. 'Goodness no! That would be scandalous.'

'Sorry,' Katie muttered. 'Even now, I keep forgetting what you can and can't do. So what's the plan, Grace?'

Grace twirled a long red curl around her finger. 'Miss Nightingale has suggested I train with her. There is a new corps of nurses at St Thomas's Hospital. All very respectable, even though Father would have died of humiliation.

'But that sounds terrific,' Katie said. 'Have you told James?'

While Katie remained at South Street, her correspondence with James and Alice had flourished. Grace nodded happily. 'James is the man of the house now, and he approves the plan. I will board with Miss Nightingale. Katie, I realize she seems very stern, but her heart is in the right place. Did you know that she has requested I bring Riordan to stay as well?'

'Riordan!' Katie exclaimed. 'Won't little Riordan kick up a great commotion in this house of women?'

Grace laughed. 'When was the last time you saw Riordan? He's not a baby any more. He's cramming for his entrance exams to Eton. And it will be good to have Miss Nightingale's sharp eye upon him. In my opinion, he's much more interested in the theatre than his Latin or Greek; or perhaps it's the actresses that hold his attention. There's a sweet young Vaudeville singer, the Little Angel. He writes to her while she's on tour.'

Here was one more lesson Katie had learned. That life circles round and round. 'I wouldn't worry about the Little Angel,' she told Grace. 'If Riordan has truly chosen her, he's chosen well.'

And so they worked and talked and wrote. But most of all Katie thought. She didn't sprawl on the sofa now, or complain of boredom. There was so much to do, and when she did have idle time, there was even more to think about. She laid out her adventures and ideas, and came to some conclusions. It was as if everything around her, and inside her, was in preparation for something new.

It happened so gradually – even Katie couldn't tell when it had started. She only knew when she was ready. One day she realized: the Little Angel had been right. Katie didn't need letters, or snow globes, or walking sticks to make things happen. She *was* getting older, and she *could* make her own choices. She needn't be yanked, or pulled or pushed through time. And she could stop herself from falling. She needn't say goodbye to her friends: Princess Alice and James O'Reilly, the Queen and her ladies, Mary Seacole, Florence Nightingale and Bernardo DuQuelle – they would always be with her. Instinctively she knew this, and this time she would not forget.

Instead, Katie put her arms around Dolores and simply decided. She would go home to Mimi and quit whining about her crazy pop star behaviour. Mimi was . . . Mimi, and the fates were not handing Katie any other mother. And at school she would try and make the best of Neuman Hubris; at the very least they had great computers. If she put some work in, she might find school more interesting. As for friends, she finally understood: if she stopped trying to be so clever in that mean kind of way, maybe people wouldn't think she was so weird and snooty. She would be her own person. And she would try and be a little bit kind. How hard was that?

But most of all, life wasn't just about *her*. It all became very clear as she spun through time with her arms wrapped around Dolores. Katie laughed to herself. For years James had questioned her, 'How do you travel through time? What does it feel like? What do you see?' She'd never been able to answer. It had always been so fast and confusing and painful. But this time, it was like swimming in a pleasant, clear sea, or floating in a vortex of warm air. This time she understood.

Katie could see hundreds of children swirling around her. Some were very young and some, like her, were almost grown. She could pinpoint the Tempus Fugit. They flew with their arms out, laughing and free. Others fell through time, the Tempus Occidit, angry and frightened. And then others were blindfolded, trancelike, unaware of what was happening. They didn't understand the power they had and the choices they could make. 'That was me,' Katie thought. 'I was blind, but now I can see.'

Epilogue

Another Christmas

Time went on, minute to hour to day. Katie did remember, but she did not regret. In many ways, it was a relief to be back in a methodically timed world. A year had passed since she'd unwrapped the snow globe. It was another Christmas. Katie looked around Apartment 11C. Silent night, she thought. All is calm. All is bright.

George buzzed from downstairs. 'Warning!' he bellowed into the intercom, 'Dolores is on her way up.' Katie smiled. Dolores thought she was so smart, but she had forgotten everything. She could never understand what had happened the year before. She'd missed Christmas completely. One minute she'd been talking to Katie, the next . . . it made no sense. Sonia and Tyrell had been worried sick.

Last year's Christmas had been rotten for Mimi too. FOREVER YOUNG! had bombed in the shops, not even making the top twenty in fragrance sales. The media had sniped that it smelled of embalming fluid and started referring to Mimi as 'Forever Pickled'. After a bit of rehab at an ashram in Malibu, Mimi had decided to embrace her age. There was only one possible career move: the theatre. So much more distinguished for an older woman.

Mimi had quickly become the toast of the town, much celebrated for accepting the slings and arrows of time, albeit with many, *many* trips to cosmetic surgeons and holistic gurus. Katie saw a lot more of her. It turned out the theatre was harder than learning one catchy pop song – all those words in just one play. Mimi had a memory like a sieve, but Katie had a way with words. She rehearsed with Mimi relentlessly. This career was going to stick.

The bell rang and Katie opened the door. 'You think she'd leave me with a key.' Dolores started to grumble the minute she got inside. 'But no, out of sight, out of mind; or maybe that Mimi thinks I'll break in and steal something. It's not like I never had the opportunity . . . now if I'd really wanted to take something . . .'

'Hey Dolores,' said Katie.

'Hay is for horses,' Dolores snapped, and gave Katie a big hug.

Dolores didn't work there anymore. She might not remember, but inside her the adventure had left its mark. She was training to be a missionary and was planning to go to the Sudan. 'I don't know why or how,' she'd told Katie. 'It just came to me, like a vision I had to follow.' None of this had made Dolores any more modest or demure. She spent a lot of time bragging about divinity school and how she was top of her class. They all might be pretty religious, but Dolores was certain: she had more God inside than the rest of them. Sometimes Katie smirked to herself when she thought of it. If those Baptists knew just what Dolores had been through, they might call in an exorcist.

This year Christmas was going to be great. And tonight was special: the opening night of the Christmas Spectacular at Radio City Music Hall. 'It's not Strindberg, darling,' Mimi had said to Katie. 'It's not Ibsen.'

'So what kind of part is Mimi playing?' Dolores asked, adjusting her new beret in the mirror.

Katie looked a bit sheepish. 'She's the Queen of the Fairies. And no, Mimi's not exactly doing Shakespeare, but she does get to make an entrance on a twenty-foot sparkly star.'

'What kind of queen? What type of fairies?' Dolores asked suspiciously.

'It's a pantomime kind of thing,' Katie said defensively. 'You know, like in England – the men dress up like women.'

'I haven't ever been to England, and from what you say, I won't ever be going,' Dolores retorted.

Katie smiled to herself, thinking about Dolores, and England. 'Look Dolores, Mimi's got a back-up chorus of a hundred men in drag. You're not a missionary yet. You're coming. Mimi went to a lot of trouble to get us these tickets on opening night . . .'

Dolores applied some rather wonderful orange lipstick. 'Is she doing the high kicks?' she asked, 'like the Rockettes?'

'No, Mimi will not *do the high kicks*. It's in her contract that she will *not* do the high kicks. Now come on, we're running late, we're out of time.'

The intercom went again. George was having a busy night. 'Is that Katie? You've got a visitor down here.' Dragging Dolores out the door, Katie ran to the elevator and pressed the button three times. She couldn't wait.

From behind the front desk, George made his introduction. 'Mr Reilly Jackson,' he announced, smiling broadly, as if the young man hadn't stood there, in this lobby, in New York City, waiting for Katie hundreds of times.

'Actually, it's Reilly O Jackson,' the young man said. And he was grinning too. It seemed to be catching.

'O brave new world, that has such people in't.'

Reilly recited as he handed Dolores a box of chocolates and kissed her on the cheek. 'Merry Christmas' he said. Dolores harrumphed, a rather fake, very happy harrumph. Taking Katie by the arm, Reilly kissed her too. 'Did you like your Christmas gift?' he asked. 'I'm sorry I made you open it early, but I can never wait.'

'I can never wait either,' she admitted, thinking of the snow globe. 'I love your gift,' she said. 'I'm wearing it tonight. I might never take it off.' She fingered the large golden amulet, shaped like a flask that hung around her neck. Reilly O Jackson might think this flask was something new that he had bought for Katie in a store, but Katie new better.

'I'm sorry it's empty,' Reilly said apologetically. 'I would have put perfume or something in it, but I wasn't sure what you'd like.'

Katie looked down at the flask and remembered. Mary Seacole and the Crimean battlefield – she'd held her golden amulet over Jack O'Reilly. She had promised Katie they would meet again.

'It's perfect as it is,' she told Reilly. 'It's already full. It's full of you.' Reilly blushed.

'You should save that kind of snazzy talk for your stories. I only hope someday you'll let me read them. I know they'll be great.'

How could she ever have been bored? The snow, the night, the friends, the fun. 'We have so much time!'

she cried, out of the blue. Reilly seemed to understand, though Dolores looked rather annoyed.

'I thought you said we were out of time.'

'Their time, our time, passing time, all time, no time, out of time,' Katie chanted dreamily.

And now Dolores was decidedly vexed. 'Katie Berger-Jones-Burg. You might not be a child anymore but you sure do talk some childish nonsense.'

Reilly O Jackson lightly touched the amulet around Katie's neck. 'I think she talks great sense,' he said.

Katie laughed; she thought she would never stop.

Dear Reader,

The Queen Must Die, *The Queen at War* and now *The Queen Alone*. This is the final book in the *Chronicles of the Tempus* series. I feel like James and Katie, standing on the pier, waving goodbye as my books, my characters – and my wonderful readers – sail away to other adventures.

This has been such an interesting series to write, as each book contains three very different worlds. Katie lives in our time, in New York City. I found Katie easy to write, as she bears a strong resemblance to me. (Though my own wonderful mother is *nothing* like Mimi!)

Princess Alice and James O'Reilly are true Victorians. Over time I've read many of the real Princess Alice's letters to her mother, brothers and sisters. Katie is very lucky. I would have liked to be best friends with Princess

Alice. Queen Victoria, Prince Albert, Mary Seacole and Florence Nightingale are all important historical figures. Though the twist in Florence Nightingale's tale is pure fiction (or at least I believe so . . .) James O'Reilly comes from my imagination. To me, he represents the best of the Victorian frame of mind: a belief in science and medicine, hard work and progress. James might not always be charming, but he makes the world a better place.

As for the rather supernatural world of the Verus and the Malum, Lucia and Lord Belzen – they *might* just be the most real characters in the trilogy. Good does coexist with evil. And the battle continues.

My favourite character, though, is the one who lives in all three worlds. Bernardo DuQuelle has to learn to be human, and he does this with keen observation and quite a bit of clever commentary. It strikes me that he would make an excellent writer!

If you have any questions, I'd be delighted to answer them. You can follow me on Facebook and Twitter, or contact me by email: kasquinn@hotmail.com

Bon Voyage
K. A. S. Quinn